Re:ZeRo

-Starting Life in Another World-

"Yes, so we shall. With your eyes, I shall strike him down, Subaru Natsuki—my friend."

"Doesn't feel too good to have my fate and yours be one and the same— Let's get this over with."

"Why...?"

"—I love you, Emilia."

He told her the one and only thing that gave his life meaning, even when covered in all those wounds.

"Rem Natsuki"
Fragments

Re:ZERO -Starting Life in Another World-

The only ability Subaru Natsuki gets when he's summoned to another world is time travel via his own death. But to save her, he'll die as many times as it takes.

CONTENTS

Re:ZeRo

-Starting Life in Another World-

VOLUME 9

TAPPEI NAGATSUKI
ILLUSTRATION: SHINICHIROU OTSUKA

NEW YORK

Re:ZERO Vol. 9
TAPPEI NAGATSUKI

Translation by Jeremiah Bourque
Cover art by Shinichirou Otsuka

Re:ZERO KARA HAJIMERU ISEKAI SEIKATSU Vol. 9
© Tappei Nagatsuki 2016
First published in Japan in 2016 by KADOKAWA CORPORATION, Tokyo.
English translation rights reserved by YEN PRESS, LLC under the license from KADOKAWA CORPORATION, Tokyo, through Tuttle-Mori Agency, Inc., Tokyo.

English translation © 2019 by Yen Press, LLC

Yen On
1290 Avenue of the Americas
New York, NY 10104

Visit us at yenpress.com
facebook.com/yenpress
twitter.com/yenpress
yenpress.tumblr.com
instagram.com/yenpress

First Yen On Edition: February 2019

Yen On is an imprint of Yen Press, LLC.
The Yen On name and logo are trademarks of Yen Press, LLC.

Library of Congress Cataloging-in-Publication Data
Names: Nagatsuki, Tappei, 1987– author. | Otsuka, Shinichirou, illustrator. | ZephyrRz, translator. | Bourque, Jeremiah, translator.
Title: Re:ZERO starting life in another world / Tappei Nagatsuki ; illustration by Shinichirou Otsuka ; translation by ZephyrRz ; translation by Bourque, Jeremiah
Other titles: Re:ZERO kara hajimeru isekai seikatsu. English
Description: First Yen On edition. | New York, NY : Yen On, 2016– |
Audience: Ages 13 & up.
Identifiers: LCCN 2016031562 | ISBN 9780316315302 (v. 1 : pbk.) |
ISBN 9780316398374 (v. 2 : pbk.) | ISBN 9780316398404 (v. 3 : pbk.) |
ISBN 9780316398428 (v. 4 : pbk.) | ISBN 9780316398459 (v. 5 : pbk.) |
ISBN 9780316398473 (v. 6 : pbk.) | ISBN 9780316398497 (v. 7 : pbk.) |
ISBN 9781975301934 (v. 8 : pbk.) | ISBN 9781975356293 (v. 9 : pbk.)
Subjects: CYAC: Science fiction. | Time travel—Fiction.
Classification: LCC PZ7.1.N34 Re 2016 | DDC [Fic]—dc23
LC record available at https://lccn.loc.gov/2016031562

ISBNs: 978-1-9753-5629-3 (paperback)
978-1-9753-8315-2 (ebook)

1 3 5 7 9 10 8 6 4 2

LSC-C

Printed in the United States of America

PRoLoGUÆ

RE:START

It was dark. An entire world of nothing but darkness.

He was tossed into a hazy world, seemingly floating in water with no sense of left or right, up or down.

His body was unable to move at all. He couldn't feel his hands or legs, and he doubted his eyes and ears were functioning.

With his mind so dazed, any thoughts he tried to formulate simply slipped out of his brain.

Where is this? Who am I? What happened to make it like this?

What little consciousness he held on to resulted only in ramblings that made the darkness flicker ever so slightly.

"—I love you."

In that pitch blackness, a voice penetrated deep into his heart.

It hung in his unhearing ears. It reached what should have been his still, unbeating heart. It found his soul, which was still unsure of its own existence.

He wailed as the voice touched him directly, its wild, mad emotion pressing in on his heart.

*   *   *

The voice was so terribly fleeting. The whispers wrenched his heart, filling it with such longing that it threatened to shatter.

Hearing words lovely enough to scorch his soul made him feel like he would go mad.

If I had fingers, I would touch you.
If I had a mouth, I would call your name.
If I had arms, I would embrace you.
If I had feet, I would run to your side.
If I had a body, you would never be alone again.

But none of these wishes could be granted. He had no fingers, mouth, arms, feet, or body to give.

The feeling was the same… In fact, it was a passion even greater than what he'd felt before.

The warmth he received magnified his yearning, his emotions many times over, until finally they became sins.

Sloth, because I cannot wipe away your tears.
Lust, because I want us to melt together and become one.
Gluttony, because I want to consume you, to take all of you for myself.
Greed, because I want to have everything that I love.
Wrath, because I cannot forgive the absurdity of it all.
Pride, because I scorn everything that is not you.

Jealousy, because that is all I feel for the world that embraces you.

With this realization, the world shrouded in black was filled with an overwhelming sensation of love.

That instant, the supposedly empty space warped, then shattered as irreversible time began to flow backward.

It was simple. He understood that he was starting over.

Where he had ended in darkness, light was born, and if he walked toward it, the world would greet him once more.

"*—I love you.*"

He turned his back on the voice and walked forward. He wanted to turn toward it, but he held fast.

However, surely, one day he would take her hand.

"*—I love you.*"

The lovely voice called out until the very end, when Subaru Natsuki—began anew.

CHAPTER 1

THE GOSPEL KNOWN AS WARMTH

1

"—Hey, kid?"

"Ah?"

Subaru's mind was roused by the abrupt calling of his name along with the sensation of his shoulder being shaken.

The image of the world around him changed in an instant, almost like someone had switched camera angles in his brain. The sudden influx of information startled him, making Subaru feel dizzy as he blinked several times.

The next moment, the unfathomable shock known as *comprehension* coursed through his entire being.

"No way…"

Subaru put a hand to his forehead as he listened to the sound of his heartbeats pumping blood through his body.

Subaru had experienced a blank of several seconds interrupting his thoughts a number of times before. It was the result of "Death"— the time between the erasure and resurrection of Subaru Natsuki.

He'd died. He'd *died*. "Death" had greeted Subaru once more.

Moreover, Subaru had lost his life in battle against that wily bastard Sloth.

"..."

After overcoming many hardships, much suffering, in the end he'd still lost his life.

He'd defeated the White Whale and, after that, reorganized the expedition force, bringing it with him as he traveled to Earlham Village to fight the Witch Cult.

At the end of that anguish, all that joy, sadness, and anger, had all come to naught—

"—*Nom*."

"Ugyaaaaah—?!"

Subaru had been covering his face with his hands, cutting himself off from the world, when he was suddenly assaulted by unexpected sensations.

The feel of hot breath and his earlobe being pinned between two hard points sent the astonished Subaru tumbling to the ground. Wide-eyed from the exceptionally soft sensation, he noticed yellow eyes gazing down at him with a teasing look.

The owner of those eyes touched a finger to their lips coquettishly as a wry, beautiful smile appeared.

"The teasing was because you were staring into space, but what a wonderful reaction, *meow*. Ferri enjoyed it so much that this might become a habit..."

The sight of his flaxen kitty ears flicking as he continued speaking lightheartedly left Subaru listening with his mouth agape. Eventually he swallowed and called out her—or rather his—name.

"Is that you, Ferris?"

"Who else does it look like? Maybe you're not just daydreaming, but hallucinating, too? You could have swallowed some White Whale mist... Should I give you a proper examination?"

"...Nah, I'm all right. I just felt like asking. Right, what I was asking about...?"

As Ferris peered at him in concern, Subaru shook his head before taking a deep breath and examining the area. Ferris was seated directly beside him, and around Ferris, many others—no, properly speaking, they were in a circle with Subaru at the center.

Beneath his feet lay the grassland. It was clear from the dawn sky above that the sun had not risen yet. With everyone's gaze focused on him, Subaru sensed a ferocious bestial presence hovering to his left.

"…Were you the one who spoke to me first?"

"—? What are you talkin' about, bro? You had a crazy look in your eyes. Pull it together."

The dog face of Ricardo, the large-framed beast man, grimaced with a suspicious look. Subaru, realizing from the exchange that Ricardo had seen his face the instant he Returned by Death, scratched his cheek as he looked over everyone's face once more, nodding as he spoke again.

"That was seriously bad for my heart. I mean really, I thought I was back in front of the fruit store again."

Exhaling like a deflating balloon, Subaru let the tension out of his shoulders as his palm brushed the ground. The cold dirt, fresh grass, and raw earth under him meant he definitely wasn't in the capital.

This was the Liphas Highway, where they'd held a general briefing right after defeating the White Whale.

In other words…

"The save point…got updated, huh?"

It felt like he had narrowly avoided a terrible fate, but it wasn't something he could laugh at. Still, the silver lining brought him relief.

2

When it came to worst cases, some were worse than others.

Having fought the good fight, only to gain an empty defeat and Returning by Death, was undoubtedly a worst case. But there could have been something even more terrible—namely having no change in restart point and returning to a moment before he managed to defeat the White Whale. Compared to that, this worst case was not the most horrific possibility.

At the very least, they had beaten the White Whale, fulfilling the Sword Devil's fourteen-year ambition.

"—"

"Sir Subaru, are you all right? Your face appears rather pale."

Wilhelm, the Sword Devil, stared at Subaru and expressed his concern. "It's nothing," said Subaru, shaking his head immediately, tightening his disjointed thoughts and slackened cheeks.

Even though he was still reeling mentally after only just enduring a Return by Death, he couldn't simply use that as an excuse. After all, Subaru and the others were in the very middle of a critical discussion—the briefing to decide what countermeasures to take against the Witch Cult.

"If you are no longer distressed, let us review the situation."

Raising a finger, the elegant knight Julius restarted the meeting. Scholarly wariness and righteous indignation resided in his almond eyes as he requested they carry on.

"From this point onward, we shall proceed to the Mathers domain to oppose the nefarious Witch Cultists lying in wait. Ideally, this will result in their annihilation and the slaying of the Archbishop of the Seven Deadly Sins commanding them. However, what we must prioritize is the safety of the innocent people caught up in this incident, and in preparation for that—"

"For the getaway, we have called on the traveling merchants Anastasia and Russel to help us. The messenger we sent to communicate the alliance and the rescue operation should have arrived at the mansion already... Sorry, I'm all good now."

Subaru thanked Julius for giving him time to calm down and fully rejoined the conversation.

Thanks to Julius summarizing the topics at the assembly, Subaru could grasp exactly how far things had proceeded before his Return by Death. Apparently Subaru had already explained Witch Cult Hunting Made Simple, as well as the insurance he'd procured.

However, he had already learned from the last go-around that his attempts to secure insurance would transform into deadly poison. The letter of goodwill they had sent had turned out to be blank, which had sown distrust. Meanwhile, inviting the traveling merchants to participate had left them open to infiltration by Witch Cultists.

He needed to implement new countermeasures as quickly as possible, but—

"Your face suggests that…something is amiss?"

"What are you, a doctor? Stop looking at people's faces and figuring out everything they're thinking, geez."

"Want the actual doctor sitting right beside you to examine you from head to toe instead? I wouldn't mind…"

As Subaru sank into thought, Julius and Ferris sandwiched him from both sides as they pointed out his troubled expression. Inwardly Subaru ground his teeth at their persistence.

He certainly did have an issue on his mind. However, he couldn't come up with a good way to explain it.

He had to warn them about the Archbishop of the Seven Deadly Sins' dangerous Authority, and a number of new problems on top of that, but how could he explain these things in a way his comrades would believe?

"—No, this is wrong. It's not good enough. Right, I…forgot some things again."

"Hmmmm?"

When Subaru firmly shut his eyes, the words he found within himself caused Ferris to cock his head in confusion. Julius remained silent with his brows knit as Subaru rued the extent of his own stupidity.

How many times would Subaru Natsuki make the same mistake before he moved forward?

"—"

He opened his closed eyes and looked around at the faces of the fifty-odd members of the expeditionary force. Subaru's silence had brought tension to their gazes, but they harbored no doubt. What they felt was not fear, but anticipation. There was no sense of despair, only hope.

After everything that had been spoken, after all the help that had been given…

In the end, Subaru had even gotten this far only thanks to the support Rem had offered him.

"...I believe you have immersed yourself in sentimentality enough?"

Julius sensed the change in Subaru's demeanor, and his light-hearted prompt invited a change in subject. The man really got on his nerves, but for a short moment, Subaru felt nothing but gratitude toward him.

He felt equally grateful for the comrades who granted him their own thanks and trust.

"Sorry for being all indecisive earlier. Actually, I have to add to my explanation about the Witch Cult...... No, that's not exactly it. I realized some things for the first time. I want to speak to all of you about those issues."

He didn't have to worry about how to come up with a good explanation. That was a waste of time.

All he had to do was not hold anything back, tell as much of the truth as he could, and they would respond with their faith in him.

Even if Subaru could not reveal the nature of Return by Death, he could uncover the things he learned as a result of it. This was the one way he could share what he knew of the future with his comrades.

And they would accept his preposterous tales in complete seriousness.

All because understanding and trust were the greatest weapons in Subaru Natsuki's arsenal.

3

Subaru had gleaned a number of new facts from his most recent confrontation with Petelgeuse.

One was that a Witch Cultist infiltrating the traveling merchants hired for the evacuation had delivered a blank letter of goodwill to Roswaal Manor. Another was that Petelgeuse Romanée-Conti's Authority included the worst power imaginable.

In particular, one aspect of Petelgeuse Romanée-Conti's power—Possession—posed the greatest obstacle to the expeditionary force's efforts to take down Sloth.

"Anyone know about…a power to overwrite someone else's mind with your own, letting you mentally take them over? Some sort of magic that can do something like that?"

Much of the magic in this new world Subaru found himself in had effects beyond anything he could conceive.

The basics of magic began with the four elements; then there were a great many other things, like Beatrice's Passage, Roswaal's flight magic, the mutant aberrations of magic called curses, and the special abilities known as blessings, too.

In a world where such incredible abilities existed, Possession had to be possible, too.

It was with such hopes that Subaru put the question to his lips, but—

"Overwriting another person's mind with your own? That's nothing but a stupid, unbelievable idea, *meow.*"

"…Gimme my greatest weapon back."

"What are mew talking about?"

Though Subaru had brought up the subject with courage, the way it was laughed off so quickly was a major blow to that foundation of trust.

When Subaru pouted and gave Ferris a resentful stare, Ferris was merely baffled. Cutting in, Julius adopted a thoughtful pose and spoke.

"Given the topic at hand, you believe it's possible the Archbishop of the Seven Deadly Sins employs a strange power along those lines… Am I correct?"

"Yeah, you've got it. I decided to call it Possession, but that's not far off from what actually happens. He survives by moving from body to body. That explains how he shows up in so many places at once, right?"

"＿＿＿"

From the long silence, Julius seemed to be mulling over Subaru's explanation. But whether others doubted it or not, it was a fact. Having shared his own body with that very madman, Subaru could firmly confirm that much.

His mind conquered people's flesh, stealing control for itself. Without any doubt, Petelgeuse Romanée-Conti was a spiritual entity that grafted itself to the bodies of others—a repulsive, wicked ability.

"In the past, I have seen references in old tomes about research on similar phenomena. It was reckless research, but…"

"Really?"

When Julius, a hand still over his own mouth, offered up that morsel, Subaru bit. The handsome man plumbed the depths of his memories as he deftly summarized what he could recall from the tome.

"It was research on lost magic, or perhaps a related record. The world lost many things in the immediate aftermath of the Great Catastrophe four centuries ago. This variety of magic seems to have been among what was lost. Gone without a trace, save in records, there was a description of an ability similar to what you describe."

"Well, don't hold back. What was the similar lost magic?"

"A technique for soul…transference."

As Subaru drew closer, Julius revealed something that sounded far removed from magic. However, Subaru did not miss the look of disgust that came over Julius's face as he spoke of it.

After firmly declaring the research abominable, Julius closed his eyes and continued.

"The phenomenon itself is exceedingly simple. Everything comprising the caster's soul—his memories, experiences, and most likely, elemental character and destiny—are seared onto the soul of another person."

"Meaning, it…is possible to overwrite the memories and mind of another person, then."

It was like doing a copy and paste with a computer file. It treated human memory like a file, overwriting it with another person's file-like soul, blotting out the old and saving the new.

That way, the discarded soul would be lost, and the overwriting soul would remain.

"But it does not exist in reality. The magic is lost, the ritual is theoretical, and the difficulty is of an almost unheard-of level. Reproducing the feat would require magical genius and tenacity beyond the ability of mortals. I simply cannot believe this Archbishop of the Seven Deadly Sins possesses such intellect and skill."

"Hey, man, not believing it exists isn't a real reason to reject the idea, especially since this is the Witch Cult we're talking about."

"Subawu, you're getting too worked up. Julius has things to say, too."

The influential Julius rejected his hypothesis, which made Subaru snap at the knight until Ferris chided him for it. Subaru proceeded to put on a guilty look and said, "Go on," prodding Julius to continue.

"Sorry. It is a bad habit of mine to take my time reaching a conclusion. Even if we put aside the fact that the ritual has been lost, there are a great deal of obstacles for the technique we've been discussing. First, the souls that the caster can affect are fairly limited. The technique is not the kind that allows the caster to transfer his soul to any random person he touches."

"Well, of course not, *meow*. Memories are a bit out of my field, but overwriting individual Gates is no trivial thing. It's probably…limited to blood relations, *meow*?"

"A limitation to blood relatives would be extremely desirable. As Ferris said, the soul being transferred would bounce off the Gate if it is not highly similar. Besides, even when one soul is laid over another, the original soul's influence over the body will remain. There would be a constant concern about the body being compelled by the mind."

"…It sure does sound like magic that has a lot of downsides."

Hearing the pair's opinions, Subaru could understand why the objections were numerous.

Subaru could not dismiss out of hand the possibility that Petelgeuse was an exceptional magic user capable of employing lost magic, but it was pretty much impossible that his choice of bodies was limited to blood relations.

The fact that he had successfully possessed Subaru shelved that premise completely.

"However, it is too soon to dismiss a completely different method."

"Will you make up your mind?!"

"I am offended by your outburst. I stated that I know of similar magic as a prerequisite for further discussion. Besides, even if it is not the exact same technique, there are surely important clues we should consider."

"…Such as?"

"Naturally, I mean the possibility that the conditions for Possession are just as strict as those for soul transference."

Julius's assertion made Subaru's face scrunch up, but he immediately grasped the point. If soul transference was invariably limited to blood relatives, then Possession might have similar restrictions.

"We could deduce that the technique is limited to fellow Witch Cultists…and a select few at that."

"You mean those finger people…?"

"It is a title in poor taste when referring to spare bodies. I suppose that suits an Archbishop of the Seven Deadly Sins well."

Julius agreed with Ferris's conclusion, a fact that made Subaru gaze in astonishment. In such an incredibly short time, the two had worked out a plausible theory about how Possession operated. Even if the pair were the brains of the operation as well as the most versed in magic out of all the members of the expeditionary force, the results were beyond Subaru's expectations.

And simultaneously, a plan to truly hunt down the Archbishop of the Seven Deadly Sins of Sloth took form. Namely—

"If we take away all the archbishop's extra lives…in other words, destroy all his fingers…"

"…He would lose the chance to possess anyone. That's when the archbishop will face his end."

The way Julius firmly finished the thought made Subaru feel both deep admiration and a sense of defeat from the bottom of his heart. The difficult situation had made him start to lose all hope, but thanks to them, he could finally see the light in the darkness. After all, it was a solution that was neither contradictory nor disputable.

"In conclusion, we will prioritize eliminating the fingers lurking in the forest, then settle matters with Sloth."

Julius's declaration drew the meeting to a close. The faces of the expeditionary force members seated around them surged with determination and resolve. Great strength can be found when a person's ability and mission are one and the same.

When the members of the expeditionary force rose, their morale was as high as when they had done battle with the White Whale.

"—Everyone, there's just one more thing I have to tell you."

It was then that Subaru called out, drawing the attention of the impetuous warriors who were ready to venture forth.

When those intense gazes turned his way, Subaru endured his genuinely apologetic feelings to discuss something he was obligated to explain.

Namely—

"Sorry, but it's not just the fingers. I'm probably a target for the archbishop's Possession ability, too. What do you think we can do about that?"

"Huh?"

It had been the direct cause of his latest Return by Death, and the final hurdle he'd had to overcome.

Once he shared that pitiful fact, they began to devise a countermeasure.

4

In the end, their departure time arrived before the "Witch Cult Countermeasures Conference" reached a definite conclusion.

Subaru wanted to continue hammering out a plan, but if they didn't make it to the battlefield in time, that would be putting the cart before the horse—so to avert that, Subaru gave Julius a suggestion.

"Hey, Julius. With the magic of your spirit groupies, you should be able to link together the minds of people within its effective range, right? Can't we use that to discuss this on the move?"

Subaru was basing this query on his experience with Nekt, the mind-sharing spell he had experienced from the last loop, as if it were his own wonderful idea. At the time, Julius had used the spell to link all of the expeditionary force's minds to quickly deal with Ram's surprise attack. It had to be possible to use that to hold a meeting, too.

Subaru's proposal made Julius look at Ferris with mild surprise. "He didn't hear it from Ferri, okay?" said the kitty-eared knight in response to his gaze, waving a hand as he headed for his land dragon.

"What did Ferris mean that it wasn't from him?"

"...It's nothing. I did not think that you knew I was a spirit user. I was merely wondering where you might have learned that."

"Ah, right. This is where the spirit knight thing first came up..."

That Julius had identified himself as a spirit knight was information Subaru heard close to the end of the last go-around. At the point where he was currently, Subaru shouldn't have recognized Julius as anything more than a first-rate knight.

But it was a rare opportunity to take Julius off guard. Subaru put on a smug face.

"You're just more famous than you think. Well, the price of fame didn't have anything to do with me noticing you quietly stuck one of your quasi-spirits on me."

"So you were aware of even that?"

This time, a look of unconcealable distress was plain in Julius's gaze. The reaction made Subaru smile, but right after, he turned his head aside.

That was because, for an instant, Julius's eyes, which stared at Subaru, seemed to endure a wave of deep pain.

"Certainly, as you have pointed out, I placed one of my flower buds on you— Ia, come on out."

But he immediately concealed the wave of emotion behind his usual composure.

Beckoned by Julius's hand, a red light leaped from Subaru's hair. It was more flicker than flame, more warmth than light, one of the six quasi-spirits accompanying Julius.

"This is Ia, quasi-spirit of fire. I had her follow and watch over you."

"That's fine, but tell me about stuff like this. I'd panic if some emergency happened and she jumped out all of a sudden."

"There is no need for concern. The buds are quite capable. It would never come to something like that."

"Thanks for sharing your sappy love story. Now, setting that aside—"

When Subaru complained about planting insurance on him without permission, Julius was slightly apologetic. Subaru took it in stride until he realized something didn't fit.

Julius sticking Ia on him matched the events of the last go-around. His memory of the spirit saving him from the dragon carriage explosion was still fresh. But besides that, he remembered something odd where Ia was concerned. And as he realized that—

"Julius. Under what conditions could Ia be shoved out of me against her will?"

"…I am not quite sure I follow your question."

"This is important. The answer has a direct impact on the plan to take on the archbishop."

Faced with Subaru's firm statement, Julius discarded his momentary bewilderment and answered.

"Attaching Ia to you means, from a spirit user's point of view, a provisional pact. Forcibly breaking the pact would mean that you, the provisional contractor, have rejected her, or perhaps…"

"Perhaps?"

"A superior, formal pact displaced the provisional pact."

In that instant, he gave the answer Subaru truly wanted to hear.

Perhaps Julius realized it while speaking the words, because his amber eyes held a glint of comprehension. "It couldn't be," the knight said immediately after, shaking his head as if to deny it. However…

"A famous detective once said, 'Once you eliminate the impossible, whatever remains, no matter how improbable, must be the truth.'"

"It has the ring of truth. But if it is so…what is to be done?"

"This is the final piece. I wanna hear the rest along the way. Like which people fulfill the conditions, and which don't."

"Understood. Let us do exactly that."

Julius nodded, keeping his words concise as he stuck Ia on Subaru once more and headed to his own land dragon. Subaru felt the warmth of the quasi-spirit on top of his head as he mounted his favorite, pitch-black dragon—Patlash.

"We've used up a little more time than before. Gonna have to go all out, Patlash."

"_____"

As the land dragon took in Subaru's words, the side of her refined face made it seem he'd stated the obvious.

Then the expeditionary force resumed its march along the Liphas Highway, heading for the Mathers domain.

"—Nekt."

Julius used the mind-melding spell once they were under way, affecting the entire expeditionary force. The results of the spell were truly as Subaru had envisioned.

But—

"Ah crap, I completely forgot."

Sorry. I didn't think my tuning with Ia and Nes would be in error… There's also the fact that Ia seems rather fond of you. Perhaps you have a high compatibility with spirits.

"Save that stuff for later. We can take our time with that talk once everything's over."

Subaru accepted the telepathic apology, pressing his fingers to his temples as his ears continued to ring.

Just like last time, Subaru was reeling from the onrush of everyone's brain waves the instant Nekt was activated. It was Subaru's own fault for forgetting all about that side effect.

Julius adjusted the signal to more tolerable levels, allowing Subaru to focus on the flow of the conversation.

"So for the plan of attack against the Archbishop of the Seven Deadly Sins…how shall we proceed?"

Unlike with speaking out loud, there wasn't a good way to differentiate voices conveyed directly via thought. In spite of this, it was possible to tell the sender of thoughts thanks to their individual character.

The thought Subaru had just received was a deep blue, but concealed scarlet passion within it—Subaru could instantly tell it was Wilhelm who had spoken.

The Sword Devil was riding alongside on his land dragon, the grave look on his face radiating hostility toward an unseen madman.

"If Sir Subaru and Sir Julius's conjecture is correct, we must carefully consider our method of attack. Invisible magic hands and the ability to take over another's body are both major obstacles."

"Yeah, they sure are…"

The Archbishop of the Seven Deadly Sins of Sloth had two powers they needed to overcome. He had Unseen Hands and Possession at his disposal, but the expeditionary force had solid leads on ways to deal with both.

The main issue at hand was that the method to tackle one power left them vulnerable against the other.

"I'm the only one who can see Petelgeuse's Unseen Hands. That means if we go at him in a frontal attack, it's no good unless I'm around. But I'm also a target for Possession. If I'm there and he takes me over, we'll lose our chance to stop him from getting away anyway."

"…Sir Subaru, I actually have a proposal about that. Would you care to listen?"

As Subaru sank into thought, pondering "out loud," Wilhelm interjected with an air of confidence. His words aroused hope throughout the expeditionary force, making Wilhelm give a firm telepathic nod.

"Concerning the archbishop's invisible arms, I thought of a simple

way to expose them to the naked eye. First, we would scatter a large amount of dust, or possibly dirt, around the Archbishop of the Seven Deadly Sins."

"Ah, I don't think we can rely on that, meow."

Though Ferris casually inserted himself into his explanation midway, Wilhelm paid no heed and explained to the very end. Subaru had already seen his plan in action once before: a Wilhelm-style dirt screen to hold Petelgeuse's Authority in check. Knowing the results from the last go-around, Subaru knew that Wilhelm's proposal could work.

The problem was that it was such a superhuman feat, only Wilhelm could pull it off. Indeed, all the expeditionary force members found the suggestion too challenging, with even Julius and Ricardo communicating telepathically that the feat was beyond them.

"*I believe anyone can do it with enough practice, but...*"

"*Yes, yes. But we don't have fifty years to spend practicing. Aside from proving that Old Man Wil is inhuman, what'll we do?*"

Callously ignoring the dejected Wilhelm, Ferris prioritized moving the conversation forward. Subaru felt bad for Wilhelm, but Ferris had made the right decision.

Subaru mulled over Ferris's question. "Guess that decides it," he muttered. "Yeah, let's go with the original plan for dealing with the Witch Cult and the Archbishop of the Seven Deadly Sins, plus the issues at the mansion and the village. That's probably best."

"_____"

All the members of the expeditionary force reacted to the conclusion of the telepathic Witch Cult Countermeasures Conference.

Sympathy, concern, trust, anxiety—there was a crush of various emotions, but the general consensus was to respect Subaru's viewpoint. They would proceed as originally planned.

"*—To confirm, you are truly all right with this plan? You won't have any regrets?*"

When Subaru was still feeling unsure of himself, Julius was the only one to raise the question. Though it was an inelegant method, this exchange served as a necessary ritual to dispel the expeditionary force's hesitance.

Plus, that it was Julius, of all people, who brought up the topic meant this was an expression of his knightly beliefs.

"Don't be ridiculous. It's my plan and my idea. I'm not gonna turn around and say, *Oh no, maybe we actually shouldn't*…though Emilia is probably gonna be super mad at me when we do this."

With closed eyes, Subaru pictured a lovely girl with silver hair.

It had been only a few short hours since he'd left the world where he'd gazed upon her with unrequited love, his wish for a one-sided reunion having been granted. Even so, the serene sight of the her face and the sound of her lovely voice were undiminished.

It was because he could still vividly recall those things that he was able to hold firm in his decision.

"I'm happy everyone's worried, but don't give me the chance to say I wanna stop. If you thought that I had managed to squeeze out any courage from myself, you should know that it's actually all on loan."

The success or failure of the operation would be decided by Subaru's will, but he knew that they would never keep questioning his resolve for such a callous reason. That was why he could bear it.

"Besides, I'm optimistic that everything'll be fine once we reach the last part. The road that leads there is a little treacherous, but that's all. When you think of it that way, it'll be an easy win, right?"

"…*Subawu, choosing the words* easy win *means you're actually a big shot and I just never realized, right?*"

"Don't be stupid, I know I'm small fry. I might be optimistic, but I need all of your strength so I can share a passionate embrace with Emilia at the very end, all right? Come on, guys, just think of yourselves as my cupids and gimme a hand, okay?!"

"*I am still not quite sure on what basis you made that claim—but you have made your resolve clear.*"

Julius spoke for everyone when he approved of how Subaru's lightheartedness had swept away the heavy, stifling atmosphere. As that brought the meeting to an end, Subaru shifted his eyes to the road ahead, toward the edge of the plains.

Past that boundary, the grassland came to an end, and Subaru would soon be able to make out the treetops of the forested region beyond. Once they left the plains and took a few woodland roads, they would arrive at the Mathers domain.

His heart beat loudly, throbbing as if it might crack, yet even so, Subaru continued to look.

"_____"

"Ho-ho? What, you're worried about me? That's adorable."

Freed of the briefing now that everyone was no longer telepathically speaking, Subaru found Patlash's head turned toward him with a pensive look. Subaru showed her a strained smile as he stroked her neck. Then he rummaged in the sack affixed to the land dragon's saddle, locating something by touch alone.

What he found was a tool that would play a critical part during the operation. After all that time, an ache still ran through Subaru's chest when he recalled how it had passed into his hands.

In Subaru's mind, it was because of that pain that he could move forward, thrusting his fear and anxiety aside.

"This time, I'll make things right."

"Of course, that's what everyone intends to do. It'll be all right. The plan was devised so scrupulously, there is no reason to think of failure. Our preparations have been meticulous. Also, once this is all over, I would like to have a toast with you."

"Stop saying so many things that sound like famous last words—!!"

Subaru shouted at Julius, who was riding alongside him, presumably ignorant of the concept of death flags.

Those yells echoed loudly, ringing in the air as though they could even be heard in the Mathers domain, which was still far, far away.

5

When the light of day reached her sleep-deprived eyelids, Emilia rose with a light headache.

* * *

"It's…morning already…"

Emilia sat up in bed, blinking several times. She brushed her silver hair away from her forehead, briefly lingering on the boundary between sleep and consciousness before letting out a frail murmur that mirrored her thoughts as it floated to the surface.

She hadn't slept much for the past several days.

Last night, she had gone to sleep several hours after sunset again. After entering the forest at night, using her power to reweave the wards that kept demon beasts out, Emilia had probably managed to get only a couple hours of sleep.

Her head felt heavy and her thoughts sluggish, as if someone had plunged them into mud.

Emilia had never been much of an early riser to begin with, even before the numerous issues that had occupied all her time for the past several days. While fatigue and anguish were constantly whittling her mind away, there was no helping it.

It had been a week since the candidates for the royal selection had assembled at the palace, and a week since she had demonstrated her determination.

After that, Emilia had returned to the manor and spent five days acting as the representative of her faction.

The pressure she'd felt during those scant five days had been more than enough to overwhelm her.

"I thought I understood… I really thought I did."

Emilia strongly gripped her bedsheet as she lamented her incompetence.

In the blink of an eye, she recalled the events of the last week in the back of her mind.

She had been called to the capital, faced the other candidates, declared her conviction with all the eyes of the court upon her, and then—

"—Subaru."

As Emilia spoke the name of the boy she'd left behind at the capital, she lowered her eyes, enduring the pain.

She thought of that cheerful, sensitive boy who was always desperate to help others, and just a tiny bit delusional, wondering what he was doing at the moment.

The intense argument between them at the palace, as well as his pained expression, like an abandoned child's, were seared into her retinas. Those images had been burned into her conscience over and over.

In the end, his tortured face, the things that he'd spoken, the words that he hadn't wanted to hear but heard anyway—Emilia felt that no one could be blamed for those things…except for herself.

"…But it's for the best, isn't it?"

The clash of their inner thoughts had resulted in the two of them going separate ways. However, Emilia did not think that explosion of emotion was something that should have been avoided. In fact, it was better for them to follow different paths. The place where Subaru belonged was not by her side.

After all, Emilia was a half-elf, the object of everyone's hatred.

Anyone who stood by her would bear the same hatred from simply being associated with her. That kindhearted boy would be no exception. Indeed, it was because Subaru wanted to be by her side that he had been so terribly hurt, in both body and spirit, during his duel with Julius.

She didn't want to subject him to that, to make him go through such a thing again.

Over the course of their quarrel, she thought Subaru had to have seen his mistake.

Emilia's one regret was that, at the very, very end, she had let her true feelings slip.

Namely, the hope that Subaru, of all people, could set her existence as a half-elf aside and treat her as a normal girl…

—It had been a fickle, fleeting, futile, selfish hope.

"Subaru can't see me as anything but special… That's what he said."

She despaired at her own selfishness, pushing him away, hurting him, only to look to him for salvation.

Such shallowness was unforgiveable, half-elf or no.

"Lia, you're furling your eyebrows. You're ruining your adorable face."

A voice suddenly spoke to Emilia as she held her knees while still in bed. When she glanced up, there was a little cat spirit with gray fur. Emilia smiled slightly as she offered a greeting.

"Good morning, Puck. You're up early today."

"Good morning, Lia. This morning there was…something to take care of."

"—? Did something happen?"

"Mm, if I said I was making an effort to sleep early and get up early…that would be a lie. It's because I'm really worried about you, Lia. It's been one thing after another, especially yesterday."

Emilia lowered her eyes at Puck's uncharacteristically awkward reply.

…The events of the previous day had contributed a great deal to Emilia's current mental fatigue and lack of sleep. The bitter memory of the nearby villagers rejecting whatever she had to say or offer bubbled up in her mind.

Their fear and disapproval had not been enough for them to hurl cruel words at her, but their gazes alone had already cut deep into Emilia's heart.

"…I knew…that would happen."

"You also know what falling is, but you still hurt and bleed when it happens. If you ask me, simply knowing the result isn't the same as actually experiencing it for yourself."

When Emilia used a childish excuse to push past, Puck mercilessly cut off her escape route. But this wasn't something Puck did maliciously. Puck, in his own way, was urging Emilia to stop running from the truth as well as hiding her feelings.

"Puck…"

"Mm?"

"Puck…what do you think I should do? How should I… No, not just me, how can everyone get along better? How do I get everyone to…?"

"—Lia, maybe you should just do what you like? I'm on your side no matter what happens, Lia, and anyone who gets in your way is my enemy."

Though it was a promise from her surest ally, in that moment, the words offered Emilia no comfort.

It was the answer she'd expected. Puck would support Emilia unconditionally, but that didn't help with her problem. In the end, Emilia would have to rely on her own judgment.

Puck's entire value system was centered on Emilia; everything and everyone else came second.

"You're not going to turn your back on that village no matter what, are you? The pink-haired girl headed to the village again this morning. Maybe waiting for her report is all you can do?"

"...Ram went to the village? But she hasn't had any rest for a while either..."

"I'm telling you, that girl's doing a lot better than you are, Lia. She finds places to take breaks from her work. At the very least, she can handle herself."

She shrank a little. Puck's rational assessment of Ram of course implied that Emilia was wholly incapable of taking care of herself. As it happened, Emilia found herself relying on Ram that very moment.

For the past several days, Ram had been executing a portion of Roswaal's affairs, shouldering his responsibilities dealing with the mansion or Earlham Village, all while Emilia remained in the mansion.

Excusing himself to conduct negotiations with a local big shot, Roswaal had claimed he would be away for no more than a few days. The great responsibility brought worry and stress, but if she couldn't cope with that much in the span of a few days, how could she possibly hope to participate in the royal selection and be ready for what would come after?

With such thoughts in mind, she'd accepted the duty, shelving her feelings of guilt from leaving Subaru in the royal capital, then readied herself to face the days to come with atypical seriousness—but two days prior, the situation had greatly changed.

"A strange presence in the forest…?"

"Yes. Unpleasant fellows against whom even my Clairvoyance is ineffective."

Ram delivered the news in her usual calm tone of voice, but her furled eyebrows were an ominous sign.

Her Clairvoyance was the unusual ability to synchronize with the vision of others and see through their eyes. However, even this ability, particularly useful for reconnaissance and searching, had been unable to discern the identity of the presence she'd sensed in the forest.

"It's not…related to demon beasts?"

"The barrier has been redeployed. I believe it is unrelated, but… What do you wish to do?"

"Well, that goes without saying… We can't pretend nothing's happening. If we can't do anything about it, at least we can keep the villagers from falling into danger."

"Prioritizing their safety… You wish to evacuate the villagers, then?"

"That…would be best. This mansion is big enough to accommodate all of them, right?"

That was the conclusion Emilia and Ram had reached during their discussion about the forbidding presence in the forest. That Ram hadn't objected was somewhat reassuring to Emilia. As Roswaal's proxy, Ram would have mercilessly shot down any proposals she deemed foolish.

Accordingly, Emilia had walked to Earlham Village—practically next door—with some expectations. She'd convince the villagers to evacuate to the mansion, sparing them from peril. But—

"We've heard about the royal selection—as well as the fact that you are a half-elf. We refuse to follow you. Everyone has agreed on this."

An old woman acting as the village's representative spoke these words, rejecting Emilia's offer.

The obstinate reply, filled with rejection and renunciation, hurt Emilia. The fact that it hurt surprised her.

Rejection was Emilia's natural environment. She had tasted that discouragement countless times before. And yet, she realized at the same time, that pain was still felt sharply in her heart.

—Emilia had hoped it would change her.

She'd hoped that leaping into the royal selection, a great undertaking, would be the first step to changing her lot in life, and that perhaps the reactions around her that she'd taken for granted might change, too. The points of contact between her and the villagers over the two preceding months had further raised these hopes.

But Emilia had continued to deceive them about her true identity using concealment magic. Could anyone truly trust her, or allow her into their heart, when she had never shown her real face even once?

When she'd spent those days with the villagers in what she mistook for harmony, those smiles had not been not aimed toward her. They had been meant for the young man leading Emilia to the village by the hand.

Emilia had not earned anything herself. And yet, had she misunderstood even so?

"...In the end, what was I even doing?"

Once her offer was rejected, her subsequent pleas fell on deaf ears; she offered three more times, but every time she was refused. The calamity that had come from the royal capital on the heels of that despair had only added to Emilia's suffering.

"I have come bearing a letter of goodwill from my master, Duchess Crusch Karsten."

An envoy of humble demeanor had arrived at the mansion to present an envelope sealed with the lion's crest of the House of Karsten. When she accepted the letter, Emilia could only guess as to its contents.

Crusch was not only a royal candidate, but the person she had entrusted with Subaru's care in the capital. Wondering what might have befallen him, she had opened the letter in great haste—

"—But it was blank. The pink-haired girl said the message was a declaration of war. I can't blame her for being upset."

The letter itself was resting atop the room's desk. When Emilia's gaze drifted to it, Puck had discerned what she was thinking, cocking his head slightly as he recounted their discovery that the sheet was blank.

Just as Puck said, the letter had been delivered blank. There was nothing written on it—neither front nor back.

Sending a blank letter implied that the sender deemed the recipient someone not worth speaking to. However, the letter's contents, and the very act of sending such a thing, clashed greatly with what Emilia knew about Crusch as an individual.

Because of that, she had immediately suspected there must have been some mistake. She had asked the envoy what Crusch had truly intended, but he promptly asserted that he'd simply done as he had been commanded. Ultimately, Emilia was unable to find a satisfying answer.

"Let's keep the envoy under watch here at the mansion. If it comes to that, we can use him as a bargaining chip."

In spite of Ram's extreme position, the envoy was being hosted at the mansion, safe and sound. Even so, the forbidding presence in the forest and the blank letter had only worsened Emilia's mental load.

In the end, she hadn't been able to sleep well last night, either, so Emilia did the only thing she could: check the surrounding barriers to make sure they weren't weakening to ward off any potential demon beast attack.

After she made her rounds, she returned to her room at dawn, fell asleep, woke, and arrived at the present.

Rem seemed to have left her alone at the mansion, heading off to the village in another attempt to persuade the villagers while Emilia slept. Technically speaking, given her position, Emilia would normally be expected to go with her, taking the lead in appealing to the villagers to evacuate—

"But it might actually go better without me…"

A feeling of shirked responsibility prodded Emilia to rise from bed. At the same time, she was deeply anxious about the possibility she would be shunned, which would make the situation worse.

As a matter of fact, if Emilia had gone with Ram, the villagers would surely have rejected the proposal out of fear.

That was reality of the situation. Emilia continued to slam into the wall that people used against those who were seen as strange and different.

But to fight against that, maybe she should go into the forest herself—

"Oh, Lia. Someone's coming up to the mansion."

"…Ram, I suppose. I need to ask her how things went in the village."

Puck's call interrupted Emilia's thoughts. She quickly headed into the changing room.

Normally Puck was noisy about Emilia's grooming, but he hadn't been too picky for those last several days. But even this show of consideration became fuel for Emilia's growing self-hatred.

"Ahh, I'm going to visit Betty. Call me if something happens, 'kay?"

"Err, yes, all right. Say hi to Beatrice for me."

As soon as Emilia stepped into the corridor, Puck split off to see the young-looking girl who, despite living under the same roof, didn't care much for showing her face.

When Emilia thought about it, she hadn't seen the girl a single time since returning to the mansion.

"Maybe Beatrice is angry I left Subaru behind…"

Subaru and Beatrice got along rather well, so maybe she was upset.

Negative thoughts seemed to keep bubbling up without end. Emilia sighed and set off for the entry hall at a brisk pace.

She put off seeing Beatrice until later. There were many things she had to speak about with Ram.

"Lady Emilia."

Emilia arrived in the hall just as the doorway to the mansion was opening. She exhaled a little when she saw Ram through the crack of the door.

"Ram, I'm sorry for putting everything on your shoulders. I will make it up to you very s—"

"No need, Lady Emilia. More importantly, you have guests."

Ram shook her head, interrupting Emilia as she moved aside, clearing a path to the door. "Huh?" said Emilia as her eyes grew wide when figures came over the threshold.

"Lady Emilia, please forgive our sudden visit."

It was a well-aged man with a sturdy physique who addressed Emilia with a bow. Emilia squinted slightly, recalling that she had seen his tall frame somewhere before; the memory came to her right after.

"You were…the gentleman who came with Ferris once, right?"

"Yes. I am called Wilhelm Trias, humble retainer of the House of Karsten. I have come today representing my liege."

The old man introduced himself in a dignified voice before dropping to one knee in a display of the utmost respect. Emilia, blushing at the sight, rushed down the remaining stairs that separated them to bid Wilhelm to rise. However, she immediately realized that something about him was bizarre.

Smeared in blood and grime, the old man did not have the appearance she would associate with an official messenger.

"Those clothes… What happened?"

"I apologize for the unsightly display. With some luck, I was fortunate enough to encounter a trifling demon beast while traveling to the Mathers domain. My atrocious appearance is the result."

"I don't mind, but your wounds……seem to have already been treated."

"There is no need for concern. More importantly, I must properly communicate my master's will."

When Wilhelm suggested shifting the focus from himself to the topic at hand, Emilia acceded. The old man calling himself Crusch's representative reminded Emilia of the letter that had arrived the night before.

"Actually, last night, I received what was apparently a letter of goodwill from Lady Crusch. However, the letter was blank...... I was concerned, wondering if there was some kind of mistake."

"Blank, you say— I see, so it truly was blank."

"What do you mean...?"

Wilhelm's blue eyes narrowed at his learning the contents of the letter. Sensing something strange in his demeanor, Emilia remained concerned as she instinctively echoed his words. But he immediately shook his head.

"No, this is highly embarrassing, but that contradicts the letter my master originally sent. I know her thoughts well, and I assure you, there is no need for concern."

"The original... I see, it actually was a mistake? I'm so glad that she...doesn't hate me."

Emilia put a hand on her chest, relieved to hear someone close to Crusch firmly deny any ill will.

The letter had arrived directly after the residents of the village had rejected her. On the one hand, she hadn't thought it was like Crusch; on the other, there had been some part of her that worried the head of the House of Karsten was acting out of contempt for half-elves.

An anxious heart indulged in unnecessary doubts, which invited vulnerability. That was the state Emilia was in.

"I sincerely apologize for the confusion. My master, Lady Crusch, is not the sort of person to engage in such rash acts, nor would she ever deem Lady Emilia worthless or someone to be ridiculed. Try as I might, I can say without reservation that I cannot conceive of such a notion."

"Th-thank you very much... Then, um, what was the letter actually about?"

The great amount of praise left Emilia surprised, but also a little happy. Her spirits rose slightly. As they did, Wilhelm retained his exceedingly polite posture as he answered.

"Lady Emilia and Miss Ram...it is Lady Crusch's opinion that those present in this mansion as well as the residents of the village should be temporarily evacuated from the area."

The announcement made Emilia's small smile freeze on her lips.

6

Once Emilia recovered from the initial shock, Wilhelm continued his explanation.

"Of late, we have received information that a criminal group known to the kingdom has infiltrated the Mathers domain. I have come representing a unit formed for the purpose of hunting down this group."

"And those people are hiding in the forest around us... Is that what this is about?"

Emilia blinked in surprise as the truth about the unrest even Ram's Clairvoyance could not discern was revealed.

As Wilhelm gravely nodded, Ram, standing beside him, nodded readily as well. Then Ram gave her own pink hair a gentle stroke as she spoke.

"The envoy has already been taken into the expeditionary force's custody and has deployed in the village to prepare against enemy forces. But the enemy is the notorious Bandit King, so if fierce combat breaks out, damage to the surrounding area is unavoidable."

"Bandit King...! We're supposed to evacuate, then? That's why even dragon carriages were arranged for us?"

According to Wilhelm, enough dragon carriages to carry Emilia, Ram, and every single villager had already entered the village to ready for their escape. Ram, having confirmed this with her own eyes, gave her seal of approval.

"When everyone has been evacuated, our expeditionary force shall immediately exterminate them. Should the danger be swept away, you have my promise you may return to your peaceful lives."

The rest of Wilhelm's explanation contained the details of the evacuation plan arranged for Emilia and the others.

Emilia admired the unblemished goodwill, but she could not bring herself to politely leave everything to them. Of course, the proposal made perfect sense, and she had no intention of doubting them. But she also had some misgivings.

"But why would Lady Crusch do so much for the sake of this domain?"

This land was squarely within the Mathers fiefdom, plus Emilia and Crusch were political rivals for the throne. The goodness of her heart was probably not Crusch's reason for acting. Emilia suspected there was something else.

Wilhelm slightly lowered his voice as he responded to Emilia's doubts.

"This is just between us, but…we have a history with this criminal organization and cannot pretend the Bandit King is someone else's concern."

"History…with you, Sir Wilhelm?"

"Not just me. There are some youngsters who are champing at the bit to get at them as well. Besides—" Wilhelm's lips had slackened slightly into a smile, but it vanished as he continued his explanation. "My master has been recognized by the marquis as an ally for the duration this royal selection. The terms are the handing over of magic crystal mining rights for the Great Elior Forest… Does this clarify matters for you?"

"—! …I see, the rights to the forest. So that's…how it is."

Even as Emilia accepted the words that followed, they shook her a little. While Emilia had been worrying about things all by herself, Roswaal had already worked in the darkness to prepare the best possible response. It was not that she didn't trust him, but it was something of a shock nonetheless.

"…But evacuating is easier said than done. Where will we go?"

"We have thought about this as well. This is connected to the earlier matter, but we would like you to head for the royal capital, Lady Emilia. Lady Crusch is in the capital and desires a conference at which to seal the alliance."

"That is…yes, that's all right. But is it possible to bring everyone to the capital?"

The capital was about half a day's journey by dragon carriage. It would prove a difficult journey for the elderly and the very young villagers. It was also unclear how long it would take to eliminate the criminal organization, which raised her concerns about who would be able to accommodate them all.

If this issue was dire enough to justify their leaving the area surrounding the manor, then—

"Perhaps it would be best if I assisted to drive the Bandit King away sooner?"

"...Lady Emilia, I am grateful that you would offer. However, that would be..."

"I may not look like much, but I'm confident in my modicum of skill. I have a really strong spirit with me, so I won't slow you down."

Emilia was referring to Puck, who wasn't present at the moment, as she offered her cooperation in the coming battle. Her words made Ram close her eyes as Wilhelm fell into thought for a time.

She had attempted to propose something helpful, but for some reason, Emilia wasn't getting a very good reaction.

"Is there a...problem with that?"

"As a matter of...... Yes. Actually, the marquis strictly demanded that I ensure Lady Emilia confers with Lady Crusch as soon as possible. If I fail in this duty, I shall be fired."

"Roswaal said *that*?!"

Hearing that truly horrified Emilia. When Emilia stared toward Ram, questioning if it was true, Ram's light-red eyes bore into the side of Wilhelm's face, staring, staring, staring—

"...............................Yes, that is indeed what Master Roswaal said."

"Roswaal, what were you thinking...?!"

Ram had sworn fealty to Roswaal; she surely would not lie where her master was concerned. Apparently, he had earnestly worked to check any possible action, knowing that she could not defy him. The evacuation, the alliance—Roswaal probably had everything dancing atop the palm of his hand.

Seeing Emilia clenching her fists in frustration, Wilhelm breathed a sigh. The old man kept his eyes lowered as he spoke.

"Certainly, Lady Emilia, as you stated earlier, evacuating everyone to the royal capital is a difficult undertaking. Given the current situation, let us evacuate half to the capital for the time being."

"What about the other half, then?"

"Per my proposal, the other half shall evacuate to the Sanctuary. Master Roswaal is already headed there, after all, and that place has sufficient space to shelter them and should be quite safe."

"I...I see. You already have it all worked out, then..."

They had already thoroughly examined every concern and misgiving Emilia might have. They persevered, slapping down one doubt after another, until Emilia had no room left to lodge any objections.

This should have been a good thing, but the current Emilia could not help but feel tortured by an overwhelming sense of powerlessness. They had prepared answers to any question she might have, thought through whatever worries she might have, and if she did as she was told, everything would be taken care of through the goodwill of others—

"Hey, doesn't this come off as a little strange? Isn't it too good to be true...?"

"—I beg your pardon!!"

Emilia's voice, seemingly bearing the weight of her doubts, was interrupted by the sound of the door violently opening. When she looked over in surprise, a young man had staggered into the entry hall, looking like he'd just kicked the door in.

The figure was wearing a white robe with a hood that covered him up to the top of the head. He cut in front of the wide-eyed Emilia and vigorously saluted Wilhelm.

"There are signs of strange movements from the group lurking in the forest! We no longer have a moment to lose! If they move with the intent to slaughter, this entire area will become a hellish scene, a sea of blood—!"

"Mm-hmm, is that so... They seem to be moving quicker than we expected. With this many people entering the village, it was only a matter of time until they noticed, I suppose..."

"What shall we do, Captain...er, Sir Wilhelm, the Sword Devil...?!"

"Lady Emilia."

Once Wilhelm received the young man's reports, punctuated with unnecessarily grandiose gestures, he stared sharply at Emilia. Emilia understood from his razor-like gaze that time was short.

Events were already in motion. Things had become urgent enough to make her think that time spent arguing was time wasted.

It wasn't as though she suddenly had no doubts about various parts of the conversation so far. But it was a fact that Ram had sensed an ominous presence in the forest, and Wilhelm had given his word as a man under Crusch's banner concerning the incident involving the letter.

More than anything, with Roswaal currently absent, the right to make decisions for the well-being of the mansion and the village fell to Emilia. The outcome would alter numerous human fates, and because of that, she had to see it through herself.

That role was Emilia's to play at the moment. Duty had to come first.

"Understood. I gratefully accept your kindness. As for explaining to the villagers..."

As soon as she said that, Ram revealed that the most urgent matter had already been resolved.

"Lady Emilia, this has already been taken care of without much issue."

Emilia, surprised at this fact, shifted her thoughts to the household. The existence of the final resident of the mansion, Beatrice, tugged at her mind. She had thought that if they were evacuating, then naturally they had to take Beatrice with them.

"—Beatrice said she was staying behind, and would use the Passage to isolate the archive of forbidden books, so you can evacuate or do whatever else you like on your own."

"Puck?!"

Upon his sudden return, Puck explained the plans of his protégé, with whom he had already spoken. However, when the kitty landed on her shoulder, Emilia stared at him, shaking her head in disbelief.

"How can you just accept that? They said this place is dangerous..."

"In Betty's case, she's much safer inside the Archive. Besides, there's the issue of her pact preventing her from leaving the mansion. You understand, don't you?"

"...It's really unfair to use that as a reason."

Puck groomed his whiskers as he responded to Emilia's dissatisfaction. To Emilia, to Puck, and to Beatrice as well, the word *pact* bore a great deal of meaning...to the point that it left Emilia unable to find the words for a comeback.

"So that's why the girl who's like a cute little sister to me will stay behind at the mansion. It's best if you don't do anything to the mansion, either. Betty may be a sweet, gentle child...but she won't show any mercy."

"I shall take your words to heart, Great Spirit."

Wilhelm solemnly bowed in response to Puck's warning. Watching this with satisfaction, Puck buried himself in Emilia's hair. Then his voice became a whisper only Emilia could hear.

"Do whatever you want to. I'm your ally, and yours alone."

"—We will evacuate. I do not want to subject the villagers to any danger."

At her command, Ram grasped the hem of her skirt and politely curtsied, whereas Wilhelm strongly nodded.

Then Emilia turned her back only upon the youth who had brought in the report—

"That's just the way you are."

Emilia did not notice the youth's tiny murmur.

7

By the time Emilia & Co. met up at the village, the residents had already begun preparing to evacuate.

The villagers seemed to be politely obeying the expeditionary force, with nary a look of worry or concern on their faces, quite methodically proceeding with the work of loading up the dragon carriages.

"Wilhelm and the others are amazing, aren't they?"

Emilia was surprised at how, in contrast to her, they had deftly gained the trust of villagers they had never before met.

But what surprised her the most came when she heard how the dragon carriages had been allotted. When she was guided to a dragon carriage for evacuation and was directed to climb aboard—

"—Please give us your best regards, miss."

With a conflicted look on her face, Emilia stood opposite a girl with reddish-brown hair who was bowing her head.

She'd seen the face of the girl countless times in the village. The children were friendly with Subaru, but she'd seemed particularly fond of him; Emilia believed her name was Petra.

Besides Petra, Emilia was surrounded by other children with faces familiar to her. Every last one introduced themselves to Emilia, who was to ride in the dragon carriage with them.

"Err, this is strange. Is there some kind of mistake?"

As worry crossed Emilia's mind, Ram, standing right beside her, firmly declared, "No, this is the result of an exacting discussion. It cannot be helped. The balance of dragon carriages and numbers of people makes your riding with these children an unavoidable necessity, Lady Emilia."

But her reply was so contrary to Emilia's assumptions that it only served to fan her worries further.

She would be spending numerous hours with the children in the closed quarters of a dragon carriage. It was less that this worried Emilia than that she thought it lacked consideration for the families of the children riding with her. She wondered if it would simply be hard on both sides.

"You can't assign me a different dragon carriage to ride? I mean, the children would be better off that..."

"You assume anyone would be disgusted at having to ride with you, I take it?"

"—"

Emilia's breath caught at having her inner thoughts read. It was the young man in the robe, the same one who'd escorted Emilia and Ram all the way to the village, who had made the borderline offensive remark.

Emilia, surprised, drew close to the youth, whose voice sounded faintly nervous and worked up.

"Have you checked with these children to know? Or did you decide you were hated and detested all on your own?"

"I…know that without having to ask. This is for everyone's sake."

"One dragon carriage, six children…how will your desires come true if you cannot even handle that?"

"How can you possibly—"

When she began to speak harshly in a plaintive-sounding voice, the youth shifted his gaze away from Emilia to Petra. He got down on one knee before her, met her eyes, and quietly asked her, "How about it, Petra? Is the thought of riding the same dragon carriage as the miss hateful to you?"

"—!"

Emilia's cheeks stiffened, her heart pained as the cruel question fell upon her ears. It was a question with a readily apparent answer; his asking it could only be to hurt her. And even if you knew something would hurt, that didn't mean you got used to the pain.

Puck had said it. Whatever form a wound might take, the only thing a new wound carried was a fresh helping of pain. Why, in spite of that, had this young man—

"That's not true at all. I don't think riding with the miss is hateful at all."

"…Eh?"

But with Emilia frozen stiff, Petra walked over, taking hold of her limp, dangling hand. *Hot*, her fingertips felt. With Emilia unable to conceal her surprise, Petra smiled bashfully toward her.

"Miss, you're the young lady with the potato stamps, right? I saw you coming with Subaru for morning radio aerobics all the time."

"That is…"

"I could never see your face, but you seemed to be having fun.

I know, too, you know? I saw how Subaru had lots of fun talking to you. Subaru, really...... That's why I'm not afraid of you, either, miss."

"...Ah."

Listening to Petra's words, Emilia felt a pain deep in her nose, raising her voice. Heat welled up from deep within her eyes, too, and her throat suddenly caught. Her cheeks reddened, and her ears were so hot, they seemed to be burning.

"Miss, won't you ride with us? Everyone's been saying to leave you alone. But I'll hold your hand, so..."

"—Mm...mm."

"You don't have to feel lonely anymore, 'kay?"

"...Mm!"

That innocent, pure, genuine gaze, disconnected from malice and irrationality, granted her salvation.

To Emilia, estrangement was normal, persecution was inevitable, and discrimination taken for granted, so much so that she had been unable to sense the warmth in Petra's eyes and voice. That fact made her chest ache.

"Me too!" "I wanna be with the miss, too!" "Come on, quick!"

Other children made a clamor, running around Emilia however they pleased. As they did so, Ram immediately stuffed the children into the dragon carriage, a sight that got a little snort out of Petra.

"Miss, let's go, too? The others might be a little loud, though."

"...No, that's all right. It's been noisy around me for two months, so I'm used to it by now."

She shook her head, and she understood how the smile came over her as if by nature.

Holding her hand, Petra led her along. The warmth of her hand made Emilia appreciate the closeness of another person.

"Ram, take care of the Sanctuary, please. Protect the villagers well."

"As you wish. Be careful along the way yourself, Lady Emilia."

Grasping her skirt, Ram curtsied politely, nodding with a wry, pleasant smile on her face.

After that, Emilia's gaze searched for the one who had made that exchange come about.

"Allow me to express my thanks to you as... Er?"

She searched for the young man whose good offices had allowed her to break the ice. However, the white-robed youth was nowhere to be seen, leaving Emilia perplexed.

"Where did he run off to?"

Of those hearing Emilia's voice, sounding like she'd been left behind, Ram alone sank her shoulders in exasperation.

8

The figure pushed its way through the branches, trampled the grass, and kept its posture low as it mingled with the green of the forest.

Concealing himself in the dense, overgrown foliage, "he" suppressed his breathing and aura, blending in with the darkness.

The residents of the tiny settlement some three hundred feet or so beyond the forest were being evacuated and led away—so that they might escape the trial.

It was unforgivable. What threatened to occur was unconscionable. To prevent such a thing, the figure had thrown caution to the wind to observe their activities firsthand.

The figure endured feelings of unease as multiple shadowy figures, remaining concealed at "his" command, gathered close with a slight sound of footsteps.

Including the figure, they numbered four—insufficient to launch a general attack, but plenty to slow them down. It was ahead of schedule, but like everything else, this was for the sake of their exalted aims.

"He" put a hand in his pocket and placed the small mirror retrieved from it atop "his" palm. However, its role differed from that of the cosmetic mirrors possessed by girls and women; its role was to "connect" to different mirrors.

—It was a metia, a magical mirror that allowed the user to converse over a long distance with another via the mirror on the other side.

Though metia were scarce by nature, conversation mirrors were numerous among them and comparatively easy to acquire. But even among the disciples, only a few possessed them. This was an honor reserved for the fingers—those whose faith had been recognized, and who had been chosen as the Lord Archbishop's confidants.

"…"

Remaining silent, "he" poured magical energy into the conversation mirror, causing the metia to activate.

It was a process the figure had undertaken several times in the preceding few hours, sending detailed reports about the resources he'd accompanied so that preparations could be made for the trial that must come. Accordingly, an emergency situation like this absolutely had to be reported.

The figure had to communicate with its brethren about the fact that the resources' movements had greatly shifted. They had noticed the movements of "his" brethren, and were nefariously attempting to flee—

"—I see. It was a big mystery how you got in touch with the others, but I guess metia are super convenient. Although I think it's important in communication to show your face to the other party, don't you?"

"—?!"

Suddenly, one of the brethren crouched alongside peered into the conversation mirror, tossing such words "his" way.

The figure hastily looked over, and the next moment, "he" was stricken by a sense of extreme unease. The other party was right next to him, and yet the figure still could not discern the features of the other person's face. It was as if something was stopping his brain from understanding what he was seeing.

"You don't distinguish by face, you distinguish by physical nature. When it comes to that, you and I are like girls in a knitting circle wearing the same perfume. Gives me chills, you piece-of-shit bastard."

As the "white-robed" brethren spoke, he stood up, practically spitting out the declaration.

Then, in front of "him"—Kety, the Witch Cultist, frozen stiff in surprise—the brethren pulled down his hood, revealing rare black hair and foul-looking eyes with the white of the sclera surrounding three sides of each iris—three-whites eyes.

"Your sin is grave, y'know—getting in the way of my sentimental reunion with Emilia and all that."

As the black-haired youth prattled on with frivolity, a taunting, impetuous smile came over his mouth.

The next instant, the indecipherable enchantment surrounding the youth fell away. Kety's eyes could now plainly make out the youth's features, bringing his identity to light.

The features of the traitor who had led the expeditionary force to their doorstep, making a plan that he would oppose them—

"—"

With the most unforgivable of foes before him, Kety reflexively leaped to his feet. There was no need to even look at the two brethren to his sides. They would launch a combined assault on the apostate before them. However—

The instant he drew the cross-shaped blade on his hip, a lower-tone whisper grazed his ear.

"—Too slow."

The next moment, a silver flash raced into the corner of his field of vision, and the brethren to his right and left gushed blood as they crumbled. Their necks had been slashed; it was obvious the blows had been fatal. And then it was Kety's turn—

"I recommend that you do not resist. I do not intend to inflict unnecessary pain."

His efforts had been completely forestalled by the cold tip of a blade against the back of his neck.

Behind him stood a slender knight, and the aged swordsman who had cut down his two brethren. In addition, a cat-eared demihuman stood behind them, all of them brought by the black-haired traitor…

"Subaru Natsuki…!"

"Ohh, I guess it's obvious, but, like, wow, Witch Cultists really do talk. That's a big help."

Shoved against the ground with his arms pinned behind him, Kety glared up at him—the traitor, Subaru Natsuki.

The youth on the receiving end had an outbreak of cold sweat on his brow. He turned to the other three and spoke.

"Well, at least it went without a hitch. Thanks for the assist."

"I admit to half doubting you, but having read them properly this far, I cannot but admit you were correct. If they have been made to dance as you expect, our advantage shall only grow greater."

"Isn't that pretty much a given, *meow*? We started evacuating the village so much earlier than expected that it made him try contacting them in a big hurry."

As the knight and the demihuman concurred with the youth's words, Kety's head was in chaos, filled with hatred and incomprehension.

He didn't understand the meaning of their conversation. It was as if they'd known every last thing in—

"Your face says you don't get it. Well, that can't be helped. This time we're way too good at running rings around ya. Oh, and thank you for helping our disinformation efforts…not that you actually realized you were a double spy."

"—?"

"The gist is, we totally knew you were a spy. As for how we found you…trade secret. So we went through the trouble of laying a trap for the Witch Cult's scout, in other words, you."

Kety was still, eyes wide open, as Subaru Natsuki closed one eye and slowly spelled it out.

And then he stated, "Two hours. You reported to your pals that we were two hours behind schedule."

Raising up two fingers, he wagged them left and right. Kety's eyes remained wide with shock as Subaru continued. "During that time, we'll get Emilia and the others outta here. During that time, we'll crush the fingers flat. During that time, we'll prepare to squish your precious archbishop flat."

At the end of those words, a bold smile came over Subaru Natsuki. And then he issued his declaration of war.

"I'm gonna give you a real good taste of the terror of being crushed by someone three steps ahead of you."

CHAPTER 2
SETTING THE STAGE

1

Returning to the time when the expeditionary force continued its moving conference through the use of Nekt…

"We finally know there's a spy in our midst. If we can make good use of him and feed him false info, we can give Emilia and the others time to flee to safety. Don't you think so?"

"—"

Subaru spoke thus as he divulged a series of information while on the road toward the Mathers domain.

During the time the expeditionary force's thoughts were shared via magic, this opinion sent vigorous arguments flying back and forth. While nodding at their various thoughts, Subaru raised a hand and spoke.

"Hey, listen. Just like we talked about, wiping out the fingers is nonnegotiable for kicking the Archbishop of the Seven Deadly Sins' butt. That said, even just taking out those fingers is easier said than done. We have to be smart about this."

"Purportedly, making use of your physical condition would allow us to draw out and fight the fingers one by one?"

"I can guarantee it. But either way, the fact that they have a spy means whatever we do will get passed on to the enemy. Even if we take out the spy first, they'll know something's up when he misses the regular time to call, so it amounts to the same thing. So I was thinking we flip this around on them and leak intel for him to send them—fake intel."

As he replied to Julius, Subaru recalled the sight of the village being raided at the end of his last go-around. At the time, every last enemy had launched a combined attack on the village from the forest. Given the numbers of raiders, he was sure he was right in thinking so, and also that Petelgeuse had possessed the finger hiding among the traveling merchants.

—In other words, the traveling merchant named Kety, the Witch Cultist embedded with them.

One way or another, he was in contact with the fingers. Likely, unlike the other Witch Cultists accompanying Petelgeuse, he'd been assigned the duty of gathering intelligence about the surrounding area.

"That's why we should turn this back on them. If we fool the spy, we fool the whole Witch Cult."

"So that is why you wish to send Rajan and his group to the traveling merchants and tell them the rendezvous will be delayed?"

Subaru's roundabout statement seemed to clear up Ricardo's doubts, bringing him to agree.

Just like last time around, a small detachment of the Iron Fangs would be sent to greet the traveling merchants cooperating with the evacuation. But this time, those select few would deliver a rendezvous time with Subaru's ruse attached. Before the Witch Cult's spy could rendezvous with the expeditionary force, they'd dispose of a mountain of concerns he wanted dealt with beforehand, making it a race against time.

Incidentally, Subaru had recommended the fox-man and his team, casualties from the last time around, for those select few, hoping to keep them far from the fight.

"So this is less of a proposal and more an update after the fact. You have such a naughty personality, Subawu."

"It's like we're talkin' 'bout the little lady… No peaceful death down that path, y'know?"

"Setting Ferris aside, what's with Ricardo's assessment of his employer…?"

Ricardo was the one working for her, but his appraisal of Anastasia was harsh. The boisterously laughing thought that followed right after made Subaru assume it was simple lighthearted banter.

At any rate, the operation to confuse the spy was already underway. And, accepting this—

"Then our counterespionage plan is settled. Incidentally, what is the source of this information…?"

"How about I say my…nose for the Witch Cult?"

"—That is a thin basis, but I shall take that as meaning you have one. That is my reply."

Julius responded to Subaru's usual vague explanation with his own difficult-to-decipher inner thought. The thoughts he passed through Nekt were opaque compared to those of the others, perhaps because it was his own magic.

But there was no room to doubt the truth of his willingness to cooperate. So it would do for the moment.

"That's fine, but what about the issue with the letter? Leaving it at just the blank page makes things difficult."

"Ehh, why? If it's completely blank, you can write whatever you want on it? Seems convenient to— Ouchie!"

"Sis, please be quiet."

The cat siblings were the next ones to wedge themselves into the telepathic conversation. Actually, behind the telepathic exchange, a torrent of lighthearted thoughts flowed out from Mimi, but everyone was taking that in stride.

For his part, TB was paying serious attention to the operation. Subaru drew his chin in during the kitty siblings' exchange, thinking over how to deal with the blank letter.

After all, thanks to that problem, Ram had launched a surprise attack on the expeditionary force, costing it precious time. The operation was in part a race against time, so a loss like that was to be avoided at all costs.

"What should we do, then?"

TB sent over an ashen, nervous thought, wanting to hear a plan to deal with it. Others beside him also turned their minds toward Subaru, waiting for his reply.

At the center of that attention, Subaru folded his arms and told them how they would deal with the blank letter.

And that method was—

2

In the early morning, just as the world began to awaken, Ram lifted her head, sensing an indecipherable presence.

She was midway along the road cutting through open fields that stretched from the mansion to Earlham Village. Since Emilia had faced a bad experience with the villagers, Ram had left her back at the mansion on her way to prod and persuade the villagers to evacuate.

"—"

There was a slight rustle in the forest. Ram knotted her shapely brows as she sank into thought for a single moment.

Ram was a demon who had lost her horn. By nature, demons were acutely sensitive to changes in the forest and mountains. A sixth sense that differed from the other five informed her of a shift in the wind blowing from the direction of the highway.

Her small nose snorted. Ram, confirming that there was no hint of danger in the immediate vicinity, went down on one knee and concentrated on her forehead. She was activating her supernatural ability of Clairvoyance.

Clairvoyance was a secret art passed down among the demons that enabled them to synchronize with the vision of others, stealing their vision and seeing through their eyes.

Few demons had mastered the art to begin with; currently Ram was probably the only one. While it was activated, her awareness of her own surroundings was greatly diminished, limiting the places she could use it, but it was the crown jewel of reconnaissance abilities.

The master to whom Ram had pledged fealty had many enemies. For that reason, too, the supernatural ability was very helpful.

"—"

She disconnected herself from those deep feelings, concentrating the effect of her supernatural ability, and entered the vision of others.

Even where there were no people to affect, that was no hindrance so long as there were living creatures with the sense of sight. However, creatures with compatible wavelengths were limited, and in the past few days, she had been unable to grasp anything inside the forest where it mattered most.

However, that was not the case this time. She detected multiple compatible wavelengths from the direction of the highway that connected to the village. She entered one of them, seeing through its eyes.

"—"

The creature from which she borrowed that sight was a humanoid riding a giant beast of war—a great dog known as a liger. The rider was small in stature, slowly surveying the area with ferocious energy. He was not on guard, but nor was he at ease.

It was a power to see through the eyes of others. Naturally, his moving in contrast to Ram's will inflicted motion sickness upon her. Ram immediately shifted to a different set of eyes from the next compatible vision, ascertaining the situation anew.

Fortunately, this set of eyes politely stared straight at the road ahead. The height of his gaze matched that of the previous set of eyes, and he too was riding a giant dog. She could scarcely tell the difference.

"...What numbers."

However, that doubt evaporated when a great throng entered her borrowed field of view.

They were a group of forty or fifty people, each and every one armed. They galloped along the highway, tens of minutes away from the village. And she recognized the crest of the lion rampant on the armor of several of the armored men. This was the crest of the House of Karsten, proof they were of the same faction that had declared war via the blank letter the night before.

In other words, it was offensive action by a rival in the royal selection—

"Seizing on Master Roswaal's absence to make their move…!"

Ram understood that it was an emergency situation, urgent circumstances demanding an immediate decision. If their goal was to inflict damage upon the Emilia camp, they would surely occupy Earlham Village.

She had to strike before that could happen, using every means available to her…

And just when Ram gritted her teeth, ready to cut the clairvoyant connection and race to the village—

"…Huh?"

—she let out a dumbstruck voice.

Her feet, ready to set off in a sprint, stopped, and Ram's face grimaced extensively at the sight she beheld through the Clairvoyance.

It was that painful to comprehend just what she was seeing.

"—Barusu?"

A black-haired young man rode a land dragon at the forward tip of the formation, carrying a sign that he turned in every direction—as if to ensure it could be seen from front, back, left, and right.

Upon that placard was written in large characters:

THE LETTER IS WRONG. MY BAD.

3

Carrying those words in the manner of a white flag, Subaru and the rest of the expeditionary force arrived at Earlham Village without incident. However, when Ram appeared to greet them, she had a sour look on her face, and Subaru awkwardly shrank as he stood before her. *Hah!* Ram instantly snorted out as she spoke.

"First you send a blank letter, and now you appear at the head of an armed band? You do not appear to comprehend exactly whose domain this is."

"But you didn't launch a preemptive strike... That means there's room to talk about this, right?"

"That sign was a message for me, obviously. I am the only one who would understand such a thing."

Ram sighed in visible exasperation as she set eyes on the wooden placard Subaru carried at his side. An apology in huge I-script was written on the sign in white paint. This was the master plan Subaru had developed midmarch for countering the blank letter of goodwill—or rather, he'd responded with the blunt truth.

"I should beat you senseless. The characters are so sloppy that I was nearly unable to read them."

"Hey, you taught me these characters! Aren't you used to seeing them by now?!"

"Unfortunately, I forgot about them as quickly as an ingrate forgets the generosity shown to him."

"Unnghhhhh...!"

Ram's characteristically harsh statement left Subaru hemming and hawing, unable to give any retort. Watching his reaction, she folded her arms and continued her lecture.

"So? According to what I have heard, Barusu, you soured Lady Emilia's mood in grand fashion and she abandoned you in the royal capital... How dare you return to show your face?"

"You really have no mercy, do you?! I'm not gonna argue with each and every point, but here I am, daring to return and show my face! Not that I came back empty-handed!"

With a hand, he indicated the expeditionary force lined up behind him to put his exploits from the royal capital on display.

Subaru's declaration caused Ram to narrow her eyes. As she proceeded to survey the expeditionary force, she spoke.

"It is fine to boast, but as your objective is unclear, the humans of the village are on guard. I too am concerned that anything might happen... My songbird heart is nearly ready to burst."

"You mean your heart has wings sprouting from it? Doesn't that make it a really strong heart?"

"If you make too many wisecracks I shall slice that nose off your face."

"Man, it's been a few days and this reunion feels really off-kilt— Wait, my nose?!"

The savage declaration sent Subaru covering his face and backing off a step as his gaze shifted from Ram to the village behind her.

Of course, the ruckus was such that the villagers noticed the expeditionary force immediately, whereupon they turned concerned eyes toward the knights lined up in the village square. However—

"Hey, at the head of them, that's Master Subaru, isn't it?"

"It really is. That's Master Subaru speaking to Miss Ram. He's come back?"

"Ahh, it's Subaru! He's back!"

The villagers' wariness relented slightly when they realized Subaru was acting as the group's representative. Thanks to that, in their eyes, the group was upgraded from "never before seen" to "under the command of someone we know."

"And now we have to upgrade that to 'reliable reinforcements brought by someone we know'..."

"That is no simple matter. In the first place, I have not yet accepted all of this. I cannot readily believe that a letter bearing a wax seal was merely in error."

"That's part of the enemy's trap... You noticed the jerks hiding in the forest, right?"

"_____"

Subaru lowered his voice to a whisper. Ram kept silent with a sober look on her face.

It was plain as day that both the Witch Cult lurking in the forest and the blank letter incident had put Ram on guard the last time around. Subaru addressed Ram's concerns as he moved the conversation forward.

"Ferris, Wilhelm, over here! Ram, you know both of them, too, right?"

Obeying Subaru's call, the pair came over to his side. "Yes," said Ram, looking over Ferris and Wilhelm as they stood side by side; her expression vanished as she straightened her back.

The pair from Crusch's camp acknowledged Rem's posture by granting her their respect.

"I am called Wilhelm Trias. I have come as Lady Crusch's representative."

"I'm Ferris, Lady Crusch's personal knight. Old Man Wil's the captain of the group behind us, so that makes Ferri the vibrant flower, *meow*."

The austere Wilhelm and the flippant-to-the-last Ferris were a shining example of polar opposites. Ram responded to both extremes by politely grasping the hem of her skirt and making a formal curtsy.

"I graciously accept your polite greetings. I am called Ram. I am employed here, at the mansion of Marquis Roswaal L. Mathers, in the capacity of senior servant."

Ram's cheekiness in naming herself senior servant made Subaru grimace, but he held his tongue. Ram was indisputably in charge of the mansion while Rem was absent. Personally, he would have preferred she call herself *acting senior servant*, or if not *senior for a day*, then at least *senior servant for the last week*, but oh well.

"Either way, these two and the people behind us are proof that Crusch is cooperating with us. This is what Roswaal wants, too. No complaints, right?"

"If Master Roswaal wills it, Ram shall obey— It would seem he accomplished his objective in leaving you behind at the capital. Though I believe he shall have your head for the blank letter, Barusu."

"Hey, can you cut it with the violent imagery? Why do you have such a brutal thought process?"

He felt like he was back in medieval times, but Ram freshly ignored his complaints. Instead she turned toward the representatives of the reinforcements.

"So you have been traveling with my apprentice servant... My condolences."

"Though he is prone to exorbitant actions and showing too much of his emotions, Sir Subaru is a person of high promise. Even at my age, he has aided me many times."

"Ferri won't go as far as Old Man Wil, but...well, I'll just take Ram's words as they were offered. I'll say, mmm, I think he's brushed up a little, *meow*."

The assessments from Wilhelm and Ferris made Ram sigh with an even more grudging look on her face.

Though the topic was a rather uncomfortable one, Subaru scratched his cheek, glossing over how he really felt. Immediately after, he clapped his hands together and started over, explaining the situation to Ram in detail.

"Anyway, leave smashing the enemies in the forest to the expeditionary force. I want you to cooperate with that and something in a different direction. Are you willing?"

"That depends on the details. I do not wish to make a hasty promise only to have Barusu's filthy, poisonous fangs sink into me."

"Hey, the looks I give you aren't that dirty, you know?!"

"That's a boy for you, not saying it was zero..."

Faced with Ram's poison tongue, Ferris's casual banter, and stern eyes shifted his way, Subaru cleared his throat. From there, having kept them waiting long enough, he elucidated the circumstances required, both in front of and behind the curtain, to make his plan come to fruition.

"I want your help in picking where to evacuate the people in the village and to guide them there. I want to make sure not to involve the villagers while we fight the enemies in the forest."

"I understand what you are saying. However, we have no means of escape."

"I've arranged the legs to carry 'em out on. From here on out, traveling merchants with dragon carriages will be assembling here, bit by bit from every direction. We'll have the villagers get aboard and haul 'em out."

"Assembled from all directions…? How?"

"—Money. We'll just have to eat the costs, okay?"

Subaru's "insurance policy" had cost a great deal of money. The treasury paying it was Roswaal's, and on top of that, it was without his having granted permission. Ram sighed deeply when she discerned that from Subaru's manner of speech.

"…Understood. I will support your effort. It is an emergency, after all."

"Seriously?! Huge help! Worst case, I was gonna have to promise to pay it back when I make it big!"

"Only those who are fit to actually rise to prominence may promise such a thing— However, Ram's consent is by no means the end of the matter."

After giving a stern assessment about his future prospects, Ram shifted an even sterner look over her shoulder. Subaru didn't need to follow her gaze; he knew exactly what Ram was trying to tell him.

The people of Earlham Village were behind Ram, still anxious about their situation. Even if Ram was willing to lead them out, convincing *them* would prove the highest hurdle of all.

He had prior experience from the last go-around, but the result of that effort still tasted bitter in his mouth. The closest word he had to describe the emotion summoned by that memory was *fear*.

He'd only scratched the surface of the discrimination and repudiation facing Emilia.

"_____"

Time was short—precious time gained from feeding false information to the Witch Cult. And yet, Subaru hesitated, wondering what the first words out of his mouth ought to be.

"Subawu, if you can't do it, I'll…"

"—Ferris."

When Ferris tried to be considerate to Subaru, offering to speak in his place, Wilhelm called his name. A single glance from the Sword

Devil halted Ferris's gesture in its tracks. He turned his eyes toward Subaru and spoke.

"Sir Subaru, this is not a duty you may shirk... You understand, yes?"

When Wilhelm asked this in a low voice, Subaru winked once and nodded firmly.

Subaru gave Ferris a thankful glance for his concern before stepping past Ram and advancing straight into the village square. To the front were the villagers with worried faces; to his back were his comrades in the expeditionary force. He felt the tension from both stab into him.

As for the first words out of his mouth, those very important words, he still hadn't decided. But he would begin with the best word for wiping away the villagers' concerns and fears.

"Everyo—"

"—Master Subaru. Please, let us drop all pretenses. Everyone in the village understands."

However, Subaru couldn't even get that first word out.

The one speaking, interrupting Subaru's word-without-a-plan, was the cornerstone of the village—a small-statured, white-haired, elderly man. He was the one the villagers called Muraosa, a name in no way related to his occupation as village headman. Normally his demeanor made one suspect he was a senile old man, but at that moment, his voice and gaze held no trace of that whatsoever.

Subaru felt overwhelmed by the glint in his eye as the elder touched his beard and continued.

"We understand how dire things must be if you have brought such dangerous persons to deal with it. We have already heard from Miss Ram about the...suspicious presence in the forest."

"No, that's..."

"Stop trying to fool us...! We knew before anyone said a word!!"

Following in Muraosa's wake, the leader of the village's young men raised a bitter cry. The last go-around, his plea had been the trigger for the villagers to put their fears and anxieties on display. This time proved no different.

"So the ones in the forest, they really are…!"

"What's with our lord? Didn't he foresee that this would happen?!"

"Why did the lord speak in support of a half-elf…of a half-demon…?"

The young man's cry ripped the bandage off, causing the villagers to look at one another and share their fears and worries. It was the sight Subaru had most feared, and had most wanted to avoid.

It was the worst of all spectacles, for even with an intervening Return by Death, and so many valiant efforts to deal with so many things, he still hadn't known how to stop things from getting to this point—

"_____"

He probably couldn't eliminate such a deep-seated discriminatory mind-set in that one moment. When he recalled events from the last time around, he thought that a similar compromise would make things easier.

Considering the menace posed by the Witch Cult, the right decision was to kick other issues down the road. If he gained their grudging acceptance, prioritizing the evacuation, then—

"The girl I know, she acts tough, she's stubborn, hardheaded…and she worries about anyone seeing that she's lonely."

"_____"

The words Subaru spoke seemed wholly unrelated to his inner thought process.

The villagers gazed in bewilderment, wondering what in the world Subaru was saying. The members of the expeditionary force had similar reactions. However, their expressions of surprise abated as they listened closely.

They offered their ears, listening to Subaru's words.

"She always chooses to hurt herself for someone else's sake. Even though she gets hurt so easily, she always picks the path that winds up with her getting hurt. She's gentle and kindhearted to the core, she fusses over things like a little kid, she gets teary-eyed even when she hasn't eaten a green bepper, she makes such a cute face when she smiles…"

"What are you talking abo—?"

"—I'm talking about Emilia, the half-elf up at the mansion."

When someone interrupted, Subaru replied with a calm voice.

His answer surprised the villagers. The little smile coming over Subaru's lips surprised them even more. Given the circumstances, and their words of distress but a few moments before, his reaction seemed very much out of place.

"I understand why you're worried. Also that you think the cause of everything is R...Master Roswaal, your lord, and his support of a half-elf girl in the royal selection that began at the royal capital."

"_____"

"That girl's name is Emilia. Really, you all know her already, don't you? She's the girl who's been spending months alongside you."

Subaru's exhortation made the villagers exchange glances. From their reactions, there had to be recognition remaining within their memories. Even if, all that time, her face and her identity had been hidden, they'd seen her with Subaru in the village many times, and at the very least, they remembered the time they'd spent with her.

"I understand that you're all worried and scared. I also understand that when the chips are down, it feels good to blame things on something that's easy to understand."

It was human instinct to protect the mind by slamming the emotions into something nearby. Subaru could not criticize them for that. He, of all people, didn't have the right to do so.

But he chastised himself. His heart was tormented because he understood this so well. Once upon a time, Subaru had coped with pain the way the villagers were doing in the present.

"I'm sure, though, you all actually understand. Pushing your worries onto someone else won't make things better."

"_____"

"That girl is someone who smiled with everyone. That girl is someone who wants to laugh with everyone. I know. She's said so. I want you to stop ignoring that, and stop hurting her."

He had no confidence that his own voice lacked worry and sorrow. He wanted to punch himself for having the gall to say such a thing.

After all, it was Subaru who had hurt Emilia, ignored her feelings, and trampled upon her heart more than anyone.

He'd regretted it at the time. The grief had pierced Subaru's chest ever since. Maybe that was why.

He regretted allowing her to make that face. He regretted making her put on that face.

He didn't want anyone else to go through that.

"Please—I'm begging you."

Subaru lowered his head toward the villagers as he made his earnest plea.

The thing he was asking seemed completely unrelated to their most imminent problems, a waste of precious time. Even though Subaru had to speak to them about evacuating, his words were about something completely different. It was as if he was reconfirming for himself just what terrible things had been said to Emilia over and over.

"_____"

Indeed, the villagers looked conflicted, at a loss as to what reaction they ought to have to Subaru's words. Even if it had been the topic they were speaking about, the conclusion clashed with the issue at hand.

Mutual bewilderment left them perplexed. However, that was not the only thing born from it.

"—Petra?"

Hearing the sound of small footsteps, Subaru called out the name of the little girl walking to his side.

The girl with reddish-brown hair—Petra—was a village girl Subaru knew well. She responded to Subaru's call with a nod as she reached Subaru's side, turning around as she stood to face the villagers with him.

Then her next words proved that she did not only *seem* to be taking his side—she was.

"Why won't anyone listen to what Subaru's saying?"

It was guileless. It was brutally honest. That was why her chastising tore a hole into their hearts.

"Subaru's so worried, he looks about to cry. Why won't anyone help him?"

"That's..."

"When I was in trouble, when everyone was in trouble, Subaru came through, didn't he? He'll probably come through for us today, too, right? Then why...?"

Adults had too many walls up to launch the attack called "innocence" that only children were capable of. With the adults cowed into silence, Petra gazed sadly at them before grasping Subaru's hand.

"The older girl at the mansion, that's the girl always wearing white, isn't it? She was the one bringing potato stamps when we did the radio aerobics."

"...Yeah, that's right. She was the stamp girl. She wanted to mingle with everyone, but she couldn't just come out and say so. That's just how she is."

Subaru grinned as Petra's words brought him back to the peaceful days they'd spent together.

It became a ritual. Every day, Emilia would accompany Subaru down to the village and do radio aerobics with the villagers. Emilia was always watching when Subaru gave his stamp of approval with the potato stamps he'd carved himself.

These everyday scenes were the tangible bonds Emilia had formed with the villagers.

That fact made understanding and hesitation rise upon the adults' faces. But no adult grumbling or hesitation had any traction with children. Other hands rose as different children rushed over to Subaru's side.

"I'm okay with Big Sis, too!" "If Petra's fine with her, then I'm fine with her!" "We won't let Big Bro be the only one to act cool!" "Subaru's gonna cry, so we've gotta help him!" "Yeah!!"

The children made a ruckus; their voices seemed to blow the previous atmosphere away. Seeing the children lined up against them, the anxiety-ridden adults glanced at each other's faces.

They needed one final push. Faced with their indecision, Subaru

stepped forward. With both arms, he held on to the children, pulling them in as tightly as he could.

"I don't expect everyone to accept her just like that. But I want an
opportunity without you rejecting her at the start. I want you to give
her a chance."

"A chance...?" .

"A chance to be a girl you can get along with...a chance for you to
understand each other."

As Subaru elaborated on his words, his hands let go of the children he had held, freeing him to get on his knees and show that his
resolve went far beyond bowing.

"_____"

Even Ram's eyes widened as murmurs spread.

But of all assembled, it was Wilhelm, Ferris, and the other members of the expeditionary force behind Subaru who watched his
entreaty in silence.

It was enough. Though it was embarrassing, he had no reason to
hesitate.

"Everyone, there's a lot of things I'd like to say, but right now, this
is the only thing I want to ask of you. And one thing more: Let us
protect the time needed to make that chance happen."

"_____"

"Please... This is why I came back."

His voice came to a halt. The villagers were silent.

That was to be expected—as far as they were concerned, Subaru
was their savior, yet there he was, pressing his own forehead to the
ground as he made his plea...a plea to "let them" protect.

Their positions were completely reversed. But the sight of the
Subaru they knew like that was—

"—Oh geez, Master Subaru, there's just no winnin' against you."

Speaking those words, and roughly scratching his head in the
process, was none other than the leader of the young men who had
caused their eruption of worry to begin with. He had a guilty look
on his face as he walked over to Subaru and reached out with a
hand.

A dumbstruck Subaru gazed blankly as that hand grabbed his shoulder and pulled him to his feet.

Then, with Subaru having yet to say anything, he spoke.

"If you're gonna say you'll protect us and put that much into it… guess it can't be helped."

The conflicted young man's statement was as contagious as the initial worry had been. His words were the trigger for the villagers to say with quaking voices:

"It is so terrible getting old. I'm driven to tears so easily…"

"Goodness, he really is so much trouble. It's blackmail, I tell you."

Complain as they might, the warmth and relief in their voices left Subaru agape. Petra thrust a finger against his forehead, still smeared with dirt, and spoke.

"Subaru, your face is all dirty!"

Petra's words sent the uncontrollable urge to laugh spreading throughout the village.

He knew it was a stretch. He thought they'd say it was too far. And yet, they'd accepted his plea anyway.

The villagers' smiling faces made Subaru sigh with relief.

Truly, the sight was the same as on the days they'd spent to date.

"…Thanks, everyone."

"That is our line, Master Subaru."

This time, the words of Muraosa, representing the consensus of the village, nearly did bring Subaru to tears.

4

And 'twould have been a far prettier tale if the matter had ended there, but…

"Am I mistaken, or did you not actually say anything about the most important part?"

"A, aa—!"

Subaru was trying to hide his half-tearful face when Ram's impartial observation snapped him out of it. Reflecting upon her words, he realized that he really hadn't explained any of the most important part at all.

He was so focused on the parts relating to Emilia that he'd completely forgotten about the plan to evacuate the villagers.

"Oh man, I messed up…"

"Just when I thought you had become somewhat useful. It seems Barusu will be Barusu."

Feeling Ram's disappointed gaze, Subaru, unable to summon any excuse, immediately turned back around to explain things to the villagers. "It cannot be helped," said Ram to him, shaking her head as she spoke.

"I shall explain about the evacuation and accompanying compensation in your place. Barusu, return to your underhanded schemes."

"Uh, that's all right? Er, I mean, you'll be all right?"

"It is you who are not *all right*, Barusu. Can you switch to speaking to the village's humans about practical matters in a heartbeat? Your personality is hardly suited to it."

"Suppose you're right! It's embarrassing, but I'm counting on you, Older Sis!"

"—?"

Ram was basking in his respectful words when she cocked her head with a questioning look. Then she headed toward the villagers. This was Ram, blessed with a great deal of comprehension and insight. Tossing the rest of the explanation to her would doubtlessly turn out all right.

This done, the next issue was—

"—Subaru, I would like to finally move the issue forward."

Julius said that just as Subaru was switching mental gears. Subaru greeted his words with a nod and headed back to the expeditionary force's ranks. They had to shift to the next phase of the operation.

Upon his return, Ferris smiled at Subaru and casually sent a wave his way.

"Subawu, you did great with that speech~. You moved even Ferri's heart."

"Don't dig it back up! And don't lie! And really don't dig that up! It's embarrassing!"

"There is nothing to be ashamed of. You very much said it in your own way, and because of that, you moved the hearts of the villagers to such an ext—"

"Don't dig it back up! Leave it in the ground! We're talking about the next operation!"

Subaru yelled both at Ferris, clearly full of malice, and Julius, clearly devoid of malice, as he dragged the topic back.

Events to come would proceed as they'd hammered out in mid-march. Once convincing the villagers was taken care of, they'd rendezvous with the detachment with the traveling merchants and evacuate the civilians. During that time, they needed to deal with feeding false info to the Witch Cult and—

"…Deceive Lady Emilia with a forked tongue, and shoo her far, far away with the people of the village, *meow*."

"Watch how you say it! Even if it fits the plan, it sounds way too bad that way!"

"Because I can't agree with it, *meow*. Why do you need to send Lady Emilia far away? Lady Emilia has both a reason to fight, and the power to do so… Am I wrong?"

Of the entire plan, this was the only point Ferris saw fit to disagree with. Subaru and Ferris didn't see eye to eye on Emilia's place in the plan.

When he thought back, Ferris was the one who'd brought Emilia into battle during the final fight in the village. Ram seemed to have helped convince her, but Ferris's assessment of Emilia's power might have proven correct.

At least, as far as Emilia's having the power to slug it out with even Petelgeuse—

"—Even so, I don't want to let Emilia fight the Witch Cult."

"Haah, we're talking past each other…"

Seeing Ferris slump his shoulders with an exasperated air made Subaru feel bad, but he wouldn't take back his view. It was the one thing he would not budge on. Subaru's selfishness—or rather, the deep-rooted bad premonition in his chest—made him want Emilia kept away from the Witch Cult, by extreme measures if need be.

The premonition was probably founded in the look on the side of Emilia's face when she'd defeated Petelgeuse at the end of the last time around. The madman's death had made tears trickle for reasons even she did not understand.

"Ferris. Sir Subaru has his own feelings on the matter. Sir Subaru has his desires where Lady Emilia is concerned, just as you have your expectations for Lady Crusch."

"Old Man Wil..."

"It is doubtless you prefer some outcomes over others. Surely you can understand his earnest feelings."

It was Wilhelm who interjected, having held his peace during the dispute up to that point. The old swordsman's words made Ferris's cheeks tighten; he subconsciously touched the dagger on his hip.

"Just as you adore Lady Crusch, Sir Subaru wishes for Lady Emilia's well-being— A boy is concerned for the welfare of the girl he loves. It is only nature."

"Having it said that bluntly makes me feel a little blushy and pathetic, but..."

Subaru scratched his cheek, welcoming Wilhelm's support with a pathetic look. Ferris had a pouting look on his face, but he did not offer any further rebuttal. The knights around them gave Subaru warm looks as well.

"Anyway! We're gonna do this just like we worked out! We'll set up the scenario so Emilia listens to reason. Ferris, Wilhelm, I'm counting on you for some really persuasive backup!"

"Understood."

"Sure thing~!"

When the two freshly acknowledged their role as persuaders, Subaru cut the conversation off then and there. If Ram pulled off convincing the villagers, the remaining issues were relatively few. Subaru turned around and spoke.

"OK, Julius. About that favor I asked about earlier. How is..."

"—Do you mean me? I've been listening the whole time."

Everyone's breath caught as a third party's voice interjected at that juncture, the very end of the exchange. Subaru, the only one who realized the identity of the speaker, naturally looked up. And then—

"Heya, long time no see, Puck. How've you been?"

He smiled toward Puck—the little cat swishing his tail as he floated in the sky.

The presence of the suddenly appearing Great Spirit surprised the expeditionary force, putting it extremely on edge. Puck, glancing at their reaction, accepted Subaru's greeting with a stroke of his own whiskers as he spoke.

"Mm, I'm in a very good mood. Right now, I can easily dispose of an insect pestering my beloved daughter."

"This is an awkward question, but this insect to which you refer…"

"Do you really need to ask?"

Puck's eyes remained round as a ghastly, overpowering aura poured from his entire body.

That sense of antagonism made tension run through not only Subaru, but the entire expeditionary force as well. The knights, sensitive to hostility, immediately put their hands to the hilts of their swords, an understandable reaction.

Though he was bathed in their wary stares, Puck's ghastly aura did not relent as he continued, "Subaru, I have a few things to say to you. Do you know what they are?"

"…I broke my promise to Emilia. On top of that, I came back against her orders. Those are my sins, and I won't make any excuse for them."

"—"

Subaru's reply made Puck's cheeks twitch. These were Subaru's answers to the questions Puck had tossed his way—for once already he had experienced that pop quiz when he drew Puck's ire.

At the time, Subaru had been unable to say anything to the enraged Puck. He'd hurt Emilia through his own selfish actions, and as a result had let her die; he couldn't speak a single word. That was why—

"Of course you're angry at me for all that. If your mind won't be set at ease until you punish me, I'm prepared to accept and face whatever punishment you have to give...but now is not the time."

He'd broken his promise, trampled on her pleas, and Subaru had added to those sins by coming back. But he absolutely would not permit the final and worst among them—letting her die—come to pass.

"Danger's nipping at Emilia's heels. I want to do something about it. I want to take her fate of facing terrible things, grind it into sand, and blow it away. Please, work with me so I can do that."

"...You sound quite...full of yourself."

"Yeah, I'm a man who's full of himself. You didn't know?"

When Puck spoke in a low voice, Subaru closed one eye and replied thus. Hearing this, Puck folded his short arms. Then the little cat made a tiny grunt and spoke.

"Somehow...you've changed, Subaru, but at the same time, you haven't."

"That's 'cause human nature ain't an easy thing to change."

"I suppose not. Methods aside, it seems you still treasure Lia in your thoughts."

A moment after he spoke the words, the ferocious pressure that had dominated the entire area to that point abated.

Freed from the sense of menace, which had made him feel like his entire body was being frozen, Subaru sighed at length. The same went for the expeditionary force, Julius and Wilhelm included. In particular, Ferris exaggeratedly patted his own chest.

"W-we're all right now? No one's killing us all of a sudden, *meow*?"

"Relax. We're brothers in kitty ears, yes? Do I look like that mean and scary a spirit to you?"

Puck responded lightheartedly to Ferris's gloomy words, visibly puffing his cheeks up. His demeanor until a moment before had seemed like a bad joke, but one way or another, the spirit's anger seemed to have been assuaged.

"Well, I wasn't *that* angry in the first place. I've been quietly eavesdropping on the villagers for a while now, you see."

"So that's where you've been?! Then you knew what I was trying to do all along?!"

"Mm, it makes a nice story…enough that it almost softened me up before I realized it."

"Don't flip this around! Talk seriously, would you?! This whole discussion's for Emilia's sake!"

Subaru was happy that they were shooting the breeze like normal, but on the other hand, he was eager to gloss over how much it had gotten under his skin. After that, he looked over his shoulder, grimacing Julius's way.

"And you should've mentioned you managed to call Puck over. I was shakin' in my boots."

"I did not surprise you intentionally. I knew the Great Spirit was present at the same time the buds made their return… I am relieved that your conversation ended peacefully."

"Well…I do feel the same way…"

Sharing Julius's relief, Subaru slumped his shoulders in exasperation.

Calling Puck to the village was one of the tasks Subaru had asked Julius to do—to have him send his quasi-spirits to the mansion and bring Puck back without Emilia's being the wiser.

This was to gain his cooperation in the skullduggery required to get Emilia to evacuate.

"If Ram, the villagers, and Puck are all on the same page…"

"Lia won't be able to really put her foot down, huh? I really must say, though, you've scrupulously prepared."

Puck made a strained smile at Subaru's attention to detail. But Subaru shook his head at the little cat.

"We're facing the Witch Cult. Nothing's too much where those guys are concerned."

"The Witch Cult…"

The term made Puck's eyes go slightly distant. It was the reaction of someone who'd encountered them somewhere before. In point of fact, on previous go-arounds, Puck had really hated the Cult. Subaru thought that correlation went even beyond their causing harm to Emilia, but…

"—So you want to fool Lia into going with you, but how exactly are you going to do this?"

"Hey, watch how you say it! Having even you putting it like that gets a guy bent out of shape!"

However, before Subaru could inquire about that connection, Puck, back to his normal self, switched the topic.

Puck was right to want the details of the plan. Pushing his misgivings down the road and prioritizing the evacuation plan for Emilia and the others was the proper call to make.

"You know the plan from all your eavesdropping, don't you? After that…my secret weapon comes into play."

"Secret weapon?"

Puck cocked his head at the grandiose language. Meanwhile Subaru revealed his trump card: a white robe packed into his bag. Subaru immediately put the robe on; he wasn't built much bigger than its proper owner, so he had no trouble wearing it.

"Plus, that faint whiff of sweet perfume is one hell of a motivator for me…!"

"I wouldn't really call that a secret weapon, but it seems to be a robe with an odd enchantment on it."

"Certainly, one robe's not enough for me to cure Emilia's confidence issues…"

The proper owner of the white robe was, in fact, Emilia. Incidentally, Subaru said "Emilia's" because Emilia was an acid burning through his own thoughts. He'd be able to speak with Emilia, touch her, and even savor her lingering aroma. His confidence and emotional stability were both shaky.

Either way, the "Emilia's" part was a joke, but the power of the robe itself was no laughing matter.

"This robe's convenient goods handcrafted by Roswaal himself, and apparently has a Block Identification enchantment embedded in it. It's Emilia's personal property to begin with…but it's not like I stole it, okay?"

He thought back as the details of the abominable time when he'd obtained the object came rushing back. It was the robe that Emilia had thrown at him when she was arguing with him during their breakup at the royal palace.

In the time since, Subaru had always kept the robe stuffed in his bag, never letting it out of his grasp. Now it served a crucial role.

"Whatever its origins might be, what do you...... Ahh, so that is your plan."

"Now I don't have to explain, but that knowing face of yours still annoys me."

"One's nature is a troublesome thing. In my opinion, your nature is a rather complex one as well."

The words made Subaru feel like Julius was seeing right through him, causing him to demonstrate his dismay with an exaggerated snort. After that, Subaru shifted his gaze toward Puck.

"So there you have it. We'll be putting on a play for Emilia. You'll be acting, too, and I'm counting on you to help me explain all this after we settle everything."

"I'll put on an act, but make up with her yourself. That, Subaru, is up to you."

"Gnnn..."

Subaru groaned in frustration at being refused to the bitter end. He couldn't expect any cooperation from Puck in making up with Emilia. It was something he would have to accomplish on his own power.

Then that meant Puck would cooperate with everything else. Namely—

"So Puck, on that note, I have one favor to ask you."

"Mm, what is it?"

"Isn't it obvious? —Convincing the hermit back at the mansion."

Subaru winked to Puck as he spoke the words, broaching the final remaining problem.

5

"Did I think I would ever again have a chance to look upon that stupid face, I wonder?"

The instant he entered the room, the girl in charge of the archive greeted him with a sharp voice. Hearing the poisonous greeting to which he was accustomed, Subaru spontaneously broke out in a smile.

This was a mysterious room, dominated by countless shelves and the books packed into those shelves. This was an archive that existed nowhere in the world—Roswaal's archive of forbidden books, protected by its librarian, Beatrice.

Through use of teleportation magic known as the Passage, the archive of forbidden books was connected to doors in the mansion at random. That, Subaru knew already, but what truly surprised him this time around was—

"I never thought it was connected to doors in the village. You're actually a pretty incredible magic user, aren't you?"

"…If all you wanted to do was talk, you asked Puckie to do a favor for nothing."

"Right now, I wanted to get a little foothold before moving on to the main subject. Sheesh, no patience at all…"

Subaru, receiving an even harsher response than usual, made a very slightly conflicted face as he cocked his head. In contrast to Subaru, the girl in the elegant dress made a weary sigh that was incongruent with her outward appearance. The girl with creamy hair in vertical rolls had a sullen face as she sat upon a wooden footstool.

Beatrice—that was her name. She was the guardian protecting the archive of forbidden books, though Subaru's image of her as part of his busy mansion life was far stronger.

Hence, she too was someone related to Subaru whom it would be unthinkable to leave behind in the mansion.

This was the situation engendered by Puck connecting the Archive to a door in the village. More accurately, it was the result of Puck calling and Beatrice employing the Passage to make the connection.

At the very least, it gave them a chance to talk. Relieved at that fact, Subaru began to broach the subject.

"How much do you know about what's going on outside? I mean, have you heard?"

"Have I heard anything from anyone, I wonder? I am not in the habit of casually conversing with the people of the mansion to begin with…but perhaps I understand the gist of it regardless?"

"The gist being…"

"—The Witch Cult."

Unlike Subaru, carefully choosing his words, Beatrice spoke the term with disgust from the bottom of her heart.

"I am aware that those miscreants are lurking in the mansion's vicinity. Perhaps I even know that you and Puckie intend to sneak that blockhead of a girl out of this place?"

"Is that so? Well, if you know that much, it becomes a short conversation. If anything, it's a huge help."

He was surprised by her unexpected grasp of the circumstances, but he warmly welcomed the fact that he didn't need to make a long-winded explanation. In particular, not having to explain the menace the Witch Cult posed made things a very different story.

After all, the Witch Cult was like a natural disaster, a symbol of malice across the entire world—

"Anyway, the situation's just as you said. I don't deny I'm sneaking Emilia out, either. I got through to Ram and Puck, so that leaves getting you to come with m—"

"I am not going with you."

"Ah?"

Subaru tried to get things in order as quickly as possible, but Beatrice cut him off with a single sentence. Her declaration made Subaru open his eyes wide. Beatrice's eyes slowly narrowed.

Then, with eyes lacking any emotion, she continued her words.

"Did I say I am not going with you, I wonder? I do not intend to leave this archive of forbidden books, let alone leave the mansion itself. Now that you know this, would you get out already, I wonder?"

"Wait a minute! What are you sa…? You're not seeing the situation! Well, I'll explain!"

"I do not require an explanation. Betty will stay here. Does she have any intention of debating it, I wonder?"

Speaking bluntly, Beatrice let her eyes fall to the book sitting upon her lap. It was the usual sight of her concentrating on an overly large book, making it plain she was serious about not evacuating.

"Like I'm gonna back down now. Don't you dare cut off the conversation on your own."

"Betty has finished speaking. No matter how much you might arbitrarily continue, Betty's conclusion will not change. Do you have any more time to waste than she does, I wonder?"

"Ugh... If you understand that much, give me a hand and behave while I lead you out!"

"I refuse. No matter who comes—yes, no matter who comes, they shall not enter this archive of forbidden books."

Beatrice did not even look Subaru's way as she made the statement, a cold, ghastly aura flowing from her into Subaru. He understood that the feeling creeping up his spine was a side effect of the magical energy pouring out of the girl.

"—"

Beatrice was a powerful magic user. That power was not limited to the Passage alone. Perhaps, in truth, she hid such might that the Witch Cult could not defeat her. Her present poise suggested as much.

"—! Even so, I'm bringing you with me anyway."

"You are still going on about..."

"It's not a question of whether you're strong or not! You're a girl, and little, and that's reason enough! I don't need any other reason not to leave you behind where you'll be in danger, damn it!"

Cowed by the feeling of oppression, Subaru shouted and marched across the floor of the archive even so.

The sight of him advancing, and the content of his words, made Beatrice's eyes fly wide. Then the girl closed her eyes, her face looking like she was enduring suffering.

"...Betty will not go with you. Could you please stop attempting to bewitch me, I wonder?"

"I'm not wrong. You're the one who's wrong— That's my answer. We're done here."

"So obstinate. I hate that about you."

As Beatrice made that frail murmur, Subaru walked over, taking her slender arm in his hand. It was the slender arm of a little girl, no matter how powerful a magic user she might be.

He didn't want to leave her there alone. It wasn't right.

"—"

Without a word, he pulled on Beatrice's arm, leading her down from the footstool. If he led her through the door of the archive of forbidden books and back to the village, even Beatrice couldn't complain then.

"Because no matter how important this place is, it's not worth as much as your life."

"—!"

"Beatrice?"

With the door right before their eyes, Beatrice's feet suddenly came to a stop. Subaru, suspicious of her reaction, looked back—only for his breath to catch at the terrified look on her face.

Beatrice looked between the door of the archive of forbidden books and Subaru, back and forth, and finally spoke.

"...Can I truly do this, I wonder?"

"What do you mean, can you..."

"I have a pact. Betty is the guardian of this room, this archive of forbidden books, and will surrender it to no one..."

"Talking about pacts again..."

The word *pact* had barred Subaru's path more than once. Not only was Emilia bound by them, but Beatrice, too, hindering Subaru's actions.

"I'm sick of hearing about them. You stick to pacts too darn much. You've gotta think outside the box!"

"—! Can a human like you comprehend the weight of this pact, I wonder?! Just how important pacts are to Betty, to Puckie...!"

"What's this human this, human that... Hey, Beatrice, wait!"

With a face ready to break into tears, Beatrice shook her arm loose from Subaru, turning her empty left hand toward him. The gesture was the one she used when driving the pesky Subaru out of the room.

Always she unleashed her magical power the next moment. But this time—

"—*Keh.*"

For a moment she hesitated.

Thus, during that time, Subaru grasped Beatrice's arm once again.

"I've got y..."

"Aa—"

That instant, their eyes met. And when Subaru beheld the fear and despair so powerfully displayed by her eyes, the sleeve of her arm slipped through his fingers.

A second later, he was enveloped by a shock wave that knocked his feet clear off the archive of forbidden books' floor.

"Bea—"

"—Farewell."

His vision contorted before he even had a chance to call her name. The spatial distortion swallowed up his flesh, sending him beyond the door that ought not to exist as she forcibly severed the link to the archive of forbidden books.

"___"

He raised his voice. But it did not reach her. His vision was covered in light, rendering him unable to see.

Not the door to the archive of forbidden books, not Beatrice's crying face, nothing.

"—ther."

She watched as the door shut before her eyes, and the sight of the youth vanished from her vision. Then the girl hugged herself with her quivering arms, haltingly murmuring to herself.

"—Mother."

That was all Beatrice said in her tiny, tearful voice.

Her eyes were dry. Her tears had already vanished. Even so, her expression remained one of grief as she spoke.

"How much longer...how much longer, must Betty...?"

Carried by mournful steps, Beatrice collapsed upon the footstool at the center of the room. Then her arms stretched far to one side of the stool—seizing hold of the book resting upon it, clutching it in her arms.

"Mother…Mother, Mother…!"

Like a lost little girl trying to cling to her mother, Beatrice continued to clutch the thick book in her arms, calling out over and over in a sobbing, tearful voice.

But the black-bound book she clutched in her arms would not give her an answer.

6

His vision contorted, and a shock wave came. The feeling of his back hitting something hard made his breath catch.

"—Ha."

With a short snort, he softened the coming impact. He was now on his back, limbs spread wide, and Subaru's vision was filled by the blue sky; he could feel the ground through his back— Abruptly, something blocked the blue sky in his vision.

"Though you have surprised me from time to time, this has to be the most extraordinary experience among them."

"Is that so? I think your fancy-pants comments annoy me more as time goes on, too."

Subaru bounced the comment back at Julius, appearing upside-down from his point of view, with an extra helping of invective.

The place was a corner of Earlham Village, a moment after he'd been shot out of the archive of forbidden books—apparently, Beatrice had rejected him and teleported him via the Passage, returning him to the village.

Understanding that fact, Subaru got up with a great swing of his legs. Then he turned his head around and spoke.

"Damn that thickheaded loli. I'm the obstinate one? …If you're gonna make a face like that, why can't you just come with me? …Shit. If it's gonna be like this, I'll drag her out if I have—"

"It might be best to quit while you're ahead."

Subaru couldn't pull his mind away from the sad face he'd seen on Beatrice when they'd separated. However, it was Puck, leisurely appearing behind Julius, who poured cold water on his enthusiasm.

The little cat spirit touched his own whiskers, looking at Subaru, covered in dirt and fallen leaves, as he spoke.

"Covered in grime, huh? Looks like Betty was pretty rough when she threw you out."

"I hate to say this, but I was literally one step away. But I suppose I have to say that went pretty much as I expected. It really would be best if you—"

"I can't. I cannot persuade Betty. Didn't I mention I have a pact?"

"Lately, that's taken the number one spot on my list of words I don't wanna hear."

Puck's face showed no ill will, but Subaru grandly scowled toward him as he replied.

A pact made Beatrice stay behind, a pact prevented Puck from persuading her, and a pact had been the impetus for his breakup with Emilia. Pact, pact, pact—

"If you talk, Beatrice'll listen. Even though you know that, it's a no can do?"

"Mm, I can't. Besides, even if I say it, Betty still won't listen. I told you first time she sent you out of the archive of forbidden books, didn't I? I cannot save Betty."

"—"

Puck turned his eyes down slightly as he replied. Subaru closed his mouth, unable to say a word.

Staying behind in the archive to persuade Beatrice; at first Subaru had meant to entrust that task to Puck. Considering the daily interaction between girl and kitty, he was sure Puck was the right cat for the job.

But when he unveiled the idea, Puck would not acquiesce, sending Subaru in his place. And sure enough, Subaru had failed to persuade her. And yet, Puck looked at Subaru and continued. "Subaru, it is likely that if you can't do it, no one can. This is Betty's answer."

"I really don't get what you're trying to tell me..."

Subaru couldn't read the emotions hovering in those round eyes whatsoever. The little cat spirit still wouldn't reveal his emotions as his tiny shoulders slumped.

"Well, leaving Betty in the archive of forbidden books isn't exactly a bad plan, anyway. I don't think anyone would breach the Passage without Betty knowing it, and she has ways of defending herself if she's inside the mansion. Trust me, it's all right."

"So wanting to bring her out of there anyway is just me being selfish, then?"

"A selfish thing is something a real man can say and hope to make a reality. How about it, Subaru? Do you think of yourself as a real man?"

"—Great Spirit."

Julius, watching Subaru's cheeks go stiff in the face of Puck's merciless words, interjected with words of his own. When the knight called out to him, Puck curled his long tail around himself and spoke.

"Sorry, I'm not trying to be mean. I know you want to save Betty, and I am truly grateful for that."

"The Great Spirit's words are strict, but they bear the ring of truth... What now, then?"

As Puck apologetically averted his eyes, Subaru knitted his brows at Julius's words.

"Whaddaya mean, what now?"

"The traveling merchants being led by Rajan should rendezvous with us here at the village anytime now. If your assumptions are correct, the Witch Cult's spy is hidden among them. There is likely no more time available for you to use."

The plan was to feed the Witch Cult fake intel and buy time for Emilia & Co. to safely evacuate. Having a spy from the Cult in their group was a situation where any misstep would be fatal.

He felt regret about Beatrice, but he'd lost the time needed to bring that girl with him.

"Mark my words, Beako. If you'd just come out like a good girl..."

"You should save regrets for later. I was opposed to your allowing time to slip even when it would not affect the results… However, in my judgment, this is the dividing line."

When Julius pointed that out, Subaru bit his tongue, clutched his head, and stamped his foot. After that, he wrung out an "Arghh!", turning toward the wide-eyed Julius and Puck as he spoke.

"…Let's switch to putting that plan in motion. We'll group up with the merchants and evacuate the villagers. We'll talk to Emilia just as we planned. Puck, I'm counting on you, too."

"You're sure about this?"

"It ain't good. It ain't good one little bit… But there's nothing better we can do."

As he gritted his teeth in remorse, Subaru's thoughts shifted toward the mansion—the mansion within which Beatrice remained that very moment.

She was a hardheaded, know-nothing, I'll-do-it-my-way girl—and a girl who had once saved Subaru's heart.

"We'll make sure Emilia and the others escape. But we're not letting the Witch Cult lay one finger on that mansion. We're completely shutting 'em down, and then that loli can complain while I drag her out by her curls."

That's what the new Subaru would do: save everyone and take his revenge on Beatrice. So Subaru swore in his heart, brushing all hesitation aside as he looked up at Puck.

"Puck! Emilia hasn't noticed anything outside for the last close to an hour?"

"It's all right, she's been sound…well, she's been asleep. I was worried about her mental fatigue, so I drained a few handfuls of mana out of her and put her to sleep. I mean, if I put Subaru on ice upon his return, it'd be cruel to let Lia see that and go into shock, right?"

"Can you stop saying stuff to make my heart skip a beat all of a sudden?!"

Unable to tell whether Puck was joking or not, Subaru let it slide and looked back at Julius. The look of determination on Subaru's face made the handsome young man tighten his own refined visage as well.

"Ferris, Master Wilhelm, and the villagers are all mentally prepared. They merely await your signal to begin. Of course, the same goes for me."

With a strong nod, Subaru shifted his eyes to the center of the village. There he saw the villagers beginning preparations to evacuate according to the plan explained to them by Ram and the expeditionary force assisting in those efforts.

Standing at the edge of that scene were Ferris, Wilhelm, and Ram, each awaiting Subaru, each with their own role to fulfill. They were who he would bring to the mansion, pulling the wool over Emilia's eyes.

"I won't be able to tell her this was all for her sake. This is totally my own selfishness talking."

"I told you, didn't I? If you turn selfishness into reality, it's not selfishness—it's hope."

When Subaru murmured, Puck sat on his shoulder and spoke thusly. The little cat thrust his paw against Subaru's forehead. Subaru laughed a little at the nostalgic sensation.

With many hardships and the operation to deceive a lovely girl lying ahead, he thought himself pretty laid back as he spoke.

"Well, let's get this started, shall we? The evil tricks to turn that hope into reality."

And so, in high spirits, they sent Emilia away, whereupon they began setting the stage to greet the Witch Cult.

CHAPTER 3
THE SELF-DECLARED KNIGHT AND "THE FINEST OF KNIGHTS"

1

"May the grace of the spirits be with you."

Climbing aboard the dragon carriage for evacuation, those were the words of prayer Emilia left the expeditionary force upon her departure from Earlham Village. To Subaru, that grace was as powerful as any blessing.

With only the best intentions, Emilia was deceived via an exaggerated performance for her own sake and sent away from Earlham Village along with the villagers themselves. Time continued onward.

It was also after Subaru had made full use of Return by Death to capture Kety—the finger from the Witch Cult lurking among the traveling merchants.

Subaru watched the horde of dragon carriages run off as his eyes shifted to the formation of knights accompanying them. Ten knights had been selected from among the expeditionary force to escort the evacuating carriages. The chance the Witch Cult would detect the evacuation was low, but they'd sent a detachment just in case.

The dragon carriages had two destinations: the royal capital and the Sanctuary. Subaru knew nothing about the latter except the name, but the fact that Ram had given it her stamp of approval was proof enough it was safe. Their safety was no doubt far more assured than that of Subaru and the others facing the decisive battle with the Witch Cult.

After all, the greatest combat power in the expeditionary force was escorting Emilia and the others.

"Sir Subaru, I pray for your fortune in battle."

"Take care yourself, Wilhelm," Subaru said after Wilhelm brought up the rear of the detachment from atop his land dragon. Facing the battle to come without Wilhelm was akin to rolling the dice. However, where the impending decisive battle with Petelgeuse was concerned, the Sword Devil's presence was not an indispensable element for defeating the madman. For that reason, fully aware it was a reckless request, Subaru had insisted on entrusting the defense of Emilia and the other evacuees to Wilhelm, to which he had readily agreed.

"Well, Petra and the others did jump at the chance to take care of Emilia…"

The children had merrily accepted Emilia aboard their carriage, just as Subaru had asked. The children had led Emilia by the hand, making her relieved that they had not rejected her. Remembering that scene, deep feelings of warmth arose in Subaru's chest—and at the same time, pangs of guilt.

"Using happy feelings to fool Emilia into going along with the situation and escaping… I've become quite a villain, playing with people's hearts like that. That stuff about me not reading atmospheres or human hearts seems like a lie now."

Grimacing in self-derision, Subaru vigorously scratched his own head.

It was too easy to dismiss his deceiving her as his hoping for Emilia's safety. Even so, the fact was, it had put her mind at ease. Besides, asking her to ride with the children had been a calculation by itself.

"Even if the lie's exposed, as long as someone holds Emilia back…"

The gentle Emilia probably couldn't shake off the hands of people concerned for her from the bottom of their hearts. Hence Subaru had intentionally created a situation where the children would bond with Emilia.

"She'll look down on me if that part ever comes out, so I'll keep that a secret for life..."

Puck, too, had agreed that it was better that way. The spirit, his fellow actor cooperating with the performance—or rather coconspirator—would not be leaving Emilia's side.

Emilia's security was guaranteed like never before—at least, he wanted to believe that.

"Looks like the village types and the half-demon girl left already. Looks like ya did pretty good, huh?"

As Subaru collected his thoughts, he heard hearty Kararagi dialect tossed his way from behind. When he looked back, he saw Ricardo coming over, carrying his great hatchet with him. Subaru glared at the dog-man's dog face and spoke.

"Stop calling my pretty Emilia a half-demon, you half-mutt!"

"Ohh! Gettin' called a half-mutt is surprisingly humiliatin'! I'll have to remember that one!"

He let loose a hearty, sarcastic laugh, and his forbearance drained the bitterness out of Subaru's strained smile. However, Subaru's cheeks soon tensed anew as he walked beside Ricardo and turned toward the forest.

"So how'd it go? Got the job done like I asked?"

"Hey, we split up to hit them by surprise in places they never expected to be attacked, right? If I screwed *that* up I'd quit my post. Every last part went great. We kicked their asses all over the map!"

Ricardo amiably showed him the blood still stuck to his great hatchet, patting the map on his hip with his palm.

"Meaning we were right the places marked on that map were where their hideouts were."

"That's what they get for bein' so methodical with their plannin'. You did good, bro."

Ricardo bared his fangs. The original owner of the map on his hip was, in fact, Kety the Witch Cultist. Thanks to his capture according to Subaru's scheme, they'd gained both his conversation mirror and his map. The map contained a highly detailed layout of the Mathers domain, and ten places had been marked upon it.

The markers were probably for Witch Cult hideouts—and to find out for sure, Subaru had sent Ricardo & Co. to the closest marker on the map. The results had apparently been as expected.

As if to prove that information correct, members of the Iron Fangs leaped out of the forest on their ligers, merrily galloping around the village square and by all appearances unscathed.

"Yahoo! We slaughtered 'em all!"

"Sister, do not say such foul-sounding things! We took proper captives!"

The smiling banter between the siblings, smelling of blood, made Subaru pat his chest in relief. He was happy about victory, but also that no one had been lost in the process. No matter how high the odds of victory, the one sending people off to battle always had reason to be concerned. Likely those reasons had been greatly minimized because of that map.

"And besides that…luck's really fallin' your way, bro."

"—? Whaddaya mean by…?"

"The hideout you picked me to hit had this layin' around."

As Subaru cocked his head, Ricardo took something out of the cloth tied around his waist and tossed it Subaru's way. Subaru immediately caught it, and his eyes went wide at the light sensation in his palm.

This was a mirror—indeed, the spitting image of one he had seen very recently.

"A conversation mirror…and this has to be on the other end of the one Kety had!"

"Accordin' to our info, the Witch Cultist we captured was communicatin' by mirror. Now that we got this from the ones I just mopped up, they won't be tellin' the other Witch Cultists nothin'… Real convenient, bustin' up their communication network like that. Ya couldn't ask for a more promisin' start!"

When Subaru's eyes popped wide at results beyond his wildest hopes, Ricardo opened his maw in a great laugh.

If his deduction was fact, they certainly had gained even more of an advantage over the Witch Cult. But after the feeling of everything going well had been followed by his tasting heaps of bitterness the last time around...

"—"

"Hey, bro. You don't look very happy."

"...No one escaped the hideout you smashed? If even one escaped, it's all for nothing."

"Whaddaya think this sharp nose o' mine is for? Of course not. Just..."

Ricardo strongly thumped his chest, but suddenly he awkwardly lowered the tone of his voice.

"I'm sure no one got away, but it's kind of a problem if there are other mirrors."

"I knew it! What? What was it?! Some kind of fatal flaw... There's an issue that's gonna knock out the entire foundation of the operation, isn't there?! Shit! I knew things were going too well!!"

"Hey, hey, what's with the fantasies of damage?! Ya can't be a general and be a worrywart like that! Besides, there's no guarantee somethin' bad happened, so stop assumin'!"

As a pale Subaru clung to him, Ricardo retorted with an overly intimidating face. Then the dog-man wrapped an arm around Subaru's head, choosing his words to rectify the latter's stubborn paranoia.

"Look here, see? It's not like anything bad's happened. Just we can't celebrate 'till the Witch Cult's smashed flat... Ahh, seeing's faster than talkin' anyway. Hey, bring in that guy from earlier!"

As Subaru grimaced, his head still in Ricardo's grasp, Ricardo indicated for his men to bring something over. When Subaru saw what they carried, his expression shifted—first to worry, then to disbelief.

Atop a liger, a single human being was being carried in, his entire body bound by rope.

"~~!!"

When the person noticed Subaru and Ricardo, he wrung out a muffled wail. Perhaps it was an objection to the impropriety of his treatment, or perhaps a plea to spare his life—

"We found 'im in the middle of the Witch Cult roost. I think he just got captured by 'em out of bad luck, but... Hey, what's with ya?"

In the middle of his explanation, Ricardo found it odd that Subaru's eyes were nailed to the wrapped-up person. But this was surely the natural reaction for him to have.

After all, the bound man wriggling around there was none other than—

"Pfft."

Unable to contain himself, Subaru let out a small sound. He pointed to the young man bound hand, foot, and even torso, and burst out laughing.

"So you got yourself captured! I thought I was never gonna see your face here, Otto!"

And so Subaru called out the last name in the dramatis personae, excess misfortune having thus far denied him the stage.

2

After letting quite a few laughs fly at his expense, Subaru freed Otto from his bonds.

"Though I am...not particularly inclined to simply say, 'Thank you very much for aiding me...'"

"Hey, is that how you talk to the group that saved your life? You wouldn't want nasty rumors to spread, would you?"

"What kind of base villain are you?! What a person! Oh, fine, thank you very much! Thanks to you my life has been spared! Not that living brings any great comfort, damn it all!"

Half in desperation, Otto spoke his thanks to Subaru, who was bullying him with full knowledge of his precarious circumstances.

Otto had been discovered when Ricardo & Co. raided a Witch

Cult stronghold. Apparently he'd been affixed to a cross in a cave in the mountains, and he had been rescued on the verge of becoming a human sacrifice.

"Well, we can't rule out the possibility he's a Witch Cultist, so we should bring him back tied for now..."

"We're treasuring him, almost like, 'Let's keep him around just in case. It's nice to have a human sacrifice on hand when you need one'?"

"What kind of appraisal is that for someone you just met?! I haven't done anything to you, you know?!"

Red faced and bound, Otto moved his limbs around and wailed at Subaru's overly harsh words.

"Well, setting that aside," said Subaru, brushing away Otto's frustration. "So how *did* you wind up captured? If there's something behind it, go ahead and tell us."

"That is, ah...something I truly do not wish to divulge for reasons of personal convenience..."

"If you don't want to say it, that's fine— Incidentally, changing the subject, most of the traveling merchants gathered in this domain right now are heading toward the mansion of Marquis Mathers to make a little money."

"That's not changing the subject, though! I heard that so I know already, you know?! Ahh, that's right! I am the fool who leaped at the fortuitous talk of profit, first in line charging down this treacherous road and captured through his own ill fortune! Go ahead, laugh!"

"That so... Glad you're all right, then. Tch, you're making me break into tears..."

"What is with those hollow tears?! Is not grasping at a fishy story explanation enough for you?!!"

Subaru pitied Otto and his wistful, energetic confession, warmly taking in the sight of him lamenting the inhumanity of it all. Apparently, his merchant nature had spurred him into some rather impulsive actions. Subaru was relieved that the impression he'd received from their previous encounters hadn't changed at all.

Subaru's mischievous demeanor led Otto to let out a sigh of unbridled dejection.

"Goodness…what a person, after I properly thanked him for saving my life and everything…"

"Wha— I did save your life, you just don't want me to rub it in? You owe me one!"

"To be frank, I feel like this 'one' is a particularly large debt, so one I feel little desire to acknowledge!"

Otto's face scowled grandly when Subaru raised his index finger and declared him to be indebted. Afterward Subaru smiled as Otto kept repeating, "Debt, debt…" as he took it in with a look most sour.

Yet at the same time, his actions established to Subaru that there was nothing suspicious about him, relieving him of the need for extra prudence.

"—"

It went the same for Ricardo, on guard as he watched the two conversing from the side.

The mere fact that he'd been brought from an enemy stronghold made Otto's position delicate to the extreme. Considering that Kety, positioned as leader of the traveling merchants, was a spy, Subaru couldn't help but give Otto, who had gotten along well with Kety during previous go-arounds, the strictest of scrutiny.

After all, carelessly trusting him only to be betrayed would render Subaru's efforts to date all for naught…

"…Man, I've turned into a pretty disagreeable guy."

"What are you saying?"

"I'm saying I'm glad you're all right. Hey, Mimi, that's great, huh?"

"Mm? Ahh, okay! I'm happy and super thrilled you're all right, Mister Half-Bawling-My-Eyes-Out!"

When Subaru bounced the conversation Mimi's way, she divulged the circumstances of Otto's rescue. After Mimi voiced that truth, she cocked her head and said, "Isn't that right?" as Otto collapsed then and there.

"Ahh, it's no wonder you half bawled your eyes out. Don't worry, I won't tell anyone. This is between you, me, Mimi, Ricardo, and after that, the Iron Fangs and everyone in the expeditionary force..."

"Does that not make it an open secret...?"

"Anyway, there's no worry about the Witch Cult attacking this village, so you can cool your heels here. Also, my condolences over half bawling your eyes out, and my condolences about the moneymaking talk, too."

"Your condolences...? Surely you cannot mean...?!"

Otto looked around the village in shock, looking like his world had come to an end.

"Do not tell me that everyone has already been..."

"The fact that you're alive after being captured by the Witch Cult means you've been blessed by heaven... Er, no, the fact that you got captured to begin with means heaven has abandoned you. Well, live strong!"

"If you are going to console me, won't you look after me till the bitter end?!"'

With Otto breaking into tears, Subaru gave him a pat on the shoulder and looked at Ricardo. As he did so, the dog-man wrinkled his snout and tilted his head up. Apparently, even his veteran mercenary's eyes judged Otto to be an utterly harmless object of pity. Subaru thought of that as the silver lining in the cloud.

"So from here on, this'll be the front line against the Witch Cult. We've got a lot to do...but I can't think of anything you can do to help with that. Maybe you could sort out the list of the freight the other traveling merchants left behind?"

"Will you pay me a fee for that?!"

"Man, even I'm surprised. You're even more desperate than I thought. Yeah, yeah, I'll pay. Someone here tag along with Otto?"

With suspicions about him lifted, Subaru gave Otto a job to do and moved that concern to the back of the line for the moment. Instead, Subaru headed to the expeditionary force, just finished reorganizing its ranks with Julius at its head.

"You reunited with a familiar face, yes? Is that really enough warmth toward an old acquaintance?"

Julius, noticing Subaru's approach, turned toward him before he could say anything. Subaru grimaced at his words, pointing over his shoulder toward Otto, now standing facing the pile of freight.

"Behind the stupid laughs and the stupid conversation, I was suspecting he was up to something the whole time. My personality's gotten so rotten I'm starting to hate myself."

"Thanks to that rotten personality, we have come this far unscathed. I believe you should take pride in that rotten personality—though perhaps you should not express it in those exact terms."

"Your personality is pretty rotten, too. I guarantee it."

"Yes, yes, have you two rotten personalities finished speaking yet?"

The exchange between Subaru and Julius made Ferris cock his little head and smile mischievously. In a vengeful mood, Subaru grandly curled his lips and spoke.

"What is it, rotten personality kitty ears?"

"My, what a way to speak to me, *meow*. And Ferri tries and tries his hawdest for everyone's sake, *meow*!"

"And your earnest efforts have always been of great aid. So what have you learned?"

"Mm. I've managed to learn a few things about the fingers from the captured Witch Cultists."

When Julius prompted, Ferris's smile vanished as he pointed to a cabin they'd commandeered.

Ferris must have been directly checking inside the body of Kety, the captured Witch Cultist held within.

During the previous go-around, Ferris had suffered repeated anguish from being unable to stop the Witch Cultists from committing suicide. For that reason Subaru had been somewhat anxious about the examination of Kety's body, but—

"First, the cultists seem to have a magic stone embedded into them that turns into powerful poison for suicide purposes. But the fingers seem to get special treatment… Instead of poison, there's an explosion ritual embedded into them, so that when they kill themselves, they take everyone nearby with them."

"Sounds like it's not so much meant for stopping information from leaking out as for the archbishop's Possession, huh? If he needs to die so he can body swap, it's a given he'd counter being knocked out and tied up by killing himself."

"For suicide... But surely it is likely a method of external activation exists. What about that case?"

"I was worried about that, too, so I nullified the ritual and ripped the whole thing out~~!"

Ferris had a simple answer to Julius's concern. But judging from Julius's wide-eyed reaction, that had been no easy feat. Ferris continued. "Also, about the characteristics of the fingers that Subawu was so concerned about... It's not so much stagnant Gates as having weird clumps of mana. I think the presence or absence of this sets the fingers apart from the regular cultists, and that the Archbishop of the Seven Deadly Sins can only transfer into the ones with this planted in them."

"So the condition for Possession is the difference between the general members and the premium members of the club. What happened to that clump of mana?"

"I melted it and scrambled it all up. So we can't really call him a finger anymore."

"You managed all that?! That's huge!"

Subaru, his voice leaping at Ferris's report, grabbed his slender hand and vigorously shook it up and down. He had nothing but praise for Ferris's skill in checking so much in such a short time.

"*Meow meow!!* Well, it's what you should expect of Ferri, *meow*? But it's also thanks to your figuring out that the fingers committed suicide a different way, Subawu."

"No, all the credit for this goes to you. You would've had a ton of regrets if it didn't work out..."

"What the...? Ferri would never regret anything where people like *that* are concerned!"

Ferris stuck his tongue out and pried his hand loose from Subaru's shake. Subaru made a pained smile at Ferris's teasing demeanor. Ferris would never know it, but Subaru was congratulating him for winning the rematch from the last time around.

Besides, thanks to Ferris's valiant efforts, he'd largely managed to piece together a hypothesis.

"Besides, if you neutralized the conditions for Possession, that prisoner won't die, right?"

"However vile his tongue, the Gate inside his body has been set straight… We should bring him back to the royal capital and treat him as a precious source of information. He fainted from the pain of pulling the ritual out, and he's still out cold~~!"

Ferris closed one eye and guaranteed that Kety's life was safe, if nothing else. Subaru couldn't conceive of the pain of having the ritual ripped out of him. And then—

"We've finally managed to take a single proper prisoner. There's no need to take more risks. You see what I'm getting at?"

"What, you think at this point I'm gonna go soft weighing those guys against the people important to me…?"

When Ferris's eyes questioned his resolve, Subaru nodded to them without showing even a moment's pause.

To bring down the Archbishop of the Seven Deadly Sins of Sloth, the Witch Cultists had to be wiped out, fingers included. That meant a literal battle of annihilation.

And it was none other than Subaru Natsuki who would sound the signal for that battle to begin.

"…Hmm. You really have straightened yourself out, Subawu."

As Subaru clenched a fist, Ferris narrowed his eyes, murmuring as he gazed at the side of Subaru's face. The contents of that murmur brought a pained smile over Subaru as he slumped his shoulders.

"Hey, now, don't put it like that. It doesn't sound like much of a compliment."

"I'm not complimenting you. You've gone from bad to normal. Don't get carried away with yourself, *meow*."

With an adorable face, Ferris laid into Subaru until the bitter end.

He'd probably been the person to judge Subaru the most harshly of all since they'd departed the royal capital. That was probably because they both lacked the power to do battle by themselves—those who can't fight alone are stuck together, for better or worse.

While Ferris's appraisal of Subaru's weakness was harsh, it was fair at the same time, and Subaru hated that.

"Don't like that, huh? Right now, you've climbed up to *normal*. Understand?"

"Normal, huh? Gotcha. But it makes me kinda glad."

"—People don't want to have their beliefs twisted out of shape, you see. Subawu, you must *not* hesitate or go astray. So don't let anything shake your resolve."

Ferris responded to Subaru's lighthearted words with a statement in a firm voice. It thrust deep into Subaru's slightly relaxed chest, driving home just what was the source of his so-called resolve.

No, Ferris didn't have to say it. It was something he had to realize and face by himself.

"Preparations are completely in order— Subaru, we may begin anytime."

Having put the expeditionary force in order, Julius addressed Subaru to create an opportunity for him. It was not just he— everyone from the ranks of the expeditionary force and the Iron Fangs awaited Subaru's voice as one.

Their morale was high before the climactic battle, their spirits beginning to soar above the battlefield centered upon the village square.

"—"

Subaru felt that fighting spirit as he slightly tipped his head back, looking up at the sky.

He couldn't remove all uncertain elements. Even so, he'd sent Emilia and the others off, entrusting them to Wilhelm, and thanks to Ferris, they'd grasped the true nature of the fingers. Julius was awaiting his signal.

He'd done his utmost to put human affairs in order. All he could do now was smile, reel it all in, and await the verdict of heaven.

"—Let's do this. Everyone, start just like we arranged."

He lowered his gaze from the sky, turning it straight toward the members of the expeditionary force standing before him. At his urging, the warriors mounted their beasts of war without a word, acting in accordance with Subaru's words.

"_____"

"Yeah. Thanks, Patlash."

The jet-black land dragon had been standing close to Subaru's side the whole time, eagerly awaiting her turn. Subaru stroked her hard hide with his palm before mounting up like the others.

Julius's and Ricardo's mounts were to their sides, sandwiching Subaru between them. Ferris, left on the ground by himself, nodded to Subaru with a serious look as Subaru took his place in the vanguard.

Then he heralded the start of the final battle.

"Now, this time we'll settle this— Sloth, Sir Fate, I ain't goin' easy on ya."

3

Subaru had inferred several things about Petelgeuse's Possession.

First, it was the power to shift into the bodies of others, stealing them for himself.

Second, Petelgeuse's so-called fingers were retainers for him to transfer into, so as a precondition of defeating Petelgeuse, all the fingers had to be destroyed.

Third, if Petelgeuse lost all his fingers, he would transfer to a different body instead. Subaru's body was the leading candidate.

The parasite of the mind was so powerful, it was virtually impossible to resist by one's own devices— The end.

"Now that I'm writing these down, this is like, kills-you-as-soon-as-he-sees-you-level stuff. Plus he even has Unseen Hands, so you can't just laugh and say, 'Nah, nothing's that evil.'"

The Archbishop of the Seven Deadly Sins had two powers. Subaru was confident that if you didn't know them, you could challenge him a hundred times and be killed every time.

In the course of repeating while keeping his memory, searching over and over for a plan to beat him, Subaru finally saw with clarity the fearsomeness of his foe. Small wonder the Witch Cult had had such influence on the world over the course of four centuries.

Such was the scale of Petelgeuse Romanée-Conti, the madman specializing in killing at first sight.

"Well, that's what I'm here for."

The best thing for taking on a kill-at-first-sight enemy was someone for whom it *wasn't* first sight.

Thus it was Subaru Natsuki, he who had Returned by Death, who was Petelgeuse Romanée-Conti's mortal foe.

Once again, Subaru cut through the gloomy forest of overgrown trees as his feet carried him to the wall of rock.

Green covered the landscape at every turn, a world where even directional sense seemed suspect. However, Subaru's steps were certain. His senses, his feet, the experiences carved into his memory—all these things guided Subaru forward.

"Let's get this show on the road."

Smiling bitterly at the quickening of his heartbeats, Subaru murmured thus as he gave his chest two light slaps. Then he headed forward. The place had come into view.

Until that moment, Subaru had never approached that place with the resolve to fight in his heart. The last time around, he'd been buying time as a decoy; before that he'd been drowning in the bloodlust of others and the yearning for suicide.

But this time was different. At minimum, this time was different from the others.

Subaru had come to that place with the resolve to fight hardened in his heart, all so he could bring a long, long string of karma, a battle repeated over and over, to a final end.

"—It is good that you have come, disciple of love."

Subaru shuddered with joy when suddenly the forest opened and he was greeted with warm words of welcome.

When he slipped out of the woods, a sheer cliff spread straight ahead of him, rising high into his field of vision. A slender man was standing in front of the rock face with both arms spread wide. His eyes welcomed Subaru with a fiery glow.

Was it now four times he had been greeted by this sight?

No matter who it was, when you saw someone's face repeatedly, you let the person into your heart to a certain extent—but it seemed that was impossible so far as this man was concerned.

"I AM the Archbishop of the Seven Deadly Sins of the Witch Cult charged with Sloth—"

The madman stretched out his hand, bloodied from self-inflicted wounds, as his trademark line lit the spark. With his eyes drenched in madness, the man arched back, stuck out his tongue, snapping his eyes wide as he said—

"—Petelgeuse...Romanée-CONTI!!"

With a flutter of his black habit, the madman loudly proclaimed his name with a clap of his bloody hands. Petelgeuse proceeded to stamp the ground, breaking into a happy little dance as he laughed with delight.

"It is A fine day, A splendid day! To think that this day, the day of the trial, I would BE greeting a new adherent of love! I AM moved, greatly moved, moved to tears, my chest is on the verge of bursting!!"

The madman let spittle fly as he embraced his own body of skin and bones. Subaru harbored disgust for his eccentricities, but he was accustomed enough to smooth over his facial expressions in the man's presence.

On top of that, Subaru executed the operation just as agreed upon beforehand. Namely—

"Lord Archbishop of the Seven Deadly Sins! It is a pleasure to meet you for the first time!"

These words spoken, Subaru rushed over and knelt at the madman's feet. He touched his left hand to his chest, raising his right aloft as he bowed his head with utmost respect and spoke.

"I am truly embarrassed to have made it to you on the very eve of this trial! Lord Archbishop, by all means, please use this body, this soul, to fill any vacancy among the faithful, and add me to your fingers with all haste!"

Thus, with an excess of bombast, did Subaru speak bald-faced lies. He proclaimed his prepared lines with a high-pitched voice, infused his face with maximum reverence that went only skin deep, and silently awaited the madman's reaction.

"_____"

Petelgeuse made no response to Subaru's earnest plea. He said nothing. He did not move. The disquieting silence made Subaru swallow his saliva as he increased his caution and alertness concerning Petelgeuse's next move.

The silence continued for about ten more seconds before it was abruptly broken by—

"OOOH! Such, such fervent zeal from the very first meeting?!"

Petelgeuse gazed up, extending both hands to the heavens. His voice and his entire body were shaking; he had been moved to tears.

"What a disciple love has called! In all my time cursed as Sloth, I cannot recall one with such clear eyes! YOU! YOU, a pious adherent of love! How unworthy I must be to have overlooked you all this time! I ASK you to forgive my slothfulness—!"

Petelgeuse cast his limbs aside as he practically leaped onto the ground in front of the fragile-hearted Subaru. Without hesitation the madman prostrated himself on the rocky ground, banging his head against the surface several times. The merciless self-punishment made his forehead bleed, but he had such a great tendency to inflict self-harm that he probably did this much every day before breakfast.

Now that Subaru knew it was someone else's body, the disgust he felt when seeing Petelgeuse act that way was stronger than ever before.

Either way, it would not do for him to self-punish to the point of dying. Behind the scenes, the operation was quietly proceeding— messing up by letting Petelgeuse switch bodies would waste everything.

"Please stop, Lord Archbishop! Such actions bring no joy to the Witch Cult!"

"Ahh, but! Butbutbutbutbuuuuut! My very own sloth! My sin! The ugly fact ONE such as I have not repaid Her love! I possess no other way to REPENT!!"

"That is not so! The Witch Cult would rather its cherished followers repay her favor than see them hurt themselves! It is the will to carry out the trial that will surely bring it joy!"

Petelgeuse was continuing to thrust his head against the ground when Subaru used rambling speech to stop him. But suddenly the words brought Petelgeuse to a halt; he stared at Subaru, eyes wide open. With those parched eyes upon him, Subaru strongly nodded, not that it meant anything to special to Subaru.

When he did so, Petelgeuse's obsession seemed to fall away. A single tear trickled down his face as he spoke.

"Yes, it is just as you SAY."

"—?!"

He said it in an uncharacteristically gentle way. The next moment, Subaru found Petelgeuse strongly embracing him.

Subaru's throat caught as powerful, instinctive repugnance hit him, but the madman paid his reaction no heed. Petelgeuse grandly wept, wiping away neither his flowing tears nor the blood on his forehead.

"Ahh, I am wrong, I am deeply mistaken! Yes! The trial! What I require is not to punish, judge, or slay myself, but the trial! What terrible slothfulness, forgetting that while wallowing in the joy of my own wounds! I thank you! I thank YOU!!"

When Subaru turned in Petelgeuse's arms, he faced upward as Petelgeuse showered him with one-sided gratitude.

Petelgeuse wiped the blood off his brow and thrust his right hand's fingers into his mouth, the same mouth that bespoke the foolishness of self-injury, crushing the thumb, index, and middle fingers one by one.

"I am worthless if I am slothful! Diligence is the most valuable thing in this world, and in this world, sloth is the worst vice that I must abhor! Ahh, AHH, ahh, I must repay Her love!"

He was in a precarious, incoherent state in which word and deed were no longer aligned. He reflected upon self-harm as he crushed his own fingers, only to lament his rash actions the next moment.

Subaru, feeling the need to bring his mad, nigh-unbearable nature to a quick end, put his hand in his pocket. However, his palm was not greeted by the hoped-for reaction. More time was needed for the operation to proceed.

"Lord Archbishop—may I speak to you about the trial?"

Fearful of an ugly silence taking hold, Subaru took a deep breath, concealed his inner thoughts, and spoke those words. The last time around, he had failed to get anything out of Petelgeuse regarding the trial, so he was still in the dark about the particulars. A trial meant a test of some sort. The Witch Cult was subjecting Emilia to some kind of test in accordance with its dogma.

If fate bound Emilia to the Witch Cult going forward, he wanted to dig up *something*...

"Lord Archbishop, now that I have joined you, I would truly like to ask you about the trial."

"The trial..."

When the words haltingly trickled from Petelgeuse, his expression suddenly lost all emotion. Perhaps his mania from before had vanished into thin air; as the madman gazed at Subaru with hollow eyes, he put the remaining fingers—the ring finger and the little finger—of his already-bloody right hand into his mouth, crushing them with his teeth. And then—

"Yes, the trial! The TRIAL!! THE trial! We must carry out the trial and test her! We cannot fail to test this half-demon, and learn if she is a suitable vessel for the descent of the Witch!"

Subaru was bathed in a strange, shrill voice and stinky breath as Petelgeuse broke into a little dance. Subaru grimaced in shock and disgust as the madman's declaration sank in.

"A vessel for the Witch's...descent...?"

"If she passes, embrace her! If she fails, eliminate her! We must test the half-demon's capacity to accept life, whether she is suitable for the Witch, whether the Witch's love can be sealed within! And the TRIAL is how we determine this!"

The madman responded to Subaru's doubt-instilled voice with his own mad voice, raising his hands above his head in the process. The words struck Subaru like a revelation; he was horrified by the comprehension he had gained.

Vessel. Witch. Descend— If he could take the meanings of those words at face value, then…

"If the trial determines she's a suitable vessel for the Witch, the Witch will descend into her body…"

"Someday that fateful day shall arrive when the Witch is resurrected into this world—! We exist to bear witness to that moment! And for this purpose I, and my fingers, shall exhaust all efforts… This is MY love!"

Petelgeuse was moved to tears, for in his world, it was the most blessed occasion conceivable. The sight of the madman before him made Subaru sick to his stomach.

Based on all that, all the acts of savagery Petelgeuse had engaged in, all the slaughter he had perpetrated, and his pushing Subaru's heart to the breaking point had been because—

"—You people don't see any value in Emilia herself, do you?"

To them, "Emilia" was nothing more than a box into which they could stuff the soul of the Witch.

They were after a container. Their great objective—the revival of the Witch—loomed large before them. The girl's aspirations, how gentle her heart was, how hardworking she was…these things simply didn't matter.

This was at once bottomless contempt for Emilia as an individual girl and, to Subaru, whose heart was greatly swayed by her existence, a humiliation difficult to endure.

"—Monster."

Petelgeuse did not notice that for a single moment, a single word, Subaru let his true feelings slip.

He did not think of burning a village to the ground as excessive in the slightest if it was for the sake of his villainous goals. He could casually dismiss the life story of each and every person he laid hands upon, brushing their dreams and futures aside.

That was why Petelgeuse and the Witch Cult were Subaru Natsuki's enemies.

"...Lord Archbishop, I have humbly heard your esteemed views. Hearing the ideals of the Witch Cult, and your determination to win, I am truly, deeply impressed. Let's make certain this trial succeeds."

"Ohhhh! You are indeed splendid! Yes! We shall become as one, and wholeheartedly hurl ourselves toward my long-cherished desire! Since the day I accepted Her favor, my entire being, my entire spirit became rubbish devoted solely to repaying Her love... Ahhh, Satella! I BELONG to you!"

Petelgeuse approved of Subaru's superficial praise, accepting it with great delight rather than doubt.

"It is YOU, an ideal disciple, who should truly be exalted! With the favor so rich within you, should you intend to join the fingers. I shall bestow the Factor upon you without DELAY!"

"Then by all means, please make me one of your fingers!"

"I am truly delighted by your unexpected offer! BUT, BUT...the numbers of my fingers have already been filled. There must be something more suitable for the likes of you... Yes, that is IT!"

Petelgeuse was counting on his bloodied fingers when he put a hand into his habit like he'd just remembered something. What he took out of his pocket was a single black book—his Gospel.

The madman lovingly touched its cover; his breath went ragged as his eyes perused its contents.

"The words recorded in the Gospel, its entire tale of love, is what guides MY future! Accordingly, all that I am...all that I ever shall be, is recorded WITHIN!"

Froth came into the corners of Petelgeuse's mouth as he browsed the pages with a laugh.

Subaru, who had once stolen that Gospel from him, knew that the strange contents of the black book were indecipherable. But to its owner, Petelgeuse, the characters constituted a legible tale. And his actions were in accordance with its passages.

If that was true, Subaru's real enemy was whoever had written that Gospel's passages to begin with.

"Present thy Gospel."

Petelgeuse, audibly closing his Gospel, spoke that single phrase. The madman cocked his neck at a ninety-degree angle, twisted his hips to the same extent, and stared at Subaru with a neutral expression.

These were the words Subaru feared most. According to previous experience, even if a conversation had gone well up to that point, that question served to sever the flow.

If someone was a Witch Cultist, they had a Gospel—no exceptions. The black books, their origin and method of creation unknown, served as proof of identity among members of the Witch Cult.

Accordingly, Petelgeuse was asking Subaru to show his ID.

Whatever answer he might come up with would greatly influence the course of circumstances, but—

"What is THE matter?"

In contrast to the silent Subaru, Petelgeuse left his head bent at that angle, his long tongue drooping out.

All he had to do was show off his Gospel. A disturbing air began to waft around Petelgeuse as Subaru failed to prove himself even to that extent. Amid that bone-chilling aura, Subaru slowly put his hand into his pocket.

Then he thrust what he had taken out before Petelgeuse's eyes. But—

"What…is this?"

"As you can see, it's a metia, Lord Archbishop."

Petelgeuse's eyes were wide in surprise, for that which had been thrust before him was a mirror—a conversation mirror, to be specific. There was no doubt that the madman recognized it; after all, it had been in the possession of one of the madman's very own fingers. The fact that Subaru had it was throwing the madman off.

But his surprise did not end there. Before his eyes, the surface of the mirror began to faintly glow.

"Ah, it's turning on. Wow, your face is scarier than I heard!"

The adorable voice they heard over the mirror was very much out of place in the current situation. Subaru couldn't see the mirror's surface, but Petelgeuse was no doubt seeing the speaker, a certain kitty-eared knight.

It was like playing a really bad joke—but this constituted the signal for the operation.

"What have YOU... No! What have YOU people done!!"

"Now, then. Ahem. Tora-tora-tora!"

"—?!"

Ferris suddenly stated those words to an uncomprehending, angry Petelgeuse. The madman did not know the meaning of the words. Accordingly, Subaru explained them.

"It means, 'The surprise raid was a success'—"

Subaru pointed to the mirror in his hand, laughing at the wide-eyed Petelgeuse.

This was not the made-up smiling face from earlier, but the real Subaru—smiling like a little punk.

"Wh-wha—?"

"You don't look like you'll understand no matter how many times I say it. Well, don't worry about it."

With Petelgeuse thrown for a loop, Subaru continued his full, beaming smile as he raised a hand above his head.

And then—

"I can't understand what the hell you're saying, either!"

"What a—?!"

Subaru spoke fighting words as he snapped his raised fingertips. Responding to the aggression, Petelgeuse instantly shifted to a combat posture. But the movements of the sprinting figure rushing in from the side proved quicker.

"Ga, haa—"

Raising a shriek, the madman was sent flying head over heels, crashing and rolling over the rocky ground.

"—"

Watching this, the pitch-black land dragon neighed, as if to spurn the madman for having made her wait for so long.

The dragon judged the unproductive conversation to be at an end. Her roar echoed across the forest sky.

4

He felt heat from the conversation mirror as he returned it to his pocket. The operation was proceeding to its second phase.

That fact spurred Subaru to harden his resolve once more, raising a middle finger toward the madman's astonished eyes.

"As for everything we were discussing, my answer is no."

"Wh-wh-wh...?"

"If you don't get it, I'll say it so it's easier to understand: After careful consideration of your offer, there is an insurmountable clash of organizational culture between us. Therefore, though this is highly arbitrary of me, I am removing myself from consideration. I pray for your continued activity and growth hereafter...and stuff."

Subaru indicated that talks had broken off with a kind and careful explanation that was even harder to understand. With Patlash close by his side, he proceeded to gallantly mount her, taking the reins as he looked down at the madman.

Petelgeuse, confused as he looked up, belatedly came to understand, whereupon he became filled with anger at Subaru's act of violence and shouted,

"Do you comprehend what you are doing?! I am an Archbishop of the Seven Deadly Sins! An Archbishop of the Seven Deadly Sins granted the grace of the Witch! I have received Her favor, the same as y—"

"Sorry, but I'm tired of hearing about all that. The Witch can go eat shit, Petelgeuse."

"Why! Why, I ASK! Why, do you refuse Her love?! The favor of the Witch! What is YOUR reason for rejecting Her grace? I, who have abandoned all things for Her, cannot compreHEND!!"

Petelgeuse tore at his head, letting spit fly as he spoke with intense emotion. He actually seemed intent on convincing Subaru with those desperate cries.

If so, exchanging words with Petelgeuse truly lacked even a single shred of worth.

"When I look at you, I sympathize with you a bit, too. But let me tell you this."

Subaru paid the madman's delusions little heed as he recalled the intricacies and rampages that had arisen from his own heart. He'd professed that *he* was right, asserted that everyone around him was wrong, and had spent his time wailing and engaging in temper tantrums like a child.

I see. It really is unbearable to watch. This is like the horrible example everyone should learn from.

"Right now, you're the one who's crazy, and I'm the one who's right— It ends here, Petelgeuse!"

And so he bade farewell to his own mistakes.

There had been nothing tying Subaru and Petelgeuse together in the first place. The madman, too, instantly understood that it had all been a performance and a fraud. The next moment, his decision was cruel and severe—

"Violence, heresy! You shall pay for this—I shall rend YOU limb from limb and offer your soul to the Witch!!"

Petelgeuse's laments cut off in an instant. His shadow seemed to explode, spreading and swelling as it became a multitude of pitch-black arms. These objects of overwhelming density cascaded toward Subaru like a waterfall to rip him limb from limb, wring his neck, and violate his soul, just as Petelgeuse had declared. But—

"Why—?!"

"Hey, I was playing *tag, you're it* with demon beasts in these parts just two months ago!"

Patlash surmised Subaru's intentions through his unskilled use of the reins, moving more than she had been commanded. The wise dragon's movements deftly evaded the evil hands pursuing them as she leaped, escaping beyond the area of effect.

The distance between them widened. Petelgeuse could not conceal his shock at his perfect opening attack being foiled. His eyes and mouth opened wide, so much that they nearly tore, and he wailed, "Just now! Those movements! You evaded! The Favor granted unto *me*?! Impossible, insufferable! Why can you see my authority?!"

"Who knows? The Witch left her scent on my body, so go ask her. Oh, did I mention that unlike you, the Witch gave me a meet-me-anytime permission slip?"

"—! What do you mean by… You blaspheme the Witch, Satella, by feigning closeness to Her!"

"Hey, we're so close she reaches out and grabs me by the heart—literally."

Subaru added a wink, taunting Petelgeuse with a maximum of ridicule.

That moment, the madman's tolerance instantly reached the boiling point; his face went red with rage as he bit his own fingers to the core. A dull sound rang out as his teeth snapped the fingers, crushing nail, flesh, and bone alike.

Responding to his intense emotions, the shadows swirling around the madman increased in density. Their total number increased, and even for Subaru, able to see the invisible evil hands, the difficulty level had just been jacked up.

However, the one most surprised by the increase in the evil hands' numbers was Petelgeuse himself.

"The Factor granted to my fingers has returned…?! Why?! What has happened to my…?!"

"As the Witch Factor you handed out comes back, the number of hands you can control increases. Well, the answer's obvious, isn't it? Hey, do the math, Lord Archbishop! Or maybe you're just too *lazy*!"

"—! —!!"

Petelgeuse was at the mercy of consternation and rage when Subaru redoubled his taunt. When it came to getting under other people's skin, Subaru Natsuki came second to none—but an opponent like this, with zero resistance against instigation, was practically dancing on the palm of his hand.

Exactly as planned, Petelgeuse was so angry that his face was dark red, thrusting his bloodlust-infused fist toward Subaru and sending the arms to bluntly smash him flat and rip his very life out.

"Patlash—!"

The land dragon grasped Subaru's intent, continuing to evade the carpet bombing–like Unseen Hands offensive with frightening accuracy. She was so dependable that Subaru truly couldn't bow his head enough to her.

Subaru judged that they could continue to hold out against the first wave of attacks.

"Operation Stage Three, let's go!"

"Just how many petty games do you intend to play…! Against my diligence, this is all futile… Aa?!"

Petelgeuse readied himself for a counterattack, but the next moment, Subaru's action made his words choke in his throat.

"Turning your back to me… Just how much do you intend to mock me?!"

"Sorry! But your stinky breath is making my eyes burn, so I have no choice!"

With a command to Patlash, Subaru moved away from the rocky area and made a beeline for the forest. Patlash violently trampled the grass, blowing open a makeshift road like the wind itself as they distanced themselves from their foe.

"Do not think that! I shall allow you! To ESCAPE!!"

Petelgeuse shouted, but in contrast to his words, he crouched down then and there. The instant after he did so, he sat holding his knees like a gym student as a shadow grabbed hold of him, hurling the madman toward the heavens.

As if in a twisted game of catch, his body sailed with ease until another evil hand caught him. Catch, throw, catch, throw—repeating this over and over, Petelgeuse was hot on Subaru's and Patlash's heels as they fled.

It was nightmarish pursuit, and it was not only he who pursued the pair.

"Now, now, now, come forth! He mocks and scorns the exalted

Witch, violates Her trial and Her favor! Rend his flesh into tiny pieces and offer him to the Witch!

When Petelgeuse's command fell from the sky, Witch Cultists hidden in the cave under the cliff appeared in the forest without a sound. They had not attended Subaru and Petelgeuse's conversation, but now that they knew Subaru was their foe, they had no reason to hesitate. Their steps seemed to glide along the ground as they pursued Subaru and the land dragon.

Petelgeuse was above the treetops, and at their backs, the Witch Cultists were ferociously chasing them—

"Here they come here they come here they come! Patlash, hang in there!"

"—!"

At Subaru's highly imprecise command, Patlash dealt with the crisis using her own judgment. She opted for speed, crashing through the slender trees that impeded her large frame. She trampled upon roots, vaulted over a depression, and snapped leafy branches apart as she charged straight forward, heading for their destination by the shortest possible route.

"Futile! Meaningless! I shall catch up to you! Even that diligent land dragon's resistance shall be blotted out, overridden by diligence of my OWN!!"

From afar, mad shouts poured down upon them, and the tyrannical evil hands poured down like a waterfall. They aimed at the sprinting Patlash, each landing in the forest with all the force of a cannonball. Huge trees were broken at the trunk and sent flying, with dust clouds swirling up from the ground being pulverized over and over.

But, despite that waterfall, the dust cloud, and the madman's hatred pouring down, the land dragon ferociously burst through.

"—"

Patlash, neighing loudly, was not unscathed. Even so, the land dragon had slipped through the attacks, protecting Subaru and herself. She had faithfully seen all Subaru's clumsy commands through.

"Sorry for leaning on you this hard… You're the best, Patlash!"

"Howeverhoweverhoweveeeer! It ends HERE!"

Petelgeuse's cackling, laughing voice interrupted Subaru's praise for his favorite dragon's valiant efforts. Pointing beneath him, the madman was not speaking of Unseen Hands. Rather, he indicated the group of black figures chasing them.

"—"

With cross-patterned swords in hand, the Witch Cultists pursued the land dragon with unthinkable speed. The menace they posed far exceeded that of Petelgeuse's clumsy attacks.

At that rate, the Witch Cult's blades would slice apart the land dragon's scales, whittling her life away. But a moment before that could happen—

"Wah—!" "Ha—!!"

A high-pitched double roar made the air tremble, becoming a shock wave that bore through the world.

These very particular voices formed a roar wave that enveloped large trees and boulders in a straight line, rocking the atmosphere as it slammed into the Witch Cultists. Bloody mist danced in the air where the shock wave had slammed into the group.

So far as Subaru knew, only three people in that world were capable of using such voices.

"Whoaaa! You were in a super-tight spot, mister! You were totally gonna die just now!"

"You were in danger of slightly missing the rendezvous point. This is thanks to Sister's intuition."

With a great and silly laugh, the beast people siblings, Mimi and TB, lined up alongside Subaru riding their large dogs. Their roar wave having rescued him from peril, Subaru looked over to them and raised a fist.

"Hey, I was going all out back there! But thanks, I thought I was gonna bite it!"

"Ohh, thank you! You are very welcome! Yaay!"

"I understand your feelings of confusion… The man above is an Archbishop of the Seven Deadly Sins, correct?"

Ignoring Subaru and Mimi's banter, TB glared up at the sky and inquired in a tense voice. The little cat's monocle-covered eye caught sight of the madman, his habit flapping in the wind, and narrowed.

"What's that, that's amazing! That old man's all balled up and flying! Amazing!"

"I have never before seen such a creepy method of flight."

"Ohh, right! That's what it looks like to you two!"

Subaru, able to see Unseen Hands, and Mimi and TB were viewing reality differently. To the two of them, Petelgeuse, balled up like a gymnast, must have seemed to be flying all on his own, but Subaru beheld the nightmarish sight of tentacle-like evil hands throwing him again and again—well, both were awful sights, really.

"Either way, I'll deal with that one! Take care of the rear just as planned, 'kay?"

"Understood. Let us go, Sister!"

"Oh yeah! Ah! Mister, mister!"

Subaru would continue his dramatic escape from Petelgeuse while leaving subsequent Witch Cultists to the two of them. But just before changing course and departing, Mimi raised her hand to Subaru—

"If you win, it'll be really cool!"

"Yeah! Leave it to me!"

At Mimi's words, Subaru gave the little cats a thumbs-up as he leaped forward, praying they would have good fortunes in battle.

Split apart by the roar wave they'd eaten, the Witch Cultists bore down on the pair, weapons in hand. At that point other members of the Iron Fangs—Rajan and company—leaped in from all directions, whereupon general combat began.

Subaru turned his back on the clashing of swords and pointed tauntingly at Petelgeuse high overhead.

"Come on, Lord Archbishop! If you get distracted by kitties and lose track of me, you'll *never* live it down!"

"—You, you, how far, how far will you go, how, why?!"

Naturally, even Petelgeuse's cheeks stiffened as his attacks were thwarted over and over. Having arrived in the current situation from having lost himself to rage, the madman finally realized that he was in a disadvantageous circumstance. His fingers lurking in the forest had been destroyed one by one, his Unseen Hands, in which he'd held absolute confidence, had been seen by another, and that very moment, his disciples had been ambushed and split apart, and Petelgeuse was alone.

Did that situation not mean he had been dancing on Subaru's palm in every way?

"That cannot be! There is nothing! Nothing recorded of this in my Gospel! What are you, then?! YOU receive favor, and yet you belittle the Witch! You resist, you obstruct the trial I conduct, thwart my PLANS...!"

In midair, Petelgeuse clutched his Gospel, holding it high as he shouted.

His fingers had been taken away, and his authority was ineffective. He did not know it yet, but Emilia and the others had already been evacuated, so his vile acts to bring about the trial had failed before they had begun.

Perhaps, to Petelgeuse, this was what a nightmare looked like.

"What...what are you...?!"

Petelgeuse screamed at the absurdity of it all, froth rising to the corners of his mouth. Subaru calmly replied, "I'm doing this for the fourth time—when it comes to nightmares, I've seen enough to kill me."

He didn't care about Petelgeuse's confusion or his laments. Deny it all he could, it was useless. The instant before his eyes was the future he'd crossed multiple nightmares to reach—

"You truly, trulytrulytrulytrulyyyy! You are Pride—"

"My name is Subaru Natsuki."

When Petelgeuse shouted tenaciously, teeth creaking, Subaru invoked his own name.

"Knight of the silver-haired half-elf, Emilia."

"—!"

"I don't know about this Pride business, but that's the only title I need. The rest can go to hell!"

He silenced Petelgeuse with a point of his finger and his caustic words. The next moment, the forest opened all at once. Ahead, another rocky place appeared—but this was not the rocky place where Subaru and Petelgeuse had faced off earlier. That said, it was not Subaru's first visit to the spot.

There, once upon a time, Subaru had lost his life.

"What is this place…?!"

"Earlier I came to an end here. So this is the place that'll be your end— It's that kind of spot."

Arriving at their destination, Subaru commanded Patlash to slow her pace.

Chasing them through the sky, the change in scenery, and Subaru's statement made the madman wary, causing his vile visage to contort.

"—"

Petelgeuse released himself from the evil hand grasping him, carrying him through the air, and fell to the ground. The madman landed, slowly lifting his face as he stood opposite the precipice, straight toward Subaru.

"If it was YOUR goal to invite me to this place…what is it you have prepared?"

"That goes without saying. A mortal enemy—yours and mine alike."

When Petelgeuse asked in a low voice, Subaru dropped from his land dragon and declared as such. His words made the madman grimace. Subaru closed one eye. When he did so—

"—Mortal enemy? Once again, it is quite something, the ways that you address me."

The interrupting voice of a third party made Petelgeuse's head practically bounce as it swiveled around.

Petelgeuse already realized that he had been lured. On guard against a surprise attack, the Archbishop of the Seven Deadly Sins stuck a finger into his mouth, strongly biting it as he surveyed the area.

But his caution against a surprise attack was utterly meaningless.

"I did not believe I would ever have another opportunity to hear such words again."

Saying this, the speaker leaped straight down from the top of the precipice to the rocky ground below. A surprise attack seemed unthinkable to him as he landed lightly, using a finger to set his handsome hair, askew from the wind, in order.

"—"

Petelgeuse stifled his voice as his eyes widened, gazing at the handsome figure.

However, the handsome man merely stood at Subaru's side, saying nothing of the madman's threatening gaze. Subaru glared at the side of his calm, collected face, grimacing in pronounced annoyance.

"What, you've got a problem with my announcement?"

"No, I was concerned that you might be recalling previous events of which you could not be unashamed... It seems you are truly audacious. I am impressed that you would say such a thing in front of me, even now."

"How about I repeat it in your sleep so you see it in your dreams, hmm?"

"I shall pass. Once is quite enough. Should I hear such a statement a second time, it shall be difficult to sear from my memory."

Drawing his slender sword, the knight answered Subaru's biting sarcasm with sarcasm of his own.

Subaru couldn't even remember how often the sight of his perfectly kempt royal guardsman uniform and his purple hair swaying in the wind had annoyed him. It burned him that that abominable sight was so dependable that moment.

"Julius Euclius, assigned to the Knights of the Royal Guard of the Kingdom of Lugunica."

Identifying himself, Julius poised his drawn knight's sword, pointing its tip toward the madman.

The next instant, lights of six different colors rose up and swirled around Julius, demonstrating their power to the wide-eyed Petelgeuse.

"—I am the sword of the kingdom, the sword that shall strike you down."

"A spirit knight, IS it…? Just how far, truly, just how far will you…"

Petelgeuse's teeth clenched as he received those spoken words. His anger was not so much directed toward Julius for joining to battle as toward the quasi-spirits nestling close to him. On top of that, the madman glared at Subaru and spoke.

"So this, too, is YOUR doing…! Never before have I been so humiliated…!"

"That so? Well, do enjoy—this is your just deserts, y'see."

Subaru replied to Petelgeuse, in whom so much hatred seethed that he clenched his teeth hard enough to split them. Then Subaru patted Patlash on the head, commanding her to depart from the battlefield.

"You've been a big help this far. We'll settle the rest."

"—"

Patlash rubbed Subaru's head with her nose in apparent concern before slowly shifting from the rocky place to the forest. Seeing her go, Subaru took a deep breath.

"Let's do this, Julius."

"You're fine with this?" Julius inquired.

Subaru threw his shoulders back at the question. Unshakable determination rested in Subaru's eyes as he opened his mouth and spoke.

"I won't retreat, I won't bend, I won't lose. I don't wanna lose anyone else."

"I am the man who beat you terribly. Though I swear even now that I had significant reason for doing so, that is no more than self-righteousness so far as you are concerned."

Julius answered Subaru's resolve by speaking of the unforgettable karma that existed between them.

Those words suddenly stirred bitter, out-of-place memories. The humiliation and anguish of that time came vividly rushing back, as if something sharp bit deep into his chest.

"I am not digging up the past in the hopes of washing away the shame. Your resolve is weighty, formed by each decision and action you have taken along the road to this point. Accordingly, I ask you:

At this juncture, can you carry out your long-cherished desire with me at your side, not dispirited in any way?"

"—"

"Can you trust in me?"

Julius's question was extremely vague, coming off as out of place and even vaguely immature. But his meandering drew Subaru's attention to the barbs continuing to assert themselves in the deepest parts of him—a necessary ritual, so that he might turn and face them.

At the royal selection conference, Subaru had put on a disgraceful display; at the training ground, his good name was not restored, but rather smashed all too perfectly at Julius's hand, his infamy redoubled.

The devotion of one girl had continued to motivate Subaru, enabling him to rise to his feet again. And now that he stood and faced forward, there was a different girl he wished to support.

Guided by these twin lights, he struggled against fate. He wondered, how could he put the feelings from back then into words now? What kind of passion did he hold, what fierce emotions scorched within him, what colors of light burned bright within Subaru at that time, in that moment?

"I really hate you."

"Yes, I know."

"That graceful air you give off annoys me, the way you talk sounds stupid and shady, and on top of that you clearly look down at me, and now that I think about it, you kissed Emilia's hand the first time I set eyes on you. When someday I'm lavishing kisses over Emilia-tan's entire body, what, that's gonna be an indirect kiss with *you*? Gimme a break!"

When he thought back, he'd hated Julius even before they had exchanged words for the first time.

The entire sequence of events leading to Emilia's treating him cruelly began with Subaru's antagonism toward Julius. At the royal selection conference, it grew significantly; at the training ground, it exploded; and the ashes continued to smolder thereafter.

Even that very instant, they remained very hot, never ceasing to scorch Subaru's breast.

"You broke my hands and feet, cracked my skull, you even chipped my permanent teeth. Even if they all got healed up, you'd expect the trauma to be real for anyone. Do you even know what holding back is?"

"I would like to point out that was still a great deal of restraint."

"Seriously, that's 'holding back' for you? I really do hate you the most."

Subaru, the self-declared knight, had known repeated shame for his powerlessness, ignorance, and recklessness.

Julius had beaten Subaru to demonstrate what a knight was, fulfilling his role with capability and force.

Subaru couldn't help but pity himself for playing the role of comic relief, but if he set that aside, the man remained, well and truly, the knight Subaru had always wanted to be.

"I *really* hate you, 'Finest of Knights.'"

"—"

"Because of my shame, I know that you're one hell of a knight. That's why I trust you."

More than anyone in that place, more than anyone in that place in the past, Subaru intimately knew Julius's sword.

Hence, it was him to whom Subaru entrusted his fate.

For at that time, Subaru had come to know the weight behind his sword.

"I'm counting on you, Julius—everything I have, I give to you."

"—"

Subaru spoke those words to Julius from close enough for two people to shake hands.

Upon hearing those words, Julius closed his eyes. He slowly opened them a few brief seconds later. Julius beheld Subaru in his yellow eyes, nodding strongly toward him.

"Then I shall answer that shame with all my spirit."

When his sword rose, pointing to the heavens, the quasi-spirits granted their blessing to Julius's decision. The vibrantly colored quasi-spirits seemed to revolve around the sword as they danced in the sky. Among them, the two quasi-spirits colored white and black emitted the strongest light—and this increased still, strengthening and rising until Subaru's vision was practically burned away.

Then, when the light shining on the battlefield with the precipice at its back finally relented, the madman moved.

"…Has your farce finally reached its END?"

Petelgeuse, who had kept his silence while watching the exchange between Subaru and Julius, inclined his head. His eyes were bloodshot as he pointed two bloody fingers toward the pair, creating countless vile, pitch-black hands in the process.

"And just what can you do with the addition of a single spirit knight to the fray? It is absurd that any mere spirit could hinder ME, MY path, MY love, MY diligence! You shall fall! I shall tear the others to pieces! I need only commence the trial anew! For my diligence knows no slothful surrender, nor demise!"

"—"

"Ahh, AHH, ahh, Sloth, Slothslothslothslothslothslothslothsloth—!!"

His tongue stretched so far that his throat seemed unable to contain it. Petelgeuse dug wounds into himself deep enough to reach bone as he shouted his premonition of death, sending his Unseen Hands to smash the pair flat in one blow.

The evil hands rushing toward them exceeded a hundred, resembling a tsunami capable of covering the whole world, one that would swallow Subaru and Julius up like two pieces of driftwood, crushing them and tearing them into a thousand pieces—

"—Al Clarista."

A rainbow-colored glimmer flashed forth, mowing the onrushing Unseen Hands down in an instant.

The aurora borealis danced wildly, reflecting light at seemingly random angles to create blades tracing shimmering arcs. Bathed in that glimmer, the black phantasms dispersed like mist down to their roots, and the savagery they were to wreak was permanently halted.

"…What?"

"You should not act so surprised."

Julius, who had swung his rainbow-imbued blade, elegantly replied to Petelgeuse's dumbfounded utterance.

"If they can touch us, we can touch them. If mutual interference is possible, a rainbow aura imbued with the six elements can cut it."

The six types of quasi-spirits contracted with Julius all rested within the cavalier's sword, giving off rainbow hues. The glimmering aurora of his blade turned it into a beautiful and frighteningly powerful enchanted blade.

However, that wasn't what was bothering Petelgeuse. The madman resentfully shook his head, his feelings of consternation causing bloody tears to flow as he pointed at Julius and spoke.

"You, YOU cannot see them. Surely you cannot. That exceeds the fact that my Unseen Hands have been cut…! That is the problem! You, you cannot, you cannot possibly see them, and yet…beyond me, they are seen by T-TWO!!"

The fact that after Subaru, Julius could also keep his Unseen Hands at bay made his teeth shake down to the molars, his face stricken less by anger and confusion than by deep, powerful fear.

It was the fear of having his final refuge, the very foundation of his faith, ripped away from him.

For the first time, the sight of Petelgeuse like that made Subaru feel sympathy toward him as a human being—but this was overridden by a sense of accomplishment. *Take that, will you?* He truly, finally, had found an edge.

"A base villain like you who knows not the favor of the Witch cannot possibly see the grace granted unto me alone…!!"

Visibly spitting blood as he screamed, Petelgeuse was denying the reality before his eyes. Accordingly, Subaru taught him just what was happening, further pounding that reality home.

"I'm the one who sees them, Petelgeuse."

"…! What?!"

"I'm the one who sees your Unseen Hands. Julius is just seeing what I see. It feels even ickier than I expected, though."

This was the quintessence of Nekt, the magic to share one's thoughts.

Normally the magic was used to link together the minds of human beings within Nekt's area of effect, enabling simple telepathic conversations. However, it required careful use, as befitted high-ranking magic. Once Julius had explained the dangers thus: "If the empathy level is too high, the boundaries between the self and others become blurred, and beings become mixed with one another."

If you mixed two minds together enough, in other words, synchronized the senses, raising the effectiveness to its highest extreme—

"It is possible to mentally maintain two persons' senses joined as one—though I had certain doubts about your sanity when you first made this proposal."

"But we pulled it off, didn't we? When you put men and courage together, they can do anything."

Through the power of Nekt, Subaru's and Julius's senses were completely synchronized on a deep level.

That moment, through Subaru's sense of sight, Julius had to be seeing it, too—the sway of Petelgeuse's countless Unseen Hands seemingly dyeing the forest black.

Subaru was also aware of the mana coursing through Julius's entire body, and of the warm pulses imparted by the quasi-spirits that flowed into him.

The input from the five senses was doubled in the process, creating the incredibly discordant feeling of having ten senses.

"Just to get this out of the way, I don't think we can keep this thing going for all that long."

"I completely agree. Even if you beg, I shall never do this for you again."

As Subaru twisted his lips, Julius gave his words an ironic laugh as he poised his blade. With the aura-imbued cavalier's sword, even Unseen Hands, Petelgeuse's trump card, could be opposed head-on, but neither of them had any room to send a shred of pity or mercy the madman's way.

"Why you...why you, why you, whyyouwhyyouwhyyouwhyyou whyyouyouyouyouuuuuuuuu!!"

Petelgeuse wailed as his unfocused bloodlust made the shadows explode.

Evil hands beyond count scattered and flew in all directions, forgetting even to aim as forest, ground, and boulder were destroyed, shorn, and sent flying.

The shameful sight of the madman surrendering to his basest impulses was so repulsive, it made one want to turn away, but Subaru clenched his fist tighter, not averting his eyes in the slightest.

He absolutely could not avert his eyes for the remainder of the battle.

From the opening to the conclusion, Subaru had to burn the battle into his eyes for both their sakes.

"Doesn't feel too good to have my fate and yours be one and the same— Let's get this over with."

"Yes, so we shall."

The knight sliced away the pitch-black evil hands pouring down upon them; with a horizontal slash, he neatly sliced one onrushing hand in two.

Julius watched as the arms thus burned away turned into black specks, scattering only to be swallowed by the wind and carried away. He laughed and said,

"With your eyes, I shall strike him down, Subaru Natsuki—my friend."

CHAPTER 4

THE END OF SLOTH

1

The black, overwhelmingly violent torrent bore down on them head-on, but the rainbow aurora slashed it apart.

"—!"

The sword's wielder lashed out, slicing down the oncoming evil black hands one after another. The process repeated dozens of times over.

Julius's rainbow-gleaming sword was an enchanted, certain-death blade imbued with the magic of the six elements. It could even rend Petelgeuse's Unseen Hands asunder; dispersed into mist, the shadows dissipated and vanished.

Subaru didn't understand the principles at work. But perhaps it was difficult to reconstitute Unseen Hands severed by the rainbow, for the shadows grew thinner as the sword blows swept away the evil hands; Petelgeuse's rage grew thicker in their stead.

"This is not amusing. This is not a joke. This is something that cannot be! For such a method, a ploy, a child's trick! To impugn! My love! My devotion…!!"

"Not a very nice way to recruit someone…and your organizational culture looks pretty awful to me."

The madman frothed at the corners of his mouth as his inexhaustible shadow arms pounded away. However, Julius countered the evil hands with his rainbow or evaded with his movements alone. With elegant steps the knight danced across the rocky ground, performing a sword dance as he dominated the battlefield.

Even so, the evil hands knew no limits, over ten constantly bearing down upon him, pounding their malice upon him. A single sword swing could not defend against them all. Naturally, Julius's limbs took glancing hits, and a number of lacerations were carved into him.

"Ngg—"

Though he was willingly on that battlefield, Subaru's shoulders leaped several times at the sharp pain. The graze of a black finger made the pain of his thigh splitting burn into his brain. For a moment he nearly let out a cry of pain, but he bit into the flesh of his cheek and endured. He strongly clenched a fist in response to the burn of his shoulder splitting.

At that time, Subaru and Julius's five senses were completely synchronized via the magical sharing of their thoughts. Accordingly, Julius was able to see Unseen Hands through Subaru's vision; for his part, Subaru had become able to trust in the might of the magic sword in Julius's grasp.

"—"

However, putting that goodwill aside, the makeshift partnership was extremely precarious.

Thanks to their synchronization, both had been seeing double. When partnered as such, their vision would be constantly blurry, as if the left eye and the right eye were looking at completely separate scenes. And, as touch was included in the shared senses, not only were Julius's fighting ardor and exhilaration of battle acutely engraved into Subaru, but the pain he felt as well.

There was the sight of the wind grazing his skin, the touch of his leather soles trampling the soil, the taste of blood and saliva mixed together inside his mouth, the ear-ringing sound transmitted to his brain, the smell of risking his life to the utmost, living on the edge between life and death.

The numbers didn't add up. If both were bathed in the experiences of two people nonstop, it simply meant the burden was double. Taste, smell, hearing, pain, touch, sight—right then, they were all a chore.

The dilemma was like having an itch in a place your hand simply could not reach. Perhaps it was better described as having an itch on the back of someone else's head.

"To tell you the blunt truth, I really wanna end this right here, right now...," Subaru murmured, as his body pleaded for an end to the ill feeling and he wet his tongue.

The dryness from the prior moments had probably been passed on to Julius. He couldn't let other physiological responses rear their ugly heads.

It was hard to endure the awful feeling, even though he'd been the one to propose the plan. To think blurring the border between yourself and another meant randomly clawing away at the core of your humanity to such an extent.

But he did not plead for mercy. It was impermissible. And it was no one and none other than Subaru who refused to permit it.

After all...

"It seems you have grown somewhat accustomed, Subaru. Shall I increase the pace?"

"Yeah, don't worry, I'm with you all the way!"

Countless evil hands leaped at Julius before Subaru could even reply. With a posture so low you'd think his chin would chafe against the ground, he slipped under the hands, and with a lash of his rainbow mowed all the shadows away.

As those became mist, the madman sent evil hands threading the dispersing shadows, headed for Julius. But even these fell to the blow of the leaping knight's sword, beautifully blasting them apart.

"—"

Julius elegantly proceeded through the battle, but his brilliant movements slightly faltered.

Of course they did. As the handsome man flung away the remnants of the shadow coiled around his cavalier's sword, the eyes of his gallant face were closed; they had actually been closed while he was engaged in battle, unlike before combat had begun.

This was to narrow the sets of vision from two to one, to achieve victory through Subaru's eyes alone.

If they'd kept sharing their synchronized vision, the world's contours would have become vaguer and vaguer. Accordingly, Julius had closed his own eyes, entrusting Subaru with all visual information.

Julius had made that judgment without consultation. Subaru understood that his judgment was correct.

But at the same time, the true motive behind that action left Subaru indignant.

"Crazy, crazy, you've gotta be kidding me! You really are a disagreeable bastard!!"

Abandoning his own vision and making Subaru his eyes on the battlefield was putting his own life on the line, proving that he trusted Subaru not to avert his eyes from the battle.

'On top of that, inserting Subaru's vision into his nervous system was not nearly as simple as it sounded. One way of putting it was that it was like a third-person shooter, fighting on TV while watching himself from behind.

"This isn't a game, and it's lunatic difficulty, one hit and it's game over! Putting your life on the line like this, gotta be nuts... You and me both!"

"I do not believe you have the time to flap your lips!"

As Subaru kept his eyes wide open, Julius kicked off the rock wall, leaping back to rejoin the boy right at his side. With a swing and a thrust, he prevented damage not only to himself, the main target, but from the stray evil hands headed for Subaru.

During that time, all Subaru could do was sit tight, not averting his eyes, and gasp at the vivid display of skill.

A wry smile came over Julius, eyes still closed, at Subaru's state.

"You are quite a bit of trouble. I understand you are desperately trying, but perhaps you could defend yourself a little more? I cannot face the enemy head-on like this."

"I'll take those words and throw 'em right back in your face! I can barely watch you cutting it that close! Or did you miss the desperate knight I was seein' through my own eyes?!"

"I see a fine young man sad at having to keep his eyes closed. He appears to be handsome and of good upbringing."

"I'm starting to suspect you and I aren't looking at the same world here!!" .

The two exchanged banter as they leaped away from the evil hands rushing upon them the next moment. Subaru's feet clumsily slipped, whereas Julius split the wave of shadow with his sword, elegantly slipping through the gap to advance upon the madman once more.

"Amazing."

Rising up after falling on his backside, Subaru spontaneously voiced his admiration at the sight of Julius in battle. Midbattle, Julius had grown acclimated to the unnatural physical sensations with frightening speed, raising the accuracy and sureness of his sword to new heights.

It was not a feat that knack alone could achieve.

This was the experience he had gained through the pain of ferocious training, cruelly using his body to its utmost limits.

This was the end result of clashing with swords and lives in the midst of battle, honing his own skill and conviction to a fine edge.

Hence, without the slightest fear or doubt, he could swing his sword confident in himself.

"—"

Unable to avert his eyes, Subaru stared at the battle, clenching a fist in fierce regret.

He felt remorse at his incomparable powerlessness in that place, and at having spent day after day in idleness.

That feeling joined the pile of regrets that were the difference between Subaru Natsuki then and Subaru Natsuki as he had become.

It was because he was ashamed, because it burned him so, that Subaru could not avert his eyes.

"—I'll be going now."

"Yeah, get goin'."

It was not that he heard the whisper. But Subaru responded to Julius's words nonetheless.

Grazes from the hands sent pain from the gouge in Julius's back, from his thigh, and from his dislocated shoulder slamming into Subaru's brain.

Subaru gritted his teeth enough they nearly broke, for he could not avert his eyes.

Rush, leap, slide, slice back, step, jump, advance, slip under, stop on a dime, glide past, circle inward, leap sideways, twist and evade, turn around, charge in, leap up, kick, leap about—refined motions all.

"Impossible..."

Slice away, slice down, charge in, slice up, kick away, gliding slice, slam, sweeping slice, thrust, cleave, lash, swing down, knock down, slice away, charging slice, slice in—with repeated sword blows and slices, the Unseen Hands turned to dust.

"Impossible, impossibleimpossibleimpossibleimpossible...!"

Eerie black covered the whole of the sky, yet the sight of the knight carrying on his aurora-shrouded sword dance was so beautiful, Subaru lost track of reality. The scene was so surreal that it could make you forget this was a deadly duel.

That was probably because the thoughts of the quasi-spirits passed through Julius and were conducted to Subaru as well. Those girls loved Julius—and in contrast, they hated the madman. They found the madman intolerable—to such an extent that they could never accept him as one of their own.

"This cannot be! It cannot possibly be so! Why is it! How can this be?! MY Authority...! I am loved, I know I am loved, I am assuredly loved! And yet, to this extent, I AM being—!"

"You persist in illogical thoughts and actions. The fitness of your so-called Authority has diminished. More importantly, I have become sufficiently accustomed to this manner of fighting through Subaru's eyes."

As Petelgeuse vented his fury, Julius thrust his sword forward, eyes still closed.

"It is finally time to cut you down in earnest. Here, I shall strike you down with my blade, and bring the long-standing menace Sloth has posed to the kingdom—nay, the world—to an end!"

"As if you can! As if I will let you! I…I am! ONE such as I who has been bathed in the Witch's grace! Four hundred years! Striving diligently to make Her will a reality! Do you really think a fool like you and your fledgling spirit flunkies can defeat me…!"

Petelgeuse bared his blood-tinged teeth as he raged at Julius's words. But the madman's very rage gave Subaru conviction that the final piece needed for his anti-Sloth strategy had fallen into place. Petelgeuse's abnormal hatred toward spirits rivaled his infatuation with the Witch—in fact, Subaru was counting on it.

"Julius—!"

"Understood! —Archbishop of the Seven Deadly Sins, prepare yourself!!"

Julius stepped forward, advancing with the speed of an arrow. Petelgeuse opened his mouth, deploying his Unseen Hands with an incoherent shout. The evil hands spread through the sky, along the earth, through the forest, as they enveloped Julius to impale him from all directions—

"—Al Clauzeria!!"

Circling around the chanting Julius, a swirling vortex of rainbow-hued light erased all the pitch-black evil hands from existence.

The aurora burned through the world for only a second—but that second was enough. In an instant, like the blink of an eye, the encircling net Petelgeuse had wrought had completely vanished. And, in so doing, opened an unobstructed path between Julius and the madman…

"Bahaa!"

Petelgeuse, struck by vestiges of the aurora and caught in the explosions of his shadows, tumbled to the earth. His crushed fingers clawed at a boulder, and the madman looked like he was about to spit up blood as he rose to his feet.

Right before his eyes, Julius drew near, unleashing a sharp thrust aimed straight at the madman's breast.

"I shall…not…let YOU! —*Ul Doona!*"

Petelgeuse spread his arms wide, intoning a spell as he took a counterattack posture. The next moment, the earth burst upward, and stone walls, a mix of boulder fragments and black soil, enclosed the madman on four sides.

The sword bounced off the rock wall. Mad laughter welled up from the other side, and Petelgeuse let Unseen Hands fly over it, slamming from Julius's blind side to deliver a serious pummeling.

"—"

Dealing with the evil hands meant giving Petelgeuse, on the other side of the wall, an opportunity to escape. However, if he pursued Petelgeuse, he would be slain by the Authority. Either way, Julius's sword could not reach him.

That is, if Julius had been waging that battle alone.

"Blaze, fighting spirit! Howl, demon ball! I've got fifty pounds of will, right here!!"

Twisting his body, raising a leg, taking a great step forward, shoulder rotating in a full swing—with a speed not exactly that of a fastball, Subaru hurled the crimson magic crystal in his hand.

The youth was no baseball prodigy. But he had once had a burning craving for strikeouts at the nearest batting center. His pitch control, at least, amounted to second rate.

When this was combined with his concentration ability in his state of extreme observation, hitting the center of the rock wall with the magic crystal was downright easy.

"What IS…?!"

The crimson magic stone imbued with destructive energies sailed past Julius and crashed into the wall of stone—and exploded in a flash of light and great heat, burying Petelgeuse's field of vision with the vermillion flames from the detonation.

"It cannot be that this, too, was your plan from the…"

"Scorning him as powerless is the cause of your defeat!"

As Petelgeuse froze in shock, Julius's voice reached him from the other side of the flames. The next instant, Julius broke through the flames in a flying leap, burying the tip of his sword in the immobile madman.

"…aa—"

His breast thus run through, the inside of Petelgeuse's entire body was charred by the rainbow aurora.

Slammed into the rock wall behind him, impaled against it, Petelgeuse flailed his limbs. The madman spit out bloody froth, wept, and bared his teeth, as if unable to believe it.

"Ab…surd. Absurd, absurd, absurd…! This cannot…be happening…to ME…!"

"The rainbow aurora has bitten into your very soul. No matter whose body you reside in, the wicked soul within shall find no escape— Now, fall to pieces at the rainbow's end!"

At Julius's voice, the glow of the cavalier's sword increased. Bathed in that light, Petelgeuse could not unleash Unseen Hands; he could only groan in agony and writhe in the unsightly manner of an insect on the brink of death.

However, as Petelgeuse struggled, the madness in his eyes was undiminished. He had not given up on living.

"It ends not here! It cannot! It shall NOT!! My efforts are diligent! I shall not permit any thoughts of surrendering to laziness or sinking into SLOTH! That's why, by any means necessary…!"

The madman wailed, struggled, wriggled, and opened his tattered mouth wide as he tried to escape from the sword. Julius gazed in wonder at his implacable tenacity while twisting his sword, pouring destructive energy into the heart of his foe.

If his heart was destroyed, death was inescapable— Before that point, Petelgeuse made his decision.

"Having lost all my fingers, my destruction is inescapable… BUT…BUT! BUT! There is still, one vessel, that remains for me…!"

They'd gone all over the place and preemptively taken out Petelgeuse's fingers—the spare physical bodies he had brought with him. Consequently, he had to select a replacement on-site.

"—"

His madness-suffused eyes opened wide and moved around. He looked past Julius and caught sight of Subaru.

A chill ran down Subaru's spine. Simultaneously, Petelgeuse's mad laughter grew louder, deeper—

"Ahh—my brain...is shaking."

The moment after his murmur, Petelgeuse's Julius-impaled body crumpled like a marionette with its strings cut. Light faded from its eyes, and its limbs drooped, all signs of life falling from them.

The time had come. Subaru thrust a hand into his pocket and shouted to Julius.

"Julius! Release!"

"Acknowledged!"

Responding to Subaru's call, Julius released Nekt just as they had arranged. As a result, Subaru was instantly freed from the ill feeling of two layers of five senses—but didn't even have time to breathe.

For next, in place of Julius's five senses, came a foreign existence, overwriting the impudent Subaru.

Stuffed into his chest, the invisible entity robbed him of his right to control his own body—and its shrill, earsplitting laughter echoed inside Subaru's own skull.

Subaru proceeded to bend exaggeratedly backward, opening his eyes and mouth to their utmost in acclamation.

"I. Knew. It! This flesh is a vessel with the capacity to hold ME! And with no way to stop ME! No way to impede my path! AHH, ahh, you, were LAZY!"

Petelgeuse's existence felt so close, it was as if they were sitting side by side in the same brain.

This was the final stage of Possession—with his fingers lost, Petelgeuse had moved to take over Subaru's body.

Subaru had no way to resist that savage blow. He'd lost the freedom of his body as the madman consumed his mind.

"Now this is the body of YOUR friend, yes! Can a knight aspiring to noble virtues bring himself to cut it down?!"

Having taken Subaru as a hostage, Petelgeuse licked Subaru's face with his own tongue. The words caused Julius, looking ready to rush over, to halt his feet as he spoke.

"Certainly, I cannot bring myself to cut him down."

"Then—!!"

"Accordingly…"

As Julius spun the quiet word, he showed the madman his own left hand. He held a glowing conversation mirror in the hand opposite to that gripping his cavalier's sword. Subaru had passed Julius the mirror in his pocket the instant Subaru was being possessed.

Its glowing surface displayed a cat-eared knight who had been observing the battle since the outset.

"Now it is your turn, Ferris!"

"Subawu, you big fat idiot for making me do this! I'm going to rip you to pieces later!"

When Julius addressed Ferris through the conversation mirror, the latter's voice sharpened to a point. The ill omen made Subaru/Petelgeuse's eyes open wide, and in accordance with that premonition, Ferris carried out the attack.

However, with his actions having been read through Return by Death, there was nothing he could do—

"Unseen……?! GaAaaaaaH?!"

The instant he tried to unleash the Authority, Subaru/Petelgeuse screamed so much, it seemed his throat would burst. The cause was an explosion inside the body that released a torrent of unfathomably vast heat and anguish.

With a wobble, Subaru's body lost its strength and, still feeling hot all over, collapsed onto the ground. His skull felt like a sauna within which his brain was boiling, with his scalded mind cutting in and out over and over.

And Petelgeuse, sharing his flesh, had shared that very bitter taste.

"A...ga...haa... What...what...happ...?"

Having experienced the novel anguish of having his brain sterilized through boiling, Petelgeuse moaned, his confusion plain. Subaru, clawing together his mental strength, stuck his tongue out at the abominable soul that was his roommate as he answered.

"If the body you take over ain't...in good shape, you can't...do a thing, can you?"

"It cannot be...it cannotcannotcannotcannotcannnoooooottttttttt... be! YOU, you expected ME to shift to your body?!"

You bet! Subaru grandly stated as Petelgeuse expressed shock inside his brain.

They were two minds in one body. It felt odd for Subaru's declaration to leave Subaru speechless. On the inside, Subaru apologized over the conversation mirror to Ferris for foisting such a distasteful task upon him.

—For it was Ferris, on the other side of the conversation mirror, whose spell had robbed Subaru's body of its freedom.

For the purpose of healing, Ferris had interfered with Subaru's Gate, making it possible for him to make the mana inside Subaru's body go berserk through use of water magic. Indeed, it was he who had delivered fatal damage to Subaru the last time around when Petelgeuse had possessed Subaru's body.

He'd made Ferris, proud of his power as a healer, use that power to take a human life. And yet, Subaru had asked him to use that power in such a fashion once more, so as to lay the final trap.

"So thanks to that last request, this body's no good, either... So ready to give up yet?"

"Give up? Give in? As if I would surrender! At this rate, I will rob your flesh, and it will be me, by me, for me, only me—me, me, ME?!"

Beyond his normal madness and fury, Petelgeuse, in a true sense, had begun to go insane.

To so great an extent his moves had been read in advance, his plans thwarted, yet even so, Petelgeuse wailed while tenaciously clinging to his delusions; and Subaru, even as he tasted the suffering of his blood boiling within his body, hardened his resolve.

"At this rate, I'll die…and that'll be traumatic for Ferris… I don't wanna die, either, so I'm gonna settle things with you. We're just gonna do it my way…"

"*What, are…more, unto me! What more, DO you seek from me?!*"

Petelgeuse's voice shook; he was aghast at Subaru's words, words that foretold what was coming.

That moment, with Petelgeuse sitting right next to him in his brain, he knew. The madman was closer to him than he needed to be, conveying his fear and denial so much that it hurt.

The same went for him. Hence, he knew that Subaru's resolve was the real deal.

"Are you scared? Now, after all the things that you've done?"

"*All unto love! All to repay Her favor! What do you know about ME?! All YOU have done is interfere and obstruct my path! What is it with YOU?!*"

Petelgeuse knew not Subaru's true identity. He was simply afraid.

The madman did not understand whence sprung the hatred Subaru bore toward him. Subaru and Petelgeuse's lives had never crossed, not even once. At the very least, that was true as far as he was concerned.

"*Your actions are simply out of irrational resentment…misplaced to the EXTREME!!*"

"…There's no point talking to you anymore. Even among human beings, there are people you can't have a frank conversation with. That goes double if you're not even a human being."

"—"

Subaru's voice, tinged with disappointment and understanding, sent Petelgeuse into shock.

The madman's reaction was raw, for Subaru's declaration had penetrated his stupor to strike at the truth.

"What. Are. You… Are you saying…you know about ME?!"

"The fact I lured you to this rocky place should've made you imagine a nut being cracked— It's a place only for proper spirit mages and—this is flattering myself—people qualified to become 'em.'"

This was the final condition for Possession that the conversation between Subaru and Julius had uncovered—

"Forcing a pact onto a human being qualified to be a spirit mage and takin' over their bodies. That's the truth behind your Possession, Archbishop of…no, spirit, Petelgeuse Romanée-Conti!"

"You dare—!!"

When his true nature was exposed in a loud, brash voice, Petelgeuse, lurking inside Subaru, forgot his fear and shouted back.

Subaru had realized Petelgeuse's true nature when in thought in the middle of the Possession incident the last time around. The real tip-off was Ia, the quasi-spirit.

Last time around, Ia ought to have been residing in Subaru's body, but the instant Petelgeuse possessed him, she was shot out of Subaru. That unnatural occurrence led him to broaden his speculation. It was for this reason Subaru began to suspect that his hatred of spirits—and of the spirit mages employing them—was hatred of his own kind.

Petelgeuse's Possession was an irregular pact, the effect of Petelgeuse himself being an evil spirit. Accordingly, he saw spirit mages, which already had formal pacts with spirits, as his enemies. Even if he could hijack a provisional pact, he could not do so to a formal one. That was why spirit mages were his mortal enemies.

It was because of Julius's sword, and the power resting within it, that Subaru had selected him for the decisive battle—

"Wow, getting ticked at me hitting the bull's-eye. Maybe while possessing people their humanity rubbed off on you?"

"Silence! Do not! Do not compare ME to spirits! Do not put me together with such lowly beings! I am a being beyond that of spirits! I am a chosen being surpassing mere spirits, abandoning vague self-consciousness and granted an objective through Her favor! What do YOU know about me?!!"

Petelgeuse vented, forgetting all about the flesh he had taken over as his rage and hatred exceeded all limits. Ironically, the contents of his words only bolstered Subaru's deductions, and the more he denied it, the deeper he dug his own grave.

"Love has changed ME! Love has given me will, a reason to exist! This, and everything, is by the grace of the Witch! The Witch's favor! Thus! Thusthusthusthusthusthus! I must offer this body, this soul, everything to the WITCH!"

"You can save the sermon, Lord Archbishop—I'll grant you an audience, then...just for you."

"What?! With whom?! Of what do you speak?!"

"Why, the great Witch you've been waiting for."

Root and branch, Subaru's statement blew Petelgeuse's fierce emotions away.

What remained was shock and bewilderment, and for the first time, Subaru had a glimpse of the underside of Petelgeuse's madness.

As the mad thoughts went blank, Subaru turned toward them, choosing that moment to be the one to draw near.

"—I've Returned by Death..."

The instant he spoke the forbidden words, the world lost its color, and all motion came to a stop.

And then it came for Subaru.

2

The world that greeted him was dominated by darkness, and darkness alone.

It was a hazy space, a world of nothing, an empty vacuum where even his own body did not exist.

Whether his body existed or not was unimportant; it was a world where existence or nonexistence held no meaning, a world where you knew not if you even had a soul.

There was a sense of oblivion alone, and there was a blissful, familiar feel to that oblivion. If he could feel anything at all in that place, he could somehow make out his own existence.

Within that darkness, where even his mind was hazy, there suddenly came a change, and the world's ambiance shifted.

"—"

In that world without light, there was a pitch-black figure blotting out even that darkness.

It was a woman. He could grasp that at least.

Her face and the contours of her body were so uncertain, he could not be sure of anything about them. And yet his heart seethed.

This chance meeting with her—no, not a chance meeting; this was a reunion.

This was blessing, this was grace, this was gospel—this was true love.

His lack of fingers irritated him. He wanted to walk over and take her hand that very instant.

His lack of a mouth irritated him. He wanted to lavish words upon her to express his feelings.

His lack of a body irritated him. If she so desired, he would offer her blood, bone, flesh—all of it.

His being only a soul irritated him, for he had but that single thing to offer her.

"____"

As before, she continued to hold her silence. But her mind had certainly shifted in his direction. That was enough. Being in a world where she paid heed to his existence felt as good as if he had ascended to heaven.

And his soul, yearning for love for so long, would be hers, forever—

"—*This is wrong.*"

The voice was tinged with disappointment and despondency.

He had prepared to receive her first words with supreme bliss, whatever they might be. Yet the instant he heard her voice, it created a shadow of worry that made his entire being tremble.

Why did it feel like this? Here, in the place that would surely grant the love that he sought...

"—*You are not him.*"

Her disappointment deepened, her ardor dissipated, and finally her despondency changed into another emotion—anger.

"*Why is someone not him here, in our place—?*"

The voice shook with anger.

The angry, hateful, accursed words rejected the soul, ripping it into pieces.

Unable to grasp the reason for her pushing him away...unable to accept the reality that she truly detested him, and that his love could never reach her...he desperately sought words of sadness and lament, a voice that he could exhaust to assuage her heart.

But he had no mouth to use to form such words, nor fingers nor a body to act out his will. All he had in that place was his soul—and she had rejected him, not permitting him to offer even that.

"*—Begone.*"

The bewilderment, consternation, and grief of his thoughts never reached her. They were meaningless, for to her he was worthless, meaningless, and idle.

Bathed in rejection and repudiation, he accepted his despair; the misery shattered his soul.

Torn away from the framework of the world, his mind was cut from it; and so he sank far, far away, the reunion he had so yearned for...severed.

The sight of her grew distant.

She, whom he had so much, so greatly, so earnestly yearned for, vanished into the ether.

But she no longer cared about such laments.

She merely gazed silently, earnestly, into the pitch blackness—

"*I love you I love you—*"

It was not to anyone present, but someone elsewhere, to whom she continued innocently whispering her love.

3

"—Aaagaah! I'm baaack!!"

Liberated from the agony he'd thought would last forever, Subaru's mind caught up to the speed of reality.

The pain of his heart's being mercilessly squeezed was the strict penalty for speaking that which was taboo. The hands wrought from black shadow—they greatly resembled Petelgeuse's Authority, a fact likely related to the Witch.

Return by Death probably had something to do with some fated connection between Subaru and the Witch of Jealousy. Or perhaps it had something to do with Subaru's being summoned to another world in the first place.

"Either way, I'll find an explanation someday... But right now...!"

Brushing his misgivings aside, Subaru moved his cramping limbs and rose to his feet. He vigorously used a sleeve to rub grimy drool off his cheek, practically gluing himself to the boulder right next to him as he climbed upward.

Then, as the foreign element purportedly in him vanished, he shifted his eyes toward the rock face.

"...How...can...this...BE...?!"

Subaru saw Petelgeuse there, crawling in a pool of blood. Having returned to his own corpselike body, Petelgeuse dragged it forward as he wept, leaving a trail of blood in its wake.

He had abandoned Possession of Subaru, breaking the forced pact, his mind returning to his own body. Having shared Subaru's body, he had to have suffered the same penalty from divulging Return by Death.

In a possessed state, pain was shared, too. Subaru had identified his comparative endurance as his final trump card against Petelgeuse.

"Worst case, I was ready to do that over and over till you tapped out...but you gave up after just once. No guts, huh?"

Wheezing while boasting of victory, the bluffing Subaru felt strength drain from his legs. But he used a branch behind him to support his tottering body, giving a snort toward the side of the face of the man standing beside him.

The knight—Julius—gave a pained smile at his demeanor, swinging his sword and turning it toward Petelgeuse.

"This time, we finish this."

There was a pale glow along the blade of his bloodied cavalier's sword as the quasi-spirits shrouded the edge in a rainbow aurora once more.

With the rainbow sword, able to cut all things, resting in his hand, Julius stared straight at Petelgeuse.

"I love…love, my love… My love is…"

Mumbling words over and over, now lacking the strength even to crawl, Petelgeuse did not notice Julius. Even if he had, it surely would not have changed anything.

Blood did not stop coming out of the wound where his chest had been impaled, and the ashen-pale look over his face was that of despair and death.

"—"

Finally, in front of the sheer cliff, the madman set his back against a boulder and turned his head.

Having lost the willpower to even act disturbed, Petelgeuse looked at Julius with a dumbfounded expression. His gaze proceeded to lower, shifting toward Subaru, standing behind the knight—whereupon he suddenly exploded into emotion.

"Why, why…WHY?!!"

Tears flowed from his wide-open eyes. The hot droplets drenched his cheeks.

These were not the tears of joy Subaru had seen from him several times; they simply reflected the extent of the rage and remorse pouring out of him. They were proof of an unsalvageable delusion—proof that the madman's dream had been shattered.

Petelgeuse wept, looked up to the heavens, tried to clench something that could not be seen, and shouted—

"O Witch…O Witch! O Witch!! I have given this much to YOU! I have done so much for You! Why, why have You forsaken ME?! Why?! Why is it?! O Witch! If it is so, then MY love… Your favor…?!"

"What you offered her wasn't your own love or faith, or even your own body. You were just offering up the people who happened to be passing by you."

Petelgeuse lamented as if clinging on, searching for salvation, when Subaru's words cut him down.

It wasn't worth listening to a word from him. Petelgeuse was just a self-righteous creep indulging in unrequited love.

Wilhelm had said as much—that it was absurd to call this love.

Shiii—!

Julius sprinted, his sword homing in on Petelgeuse's slender frame.

The only things Petelgeuse turned toward the swinging, rising sword were teary, misty, wistful eyes. A rainbow-colored sword blow struck his chest for the second time, and the torrent of light burst within him.

The accumulation of mana that was the true body of Petelgeuse— the evil spirit grafting itself to the bodies of others, feasting upon their Odo—was scorched to the core by the brilliantly colored glow.

When the cavalier's sword came out, Petelgeuse looked down, dazed, as hot blood poured out of his chest.

Then, he trained his unfocused eyes overhead, stretching a hand toward the heavens.

"—My brain...trem...bles."

From his slender shadow, he unleashed a single Unseen Hand toward the heavens above. It stretched farther and farther, as if aiming for the dazzling sun above.

However, that hand grasped nothing, heading for thin air before finally leaving a large gouge in the sheer cliff, sending large cracks running along the rock face.

He probably hadn't done it on purpose.

To Petelgeuse, it was a meaningless act. It was an impulse driven by one final delusion.

"—"

A rock slide occurred above Petelgeuse's head. Giant fragments of the gouged rock face split off and fell. Directly below was Petelgeuse, seeking the heavens, and in the end unable to grasp anything—

"She never loved m—"

The mass of rock crushed his flesh, and there was a grand sound of flesh and bone being squished.

There was a string of rumbles as dust was blown upward from the impact, and in an instant Petelgeuse was crushed, buried by his own hand under the rubble that would serve as his tombstone.

Having escaped from the peril of the rock slide, Julius walked over to where Petelgeuse surely lay. At the end of his gaze, a large quantity of blood was pouring out from under the boulders. Upon seeing this, he shook his head, returning the cavalier sword in his hand to its scabbard.

"__"

Subaru too walked forward, not speaking a single word.

Then, when Subaru stood in front of the tombstone, he made a small sigh.

It was not a sigh of admiration, or a sense of achievement, or satisfaction.

He knew that the only thing spreading within his chest was a deep sense of emptiness.

Subaru would not sully that time and place by speaking of crude concepts such as *victory* and *defeat*.

But he did voice the words that came to the back of his numbed brain.

"Petelgeuse Romanée-Conti."

That single phrase would serve as the marker for the end of that battle.

Petelgeuse Romanée-Conti, Archbishop of the Seven Deadly Sins of the Witch Cult, charged with Sloth.

He who had battled Julius Eucleus, "The Finest of Knights," and Subaru Natsuki, the Self-Declared Knight.

Before the rubble that was his tombstone, Subaru exhaled a little, and said this:

"Man, you were lazy."

CHAPTER 5
—A TALE ABOUT THAT, AND NOTHING MORE

1

Having tossed his final words toward the tombstone, Subaru turned his back upon the madman.

When he turned around, he saw Julius, one eye closed, and Patlash, standing beside him with a composed expression. Both were wounded all over, but their considerable mental strength meant they didn't let it show.

That said, their mental and physical depletion was severe, and that sense of fatigue was beyond their capacity to conceal.

"Well, not like I'm one to talk. Even if it was for just a second, I let him get in my body and all."

The side effects of Possession by Petelgeuse the evil spirit were utterly unclear. He dearly hoped he wouldn't suddenly wake up covered in blood from subconsciously self-inflicted wounds.

In contrast to such absurd thoughts, Subaru was surprised at the oddly despondent feeling within himself. This was Petelgeuse, the most fearsome foe he'd faced since being summoned to another world. Even with him defeated, the sense of loss inside Subaru's chest outweighed any sense of accomplishment.

"This has to be just burnout. I don't feel sad for him biting the dust one little bit... Stupid, stupid."

After those words to himself, he slapped his own cheek, using the pain to switch gears away from such soft thoughts.

They had defeated Petelgeuse. However, Subaru's goals did not end there. The largest task remained: patching up his relationship with Emilia.

Starting with the breakup in the royal capital, he'd allied them with the Crusch camp, defeated the White Whale, battled the Witch Cult, and used a white lie to get Emilia and the others to evacuate—once he finished all the follow-up, including explaining after the fact, only then would this string of affairs be concluded.

Beyond his overusing his body, the various events had left him mentally depleted.

"But no one's been maimed, no one's been killed. This is way better. You realize for the first time how precious peaceful days are when you lose... Nah, I thought that from the start, actually."

Even Subaru, who thought peace and security came first, could not escape irrationality's ire.

That said, the turbulent times had largely calmed. When Subaru turned his head, he shifted it from Julius and Patlash toward Petelgeuse—and then his feet stopped in midstride.

The reason: a single book resting atop the blood trail Petelgeuse had left while crawling.

"—His Gospel, huh?"

He must have dropped it in his dying moments, for the pages of the Gospel were sullied by blood and grime.

Subaru picked it up and flipped through the pages to be sure. Just like before, the contents looked like a bunch of hieroglyphics to Subaru's eyes. The latter half was filled with blank pages, and at any rate, there was no way to ask Petelgeuse about the contents now that he was dead.

"Best to just grab it and talk to Crusch and Roswaal about it later, huh?"

Furthermore, his goodwill toward Roswaal was insufficient to give him the first crack at it. His current absence spoke volumes, so in spite of Roswaal's being an ally, Subaru's trust in him was at its nadir. He wanted to hope Roswaal would make up for it later.

"—Subaru."

As the boy contemplated how to deal with the Gospel, Julius approached him. When Subaru lifted his face at the voice, Julius's brows were knotted with a grave expression.

It was an ill omen. And, as if to bolster Subaru's premonition, Julius straightened up and spoke.

"I know we just settled things here, but let us return to the village immediately. A problem has arisen."

"...I've got one hell of a bad feeling about this. What happened?"

"I have received word from Ferris."

As he spoke, he lifted up the glowing conversation mirror. The mirror's surface was connected to Ferris on the other end. Julius glanced at it, wariness evident in his handsome yellow eyes as he spoke.

"There is apparently something disturbing about cargo aboard the dragon carriages used to evacuate—Lady Emilia is in danger."

And thus, he spoke the explosive words that turned every presumption on its head.

2

When Subaru and Julius arrived back at Earlham Village, the returning expeditionary force had already assembled inside the village.

They noticed the approaching pair, thanking them for the feat of striking down the Archbishop of the Seven Deadly Sins. However, even as they grandly lifted their fists in celebration, thick tension remained in the air around them.

"Not exactly the mood for a victory party to celebrate the mission's success. If something happened, tell us already!"

"Yes, yes, of course. But first, I need to check both of your wounds."

Responding to Subaru's search for an explanation, Ferris slipped past the ring of gathered men. Ferris was smiling, but there was sweat on his forehead, and his Royal Guardsman uniform was terribly stained with blood.

When his attire took Subaru by surprise, Ferris said, "Ahh…" and nodded as he explained, "It's all right, it's not Ferri's blood. It just got messy during healing. Besides, no one here's as badly wounded as he looks. We had wounded, but no fatalities."

"That's good news… Anyway, leave me for later! Do Julius first."

"I can handle your wounds with one hand, *meow*. Looks like I need to take Julius's seriously, though."

Asserting that Subaru's wounds were light, Ferris waved a hand over them and activated his healing magic. With a ticklish feeling, the wounds were healed, and even the pain taken away, in the span of a mere ten seconds, the sort of feat expected of him.

"Okay, we're done, Subawu. As for Julius… Oh my, that looks painful. Come on, strip off your coat."

"Please be gentle."

Julius's reply was crisp, but his wounds appeared deep. It was clear from the grimace on Ferris's face as he examined the wounds that convalescence would take a fair bit of time.

"Your job's finished. Be a good boy and rest… Anyway, Ferris, the other thing. What happened with that cargo…?"

Subaru glanced at the start of Julius's treatment, his feelings distant as he changed the subject. Ferris, receiving the question as he employed his healing magic, straightened up.

"Mm, I know. But I think it's best you speak to the one who noticed first… Oh, Otto!"

Subaru's eyes went wide at Ferris's mention of the unexpected name as the crowd parted in front of him. A young, ashen-haired man practically fell forward as he leaped, slipping through the gap between the knights…

"Otto?"

"Mr. Natsuki! I have been awaiting your return!"

Otto rushed over, his breath labored. He seemed rather agitated as he looked between Subaru and Julius, patting his chest in relief that both were safe.

"First, it is good that you are safe. To be frank, I believed fighting a Archbishop of the Seven Deadly Sins to be nothing short of suicide, but... Ah! More importantly, there is something I must speak with you about!"

"Calm down! Take your time and explain. But keep it to a brief summary of the main points."

"Such difficult conditions...! Anyway, this is about the cargo. Actually, I found something odd when checking the list."

"List, you mean of the traveling merchant freight that was left in the village? What was odd about it?"

Otto lowered his voice as he hastily unfolded the list of trade goods he was holding against his chest. Then he flipped to a certain page and spoke.

"Sir Kety...I do not know if that is his real name, but the traveling merchant, Kety Muttat. It would appear he was captured as a spy for the Witch Cult, but..."

"Yeah, I know about him— I see, you knew him personally, didn't you?"

Subaru knew from previous go-arounds that Kety and Otto had come into contact with each other any number of times. Otto had to be in shock that someone he knew had been in the Witch Cult.

But Otto did not linger on that part; rather, he moved forward, drawing even closer to Subaru.

"Sir Kety being a Witch Cultist surprised me, and it is most unfortunate. But that is not the issue— You used his dragon carriage to evacuate the villagers, yes?"

"—? Yeah, I used it. Owner aside, the dragon carriage did no wrong. I didn't have the luxury of leaving a usable dragon carriage behind, so I had to use it to get everyone out."

"And the cargo unloaded from the dragon carriage is as I see recorded on this list, yes?"

"It should be..."

Subaru nodded as misgivings crept in about why Otto was so

focused on the minutiae. "I thought so," said Otto, certainty on his face as he continued to speak to the nervous Subaru, his voice hardening. "When I compared the list to the freight, there is something missing that ought to be in the village."

"Missing?"

"A large quantity of fire magic crystals Sir Kety's dragon carriage was hauling is missing—a quantity sufficient to blow seven or eight dragon carriages apart cannot simply vanish into thin air."

3

Kety's dragon carriage was headed to the Sanctuary. Rather, it was being used by the evacuation group taking Emilia and others to the royal capital.

When Subaru confirmed the distribution of dragon carriages after his talk with Otto, he came to a conclusion.

There had been three Witch Cultists hidden among the traveling merchants. Once they'd lost their owners, expeditionary force members had taken their carriages; Subaru distinctly remembered that the carriage Emilia had boarded was one of those three.

"Those magic crystals on the list...they were really loaded aboard? I just have to say, relying on a list from a Witch Cultist is a little..."

"The frightening thing about Witch Cultists is that they melt into everyday life only to become poison when you least expect it. They act as is appropriate for their false identities... You are merely closing your eyes because you do not wish to see, Subaru."

"Even here you whip out the logical...... I know. I'm in the wrong."

Julius sternly thrust reality into the nervous Subaru's face. Ferris glanced at Subaru as he prudently abandoned a reflexive retort, turning his eyes toward Otto as he spoke.

"It was Otto who noticed the discrepancy between the list and the freight...but he had another reason, too."

"Yes. All the other freight matches except for the magic crystals, after all...and actually, I have seen the crystals myself."

"You saw that there were magic crystals loaded aboard?! When?!"

When Otto named himself as a witness, Subaru pointed a finger at him in disbelief.

"It was…back when dragon carriages were being recruited for the evacuation. I was with Sir Kety when I heard the offer. Then everyone was in a great hurry to be the first out of the gate, and as they made predeparture plans for the journey……I sneaked a peek at what he was carrying."

"Man, can't take my eyes off you for a second… You really had it coming, didn't you?"

"Isn't that a little too mean?! Anyway, I saw them with my very own eyes. As for the quality…because they are absent, I am the only one who can attest to the menace they pose, but…"

As the explanation came to a conclusion, Subaru grimaced as he looked at Julius and Ferris. However, even their expressions were grave; in particular, Julius's anger toward himself was evident.

Subaru, too, understood well the anger he bore.

"Shit, I missed it! This is what I get for being a cheapskate and using whatever I can lay my hands on!"

"I checked to make sure they had no trigger via enchantment… but I overlooked that a physical trigger might have been left in the dragon carriage itself. I am sorry, this is my mistake."

"It's not your fault…it's mine for not realizing."

Julius's caution regarding magical traps was no doubt impeccable. If he was taking care of that end, Subaru had to be the one to realize there was a physical trigger.

But what hurt more than anything was that Subaru had personally experienced that dragon carriage's explosion the last time around. Back then, Kety's true identity came out when Petelgeuse used Possession on him, and Subaru and Ferris were caught in the explosion. After, when he learned that the fingers had an explosion enchantment embedded in them for killing themselves, he'd assumed that the explosion had been that enchantment at work—

"That explosion wasn't an enchantment, it was the dragon carriage's trigger…and this time, it's a dragon carriage used in the evacuation."

Rigging his dragon carriage with magic crystals was a highly effective emergency measure in case Kety was exposed as a Witch Cultist. He'd be able to inflict great damage on the expeditionary force, turning the tide of battle in his allies' favor.

Considering the monomaniacal malice of the Witch Cult, it was a scenario that was easy to accept.

"Ferris! If we rush over by land dragon, can we catch up to the evacuation group heading for the capital?!"

"That might be difficult. It's been an hour and a half since Lady Emilia and the others left... To ensure the Witch Cult wouldn't spot them, they didn't kick up a storm, but they're not moving at a leisurely pace, either."

Of the two evacuation groups, the one making a run for the Liphas Highway was relying on speed. Once that group left the Mathers domain and reached the highway, it would be even harder to catch up to it.

But if they didn't do anything about the booby trap, Emilia and the children would pay the price—

"It's still not enough? After all this, and I still can't..."

Would the fates of people precious to him be decided in a place beyond his reach?

No matter how much effort Subaru exhausted against Fate, snares were laid by this hand or that hand. It was as if all the paths for Subaru to walk had been meticulously paved with thorns.

But just as Subaru felt himself entwined by the irrationalities of Fate—

"May I speak to you for a moment, Mr. Natsuki?"

With a serious look on his face, Otto raised a hand and interrupted Subaru's unease.

Determination rested in his eyes; the frail words of before seemed to have come from a completely different person. But Subaru remembered that look on his face. On a previous go-around, when in a true sense he had met Otto for the first time, and Subaru had brought the thoroughly plastered Otto a business offer, he'd put on his merchant face just as he was doing now. In other words—

"This means you want to make some kind of deal with me, Otto?"

"What a perceptive man, something I do not mind at all. Mr. Natsuki, right now I am on the edge of a considerable precipice. The cargo on my dragon carriage is now worth less than dirt! And tragically, the opportunity to turn it all around has slipped through my fingers! To be blunt, I cannot laugh off a deal upon which I wager my life."

From what Subaru had heard, the disastrous circumstances afflicting Otto were more comedy than tragedy, but he had no time to poke fun at them. Subaru nodded, prodding Otto to continue.

Subaru's demeanor made Otto close his eyes for a single moment; then he made his proposal.

"Let us make a deal. If you accede to my conditions, I promise to exhaust all my spirit to get you to your destination—and catch up to the dragon carriage at issue."

"You can catch up to them if we leave right now?! How?!"

"Before we speak of that, I want your firm pledge that you will accept my conditions. What I am offering is my trump card, so I cannot easily speak of it…even under duress."

"Just say what your conditions are! If they're in my power I'll do whatever you want!"

After Otto carefully selected his words, Subaru grasped his shoulders, demanding to hear further.

He'd already repeated that world four times over. He'd struck down the White Whale, dispatched the Witch Cult, cleared most of the conditions for getting what he was after; having come this far, he refused to let it all go to waste.

If it was only one more step, he'd overcome it with a pinch of guts and grit.

"You decide quickly. I do not mind this, either."

Cold sweat broke out on Otto's brow as he formed a smile at Subaru's immediate decision. The negotiations taking place that instant were a seminal event that would determine the course of his life. Subaru's snap decision after the briefest of pauses surprised Otto, but he immediately tossed his conflicted feelings aside. And then—

"As my reward, I want you to arrange an audience between me and Marquis Mathers. Also, you will purchase all the oil I am carrying…and I shall name my price. How about it?"

Narrowing his eyes, Otto put on his merchant's face as he spoke, seemingly testing Subaru.

Coming out with your maximum demand at the outset and haggling down from there was Negotiation 101. Taking advantage of exigent circumstances was playing the merchant by the book.

From there, Subaru and Otto began their fierce battle of negotiation—

"You're still hung up on that?! All right, I'll buy all your oil or whatever, and if you wanna meet that perverted clown, I'll do whatever it takes! It's a deal!"

"Eh?! What the—? You're scaring me!"

The negotiations began on the same note as the previous time around, and ended the same way as well—once more, Subaru fully accepted the terms of the deal upon which Otto had wagered their fates.

Whether he would think of an unearned win through the opponent's resignation as something to be proud of was another matter entirely.

4

"I shall have Ia accompany you. She should be able to locate the magic crystals the dragon carriage is rigged with."

With those words, Julius once again handed his red quasi-spirit companion to Subaru.

Just like before, the faintly glowing quasi-spirit synchronized with Subaru's Gate and vanished from sight.

"That's a big help, but won't she get angry at your lending her out that easily?"

"It appears that Ia is quite fond of you. Besides, I wish to avoid any regrets from sending only one as ill-versed as you. I really would like to go myself, but…"

There, Julius's words cut off as his refined face bore an air of regret. But Ferris, right beside him, puffed up his cheeks in exasperation as he continued casting healing magic.

"Sit tight and stop saying stupid things. You're completely out of mana, so you're useless anyway!"

"This is what I get for borrowing the buds' power. I can only rue the limits of my abilities."

"Coming from you, that's just sarcasm. Anyway, I'm grateful you lent me the spirit. Beyond that…"

Having accepted the spirit on loan, Subaru thrust a finger at Julius, fully immersed in the last of his treatment.

"After all this is done, we're having a banquet to celebrate busting the White Whale and the Witch Cult. You're invited, so don't go dying on me."

"So if I am murdered here, you and Ferris are the culprits. It is an easy-to-understand situation, then."

"Well aren't you two getting along, *meow*. Hey, get going and catch up to Lady Emilia already!"

Glaring at the lighthearted exchange, Ferris pointed toward the entrance to the village. Taking the hint from the pair, Subaru gave a thumbs-up and set off running.

"I expect your utmost efforts."

"Just watch out, okay? I can heal you if you don't die, but if you bite the dust there's nothing I can do."

Subaru waved a hand toward the voices of support and met up with Otto at the village entrance.

Otto was preparing for the pursuit by hitching Patlash and his favorite dragon to his own dragon carriage. It'd be a midsize dragon carriage with a canopied wagon with two heads drawing it—that was how they'd catch up to Emilia and the others who'd left first.

"You have not forgotten anything? Time is precious, so let us set off."

"Yeah. I'm counting on you for route navigation and all the other little stuff, Otto!"

The two nodded to each other and climbed into the driver's seat together. In front, there was a fair bit of a size difference between the two land dragons drawing the carriage. Subaru was concerned about the slender Patlash's inferior size, but…

"Land dragons have the wind repel blessing, so a certain difference in size is not a hindrance. They are also both females, and I have not heard any particular friction between them."

Seeing the doubts on the side of Subaru's face, Otto explained thus as he took the reins. The way he used the word *heard* made Subaru let out a little "Hmmm."

"What is it?"

"Ah, nothing, I just thought that blessings are amazing things. I was thinking of them kinda like talents, but I was surprised there was a Dr. Doolittle one, too."

"A veterinarian? I see what you are saying, but blessing bearers go through considerable difficulties of their own. In particular, I could not control my language blessing very well when I was at a young age."

When Subaru voiced his admiration, Otto made something of a pained smile as he spoke of his own blessing.

The language blessing essentially allowed a person capable of conversing with any living thing. He would employ the power of his blessing to catch up with Emilia and the others—that was his end of the deal.

"At first, I was wondering how the heck you'd use this blessing to catch up with them, but…"

"I will speak to the birds and insects along the way to determine the shortest route. It will be hard on Fulfew, my land dragon, but we will charge through, be it game trails, poor roads, cliffs, or swamps."

Otto had reached the Mathers domain ahead of other merchants by plowing through paths that were not paths. As he was extremely short on luck, this had resulted in his becoming a prisoner of the Witch Cult.

Regardless, borrowing the power of his blessing—

"We'll catch up to Emilia and the rest up on ahead. Easy win."

"No, I would not deem it an easy victory…… It is quite possible we will catch up. In the first place, there is actually nothing in the terms agreed to earlier that guarantees we will catch up to…"

"We'll catch up to Emilia and the rest up on ahead. Easy win—!"

"It really puts me a bind if you say it with a smiling face like that, you know?!"

Though Otto shouted under the weight of that trust, nothing was served by weak musings at that point.

Subaru's smile vanished as he bowed his head to Otto with a serious expression.

"I'm counting on you, Otto. You're the only one I can rely on."

"…Those truly sound like last words, damn it."

Faced with Subaru's meek demeanor, Otto spoke with chagrin and sighed with an air of resignation. Then he gripped the reins and strongly issued a command toward the two land dragons. They picked up speed.

"Oh, fine, I'll do it, I'll do it! I'm making money from this, so if I work myself to the bone, I owe you that much—!"

In accordance with the desperate Otto, the dragon carriage ran at extraordinary speed, onward and onward.

Subaru, strongly sensing that speed, began to hallucinate, seeing Emilia and the others on the road ahead. It was their backs he was racing to catch up to.

But then—

"Er—?!"

With a sudden start, the dragon carriage left the road, plunging into the forest down a game trail.

The ride was so bumpy that even the wind repel blessing could not wholly protect him. Subaru stared at the trail as the dragon carriage barreled down it, beginning to take a series of literal shortcuts.

Afterward, Subaru resigned himself to death numerous times as they ran along bad road after bad road.

Having already died ten-odd times since being summoned to another world, Subaru *knew*, without a single speck of exaggeration, his rocky ride with Otto was reckless, grazing past death at every turn.

They engaged in the thoroughly suicidal behavior of running down a nearly vertical cliff, charged across an old rope bridge that seemed on the verge of falling at any moment (which, in fact, fell just after they had crossed), and when barreling through a demon beast habitat zone were pursued by a particularly fierce pack of ferocious beasts; Subaru had no time to count the number of times they'd wagered their lives.

"I'm a goner... This is finally gonna kill me for sure... End of the road...!"

"What is it? We are moving at an incredible pace. To be honest, even I did not think I could come this far... So this is the latent power of a human being with no tomorrow...!"

Beside Subaru, who was clinging to the driver's seat with a blue face, Otto was completely in a trance. His statement sounded rather precarious, but Subaru said nothing, fearful of an unnecessary question breaking his concentration.

"Besides, setting the process aside, we're making awesome time."

Punching out of the forest, they at long last leaped back onto something that resembled an actual road. There was a sign right at the edge of Subaru's vision marking the border between the Mathers domain and the highway. It had taken them half the normal time to arrive—their repeated travails had brought tangible results. Not that he ever wanted to do it again...

"The highway... Rather, cutting through the grove to the left is faster, isn't it?! That is the shortest route!"

"By grove, don't you mean forest?! Is that way really all right?! It doesn't look like there's even a game trail...!"

"—"

"Hey, answer me!!"

Otto did not respond to Subaru's shout as he sent the dragon carriage charging headfirst through the entrance to the forest.

With the die cast, all Subaru could do was hold on with both hands and pray no accident would befall them as they headed into the forest. The dragon carriage leaped as it rolled over tree roots; Subaru clenched his molars as they headed down an atrocious path once more.

The whole of his vision was buried in thick trees; one false move and they would be crashing headfirst. But the way Otto was delighted in contrast to the pallid Subaru made the latter reassess his view of peddlers.

"Is being a traveling merchant this dangerous?! Making a name for yourself in the capital's market is a lot saf—"

"Mr. Natsuki!"

Subaru was trying to distract himself with small talk when Otto suddenly interjected with a shout. The voice, infused with a sense of urgency, made Subaru look over, wondering what was up. As he did so, Otto put a hand to his ear, surveying the area around them as his cheeks stiffened.

"The forest is astir... No. The birds and insects have left in a great panic! Even Fulfew is tense... Something...something is coming!"

Otto's wary voice made Subaru gasp and look around the area. But atop a rocking dragon carriage traveling through the forest at such speed, he'd never make out anything even halfway bizarre.

Yes, if it had been halfway bizarre—

"Ugh, time is precious, but we should take measures for safety. Mr. Natsuki, please watch over the rea—"

"Nah, ain't no need for that."

As Otto tried to switch policies, Subaru spoke in a ridiculously calm voice.

Subaru's gaze was trained behind the dragon carriage, glaring at the forest scene they were leaving behind. As it grew more distant, the forest seemed to vanish from his vision, as if "it" was swallowing the forest whole.

"—"

Trees were snapped and sent dancing in the sky, brutally devastating the forest's foliage.

Just after the destruction arose, the dragon carriage raced up an incline, but *it* was ferociously heading straight toward them, heedless of the damage to the surrounding area.

"Let her fly, Otto—do *not* let him catch us!!"

"Mr. Natsuki?!"

When Otto started to look over, Subaru checked him with a hand as he transferred from the driver's seat to the wagon. Then he stood as the guardian of the wagon, baring his teeth as *it* pursued, right behind them.

"Why you— Just how stubborn are ya gonna be, you shitty bastard!!"

Subaru let out an angry shout as pitch-black shadows swelled and wriggled before his eyes.

The evil black hands stretched and erupted from a corpse, no longer a person, but a collection of delusions.

The remains of Petelgeuse Romanée-Conti consumed the forest as it pursued the carriage from behind.

5

It was repulsive. It was hair-raising. It was sinister beyond measure.

The body had been crushed under a rock slide; its right arm and the right side of its torso were both gone. Hair and scalp had been torn from its skull, leaving it dyed red, and the lower body being dragged along had nothing under both shins. Its limbs drooped, their vitality meager; this was already a mere corpse.

But the corpse had not ceased its morbid defiance, drowning in delusion as it continued its pursuit of Subaru.

"Giiiive…thaaaat…boooody…baaaaack!"

"Man, you're stubborn. Don't you remember the rough time you had inside me…?!"

Petelgeuse's shout was like a voice from the grave, chilling Subaru to the bottom of his heart.

With the body he had possessed already dead, Petelgeuse's own "death" lay right before his eyes. However, appearances aside, the use of Unseen Hands imbued the madman's movements with explosiveness. If he was left to his own devices, they'd probably collapse on their own, dissipating far away, but—

"Not easy to just wait for time to run out, huh…? Damn it all!"

Subaru gritted his teeth and glared as the madman pressed closer to the rocking wagon.

The dragon carriage was already hurtling at nonsensical speed, but Petelgeuse moved even faster. Like a lit candle on the verge of burning out, he was radiating his final, wicked delusions.

"This is a spirit? How? Aren't spirits supposed to look more—holy or something?"

"Mr. Natsuki! What is going on back there?!"

Subaru's lament was overshadowed by Otto's shout. He could not see the nightmare behind them, for it was located directly behind the carriage—leaving Otto the better for it.

"We're just being chased by a slightly huge dark monster. I think we probably ran over its tail halfway through the forest. It makes a lot of noise and its face is scary, so I recommend you don't look."

"That makes not seeing it really trouble me?! And that description was full of troubling details!!"

"Just let 'er rip! Next time you snap at me I'm taking a bite outta you!"

"*Whaaa—?!* How terrifying!"

Otto handled the reins as Subaru intimidated him and made him focus on the horrid path. But the speed of a land dragon had limits. They were done for if, God forbid, they smashed into even a single tree; consequently, the land dragons could not be hastened any farther inside the forest. In other words—

"The job of slowing you down falls to me. It's time to put on a grand finale... How many grand finales are you gonna have, anyway?! What about you makes you Sloth? You're a freaking workaholic!!"

"Wiiitch SATELLA! Give me—me—her love, love, looooooooove!!"

"She doesn't love either one of us!! There's no romantic comedy where you crush the heart of the person you like! With a heroine like that, no thank you!"

Petelgeuse lifted up his head and screamed, looking like his eyeballs were about to fall out of his skull. He had been betrayed, turned into a dead body, yet even so, Petelgeuse continued to shout his "love" toward the Witch. For the first time, Subaru genuinely saw him as pitiful.

He tenaciously yearned for a body, deluding himself with his lust for "love" from the Witch—and behind it all, he was a spirit without a body of his own, with a craving for affection and physical contact that could never be fulfilled.

Gradually rotting away from a craving that could never be sated, Petelgeuse's mind fell into madness.

No one would ever accept a being like him in the first place.

"I don't have a special attack or a super spell, but I'm taking you on anyway. I ain't letting you get past me, and no way am I letting you get to the one behind me...!"

"Mr. Natsuki, I didn't know you cared...!"

"Will you shut up a second?! I'm trying to act cool here!"

Whether Otto was flippant or serious, Subaru shut him up and turned back to face the madman.

Thanks to the amount Julius's sword had burned away, the total number of Unseen Hands was barely enough to propel his own scamper. The number of arms waving above his head, available for attack, was seven—the exact amount he'd started with.

Petelgeuse savagely clawed at the ground, kicking up a cloud of dust as he drew nearer to the dragon carriage. The evil hands swung upward, making tree limbs fly, and pounded down from the sky above, each blow splitting the earth. Black fingertips lightly grazed the rearmost parts of the wagon, digging deep wherever they touched regardless of their strength.

Subaru calculated the range was such that the next blow would land for certain. If a direct blow of identical force landed in the center of the wagon, the dragon carriage would roll onto its side, killing Subaru and Otto both.

The next move would decide the match.

"Mr. Natsuki, we are coming out of the forest—!"

At the same time Otto spoke, Subaru's field of vision, covered by green, suddenly brightened.

The dragon carriage flew out of the forest as if punching through a wall and slid down a grassy incline. Petelgeuse chased them out, clawing the ground as the mass of shadow seemed to swallow rocks and fallen trees, all becoming a twisted spirit set to consume the rear of the dragon carriage as well.

They cut through the forest and onto the highway. Emilia and the others they were chasing were not far beyond.

Subaru couldn't lead Petelgeuse before them—before Emilia. The Archbishop of the Seven Deadly Sins couldn't appreciate his goal, but he would not permit Emilia's heart to be wounded.

Therefore, accordingly, Subaru Natsuki would set his life ablaze then and there—

"We're out of the forest—no more holding back!"

"LOVE! LOVE! Love is everythiiing—!!"

Tears of blood streamed out as Petelgeuse opened his toothless mouth, laughing maniacally.

Subaru listened to his cackling voice as he sprung loose the cargo inside the wagon. He dragged one of the heavy, lined-up containers forward as the pungent scent of the liquid within clogged up his nose.

He wrapped his arms around it and picked it up. Then he hurled it at the mad, bloody laughter.

"Burn in hell, Petelgeuse!"

"—!!"

Simultaneously, the Unseen Hands stretched into the sky swung downward in a cascade of destruction.

But Subaru moved faster, before the evil hands could reach.

As the vile laughter floated in the air, Subaru hurled the pot he carried—the *oil pot*—toward the madman. The ceramic vessel crashed and shattered, the contents within spectacularly smearing the madman's corpse. The preparations were complete.

The pitch-black, evil hands were falling—to blow the dragon carriage asunder, and Subaru with it.

Heedless of that, Subaru stretched his right arm straight forward, pointing with his fingers arranged like a pistol. At the end of his fingertip was a red light—for it was there that the red quasi-spirit he had borrowed from Julius resided.

"Gonna borrow your power, Julius Juukulius."

"Whyyyyy YOUUUU—!"

"Rental Goa—!!"

It was an incomplete chant by a novice magic user to an uncontracted quasi-spirit, two incomplete things piled upon one another—but his will was focused upon that single point, granting the incantation strength.

And for it to interact with the world around him, only a spark was needed.

His mana, like a gas tank running on fumes, connected to the power of the quasi-spirit, sending a tiny spark of minimal destructiveness rushing toward Petelgeuse. And then his wicked mouth, covered in blood and oil, opened wide.

"AaaaaaAAAAA!!"

That instant, Subaru's vision was enveloped by vivid, soaring flames.

Petelgeuse's entire body was bathed in ignited oil that burned with incredible heat. Billowing waves of flame scorched the inside of his flesh, and Petelgeuse's wordless scream clawed at the air around them.

Against the spirit that was Petelgeuse, Subaru had inflicted the greatest blow possible. The elements were Otto's cargo of oil pots and Julius's quasi-spirit, granted as a safety net. All of it was borrowed—he'd simply patched them together for a very Subaru Natsuki–like attack.

"It's over for— Gahh!"

A moment after he saw the end of the match, Subaru noticed the existence of a pitch-black, evil hand lashing above his head. The evil hand was being swung like a grim reaper's scythe, its course reckless and its target undefined.

However, the arm collided with the wagon, instantly sending it flying, grazing Subaru in the process. The dragon carriage violently bounced from the impact, and the wagon that had taken the direct hit was wide open, looking like some beast had taken a bite out of it.

With the carriage gouged, Subaru was among flying pieces of wood as he tumbled deeper into the wagon. His calf was torn in the process, making him clench his teeth as the pain felt like it was setting his brain on fire.

"—Gahh! Shit, that hurts! Aw, damn it!"

Subaru's voice went ragged as he pressed a hand on the bleeding wound. But Subaru had the time neither to bandage it nor to curse his misfortune. The reason was simple: Black fingertips were grasping the rear end of the wagon that very moment—

"Giiiive MEEE, haaand it OVERRR..."

The dragon carriage heavily rocked as the fiendish, burning face of Petelgeuse crawled up into the wagon.

"—"

The thing that climbed into the wagon had abandoned a complete human form.

The missing parts—the lost right half and torn-off lower extremities—had been replaced by wriggling black hands. Of his original body, only his head was not charred red and black. Though the fire had spread to even his habit, he somehow managed to hold his body in one piece, but even so, the sheer ugliness of the being shone through...

Almost as if to assert beyond all doubt that this was a repulsive monster wearing the skin of a human being.

"You look *awful*...not that I'm really one to talk, I suppose."

Grimacing from the spasm-like pain, Subaru bore it and rose to his feet. The bleeding of his leg had not stopped, but the opponent was far closer to the brink of death than he.

Petelgeuse's entire body had been decaying even before being set on fire; he was already at death's door. He wasn't seeking a war of attrition, either. The next instant would settle it for both of them.

Subaru did not have many trump cards to play; indeed, they were few. All that Subaru had left for a weapon was cunning.

"Bo...dy—CANNOT vanish... Cannot...allow...to vanishhh..."

"Hey, I told you already, come into mine and you'll have a really bad time! Who cares about the Witch?! She's just taking us for a ride, you and me both!!"

Petelgeuse spoke with difficulty, craving Subaru's body as he repulsively crawled forward. As he raised his voice, refusing to give in, Subaru tried to break the madman's spirit.

But Petelgeuse showed a reaction to that shouting voice that he had not shown to that point.

"—Witch, Satella…"

Suddenly Petelgeuse murmured with lucidity as he lifted up his face. His visage was half-destroyed, his cheekbones raw and exposed, yet reason returned to the madman's eyes.

His disjointed eyes wavered, and one caught sight of Subaru, then the other. Together they blinked with madness.

"You are…dangerous. Danger, danger, dangerdangerdangerdanger dangerdangerouuuuss—!"

"Aaah?!"

"YOU receive, receive—ceive—ve—her Favor, yet deny her love! And YOU have driven me, me, me, meeee! This close to the point of death, death, deathdeathdeathdeathdeathdeaaaath!"

Petelgeuse's head swayed and trembled as he ranted incoherently. But behind that fury, the power of the evil hands steadily spread, consuming the wagon and stealing Subaru's foundation out from under him. If the evil hands were unleashed with nowhere to run, Subaru had no chance of victory.

The madman's intelligence had returned; he was chasing Subaru out of intellect, not instinct. With the cards stacked against him, Subaru inched away, and at the same time, a single possibility came to mind. And then—

"The Witch, Witch, Satella…SATELLLAAA! Love, love, looove! I was loved! I WAS loved!! Satella, me—Satella loved me! I shall not forget, for even an instant! Even if YOU forget, I—shall—not!!"

Tears flowed. These were not tears of blood, but real tears.

Truly, since their first chance meeting, this was the first time Petelgeuse had shouted about love while sane.

Be it affection or passion, it had dragged Petelgeuse from the brink of madness back to reality. Petelgeuse's stagnant eyes shone with the firmness of will as they glared at Subaru.

"You are dangerous! You shall someday pose a threat to the entire

Witch Cult! Before that! Before your hand can reach Satella! Here! Now! By my hand! By my diligence! To sunder myself from Sloth, and repay Her love...YOU shaaall DIE!!"

Petelgeuse shouted, and his body, unable to withstand the unleashing of the power of the evil hands, burst open and broke apart. But Petelgeuse was no longer bent on taking Subaru's body, but rather, on killing Subaru, so that a threat to the Witch Cult would not be left to fester—and thus protecting the Witch he worshipped.

These were the actions of a beast, but performed with will, with intellect...

"I'd probably have lost if you'd stayed a monster, you know."

When Petelgeuse saw what Subaru had taken out of his pocket and held in his hand, his eyes went wide.

His reaction made something in Subaru's heart cry out. But he bit back the sentiment that momentarily reared itself, hoisting his arm aloft.

Swinging his arm high, he flung the small, black book—the Gospel—at the tip of Petelgeuse's arm.

"Ahhh...Satella!"

In a daze, Petelgeuse let a low, quiet voice trickle from his mouth.

It was a voice immersed in tranquility, calling out the name of someone lovely beyond measure.

Desiring the heavens, Petelgeuse raised his left and only remaining arm toward the sky. Obeying his will, the evil hands stretched toward the Gospel, the black fingertips reaching for the book dancing in the air—and the next moment, *it* came.

He caught the Gospel just as it was enveloped by wind, just on the verge of blowing away. It was affected by the wind. Meaning it was beyond the blessing. In other words—

"—?!"

As Petelgeuse grasped the book, his body heavily bent back, bathed in ferocious winds. His feet were dragged, splitting the already gouged-out floor of the wagon; half his body was cast beyond the dragon carriage. And, as a result of being cast beyond the wind repel blessing, he was wholly immersed in turbulence.

Once upon a time, Subaru had fallen into a similar circumstance during horseplay on the way to the capital.

Without the wind repel blessing, he was taking all the wind and shaking of a dragon carriage running at full speed over horrid footing. He couldn't possibly have held out.

"—Aaah, AAAAAAH!!"

Subaru let out a great shout and put his foot down the instant Petelgeuse's balance greatly faltered. He forgot the pain of his torn leg and leaped, bouncing into the air. He had no tremendous power to turn the tide of a battle—that's why he had to make his move when it counted most.

"—"

Petelgeuse shouted something as Subaru rushed over. Subaru couldn't hear a thing. He threw caution to the wind, lowering his head for a charge, and leaped toward Petelgeuse's flank.

Unseen Hands shot out. The speed of the hands thrust out had slackened; with Subaru's concentration at its zenith, they might as well have been standing still. As he cocked his head and violently swerved his body, a fingertip grazed Subaru's cheek as he closed with his foe. The sense of oppression from the powerful evil hands was such that Subaru almost unwittingly shut his eyes.

"Wilhelm taught me two things."

Hands grazed him. Pain ran through part of the skin of his neck, cheeks, and ears, which felt like they'd been touched by hot steel. The bursting heat scalded his thoughts, and he bit down a painful cry that threatened to tear through the inside of his throat.

He dodged. He breathed. He wasn't done yet.

"That I don't have one smidgen of talent with a sword..."

The pain was scorching, but he became relaxed, at ease.

These twin elements intruded upon Subaru's mind as he looked straight before him. On the other side of the hand Subaru had dodged was another hand, snapping toward his face—

"...and the courage not to shut my eyes when I'm being smacked!!"

He shouted and ducked his head. The hair on the back of his neck got a shave as he evaded by a hairbreadth. Dead ahead, Petelgeuse's face stiffened in shock, and into the side of that face, Subaru slammed his fist.

"—!!"

The haymaker struck Petelgeuse's cheek, causing him to greatly snap backward. His body lost its footing, and Petelgeuse was hurled out of the dragon carriage. And then—

"Oooooo—!!"

Petelgeuse hung upside down in the air before being dragged back to the dragon carriage. A piece of his habit had snagged on the wagon, and his body, connected to the dragon carriage, was being dragged along the ground.

Blood scattered. Flesh exploded. As the damage piled up, even the Unseen Hands came unmoored as the being known as Petelgeuse was undone. Even so, Petelgeuse raised his decaying face and glared at Subaru, his inverted gaze brimming with hatred.

"It is not o-ov-over—it is not…o-overrrr?!"

"Nah, this is as far as you go."

As Subaru spoke to the excessively tenacious Petelgeuse, he revealed the Gospel he held in his hand—that which Petelgeuse had dropped when Subaru struck him, and the last thing the madman's heart clung to.

Subaru flipped to the latter, blank half of the tome, pressing his finger against it.

He had touched the finger to a wound, covering it in blood. With this, he placed his imprint upon the Gospel.

"Your end is right here!"

In red I-script, Subaru wrote the word *END* on the open, blank page.

When Petelgeuse beheld the sight, his tongue trembled from the blow. The fierce emotions spreading like a wave through his eyes were so complex that Subaru could no longer read any of them.

And then, before he could put his emotions into words, the end came.

"—!"

The dragon carriage bounced high up, and Petelgeuse, dragged by the wagon by the sleeve of his habit, came loose… Then the tattered habit was caught by a wheel of the dragon carriage, turning at high speed.

Pulled in by the snagged habit, Petelgeuse's body, stripped of limbs and blood, was pulled straight toward the wheel. The end was in sight. Mixed with the sound of a habit tearing, flesh and blood bursting, in his last moment, Petelgeuse looked up at his foe and shouted.

"—Subaru Natsukiiiiiiiiiiiiii!!"

His scream echoed and became his death cry.

Petelgeuse shouted Subaru's name as body and voice were swallowed by the wheel; and thus ensnared, they were pulverized, with bits of blood, flesh, and bone scattering out as his life was trampled away.

With the loss of its body, the essence of the evil spirit dwelling within was drawn in until it, too, dissipated.

"—"

One last, final Unseen Hand stretched toward the tip of Subaru's nose—

Just on the verge of grasping Subaru's head, the hand stopped; from the tips of its fingers, it fell apart and vanished. This fact revealed that Petelgeuse Romanée-Conti well and truly was no more.

"This time, rest in peace forever…Petelgeuse."

It was over. Certain of that, Subaru flopped onto the wagon.

Instantly, the pain he had been ignoring to that point came rushing back, and Subaru moaned as he rolled around in the wagon.

"Oww, this is bad, it's so bad, I'm gonna die. Oww, this is bad, this is bad…!"

Tears welled up, and the sharp pain would not relent. His bleeding wounds throbbed, and he felt like needles had been thrust inside his body. Only the physical pain of his wounds racked his chest.

He did not pity Petelgeuse. Madman, evil spirit, Archbishop of the Seven Deadly Sins—there was no point on which he could sympathize with Petelgeuse, aka Sloth. He'd run amok all on his own, and this was the result.

He'd shouted delusions of love, arbitrarily imposed them on others, and ended up secluded and alone.

No one needed to nurse pity for a man such as Petelgeuse meeting his end.

No one, save Subaru, needed to be tormented by such sentiments.

"No one was ever gonna understand you. Of course you're dead. You had it coming. No one—no one—will forgive you— That's why...I feel for you...that much, at least."

He was understood by none...unloved by the one he loved...a lonely monster.

This time, Petelgeuse Romanée-Conti was truly no more.

Nothing left of him remained in anyone's chest, anyone's heart.

...None, save the nail called "pity" driven into Subaru's chest nonetheless.

6

"Mr. Natsuki, are you all right? You are wounded to no small extent."

"Hell no, I'm not all right. I used to bawl my eyes out when the anesthesia ran out after dental work."

Subaru moved from the half destroyed wagon to the driver's seat, mumbling thus as he smeared salve on his wounds. Bandages and homemade salves seemed to be necessities of travel; he'd helped himself to what the dragon carriage held.

As Subaru, done treating his wounds with teary eyes, handed the salve back to Otto, he pointed to the dragon carriage's wagon and spoke.

"I'll put the word in to have Roswaal pay for dragon carriage repairs, too... So how much time have we lost?"

"None whatsoever. If anything, we have gained time, thanks to having two land dragons earnestly fleeing... Something really came after us?"

"Yeah, a sloth. Never heard of 'em? They're animals with long hands that make funny noises."

When Subaru played dumb, replying with a deep sigh, Otto abandoned pursuing the matter further. Subaru shrugged at the sight; then he glared at the Liphas Highway's horizon.

What Subaru yearned for was beyond that horizon, its silhouette not yet within sight, but—

"I'll catch up to you. This time, I'll save you."

"You think we will make it in time?"

"We'll make it!"

It sounded like Otto asked not out of concern, but to gauge what Subaru's resolve was made of. Hence Subaru put on a smile, baring his teeth as he replied with a hearty voice.

"Besides, I have to finally bring Rem some good news. A man has to live up to expectations."

"That is the name of a woman you've fallen for?"

"It's the name of the girl who's fallen for me!"

Subaru said it not with ardor or a blush, but simply as a matter of fact. For a brief moment, Otto was taken aback by Subaru's reply, but that expression immediately crumbled.

"Ahh, then we cannot fail to look good for her, can we?!"

With a joyful shout, Otto snapped the reins, and that sharp sound made the land dragons increase their running speed.

They ran, they ran, and the dragon carriage went, seemingly flying, down the highway—

Almost as if to reel in something precious over the horizon as it threatened to pull away.

All Subaru Natsuki could do was pin his hopes on the future.

7

The dragon carriage's speed increased, and the sounds of the wind and terrible rocking echoed inside the wagon.

"Wah—!"

"It's okay. Hang on tight. There's no need to be scared."

As the children huddled in a clump to endure the shaking, Emilia sent a strong smile their way. Seeing her smile, the anxious children muttered, "Yeah" and nodded several times over.

Such strong children, thought Emilia in admiration. Any child had worries in its chest, yet these desperately clenched their teeth, continuing to fight against fear with nary a whimper.

It was enough to make Emilia think, *I can't put on a shameful display in front of them.*

By rights, a dragon carriage was protected by a wind repel blessing. But currently, the blessing of their dragon carriage was not functioning.

There were various conditions that might cause the effects of blessings to lapse, but for the wind repel blessing, it was very simple: either the land dragon's legs had come to a halt or it had gone outside the area affected by the blessing— In this case it was the former.

Once stopped, it took time for a dragon carriage's blessing to be restored. And currently time was what they lacked.

"—"

As the wagon ferociously rocked, Emilia braced herself, strongly grasping them with her hands as she shut her eyes. She focused her ears beyond the dragon carriage's curtain-covered rear, listening to the fierce swordplay in the distance.

About two hours had passed since they'd left the village, evacuating because of a criminal group said to be lurking in the environs of the village. Midway, they'd split from the group Rem was leading to the Sanctuary, and Emilia's group was set to make good time evacuating to the capital—but the situation had rapidly changed a short time ago.

"...Lady Emilia, may I have a few minutes of your time?"

From beside the dragon carriage, then taking a short break, Emilia heard the voice of the aged swordsman guarding them speaking to her.

The individual calling himself Wilhelm Trias was a retainer of Crusch's, and even Emilia could tell that he was a man of exceptional swordsmanship behind his gentle demeanor.

The fighting spirit Emilia sensed from his hushed voice was all it took to make her brows buckle with concern.

"Has something happened?"

"It is of minor concern. Accordingly, I wish to take several men with me and eliminate that concern. I ask that you forgive my rudeness in leaving your side."

"…It's all right. What's wrong?"

"It is only driving off wild dogs, a trifling matter. We shall catch back up with you soon enough."

When Wilhelm made that statement with a polite bow, Emilia sensed that something was off. Immediately after, she realized that he had been speaking out of consideration for the children all around her.

Considering Wilhelm's duties, she could guess what he was trying not to say, and what these "wild dogs" amounted to.

"Am I not needed?"

"—"

She knew that the question she posed was an impolite way to repay Wilhelm's considerate words. Wilhelm narrowed his eyes when, even so, Emilia could not refrain from asking.

I've gotten on his bad side, thought Emilia. However, unexpectedly, the old man's lips formed a smile.

"Lady Emilia, please continue evacuating in the dragon carriage. Please take good care of the children."

The emotion contained in the smile was neither disappointment nor disdain. He clearly longed for something dear to him.

To Emilia, perplexed and unable to understand the meaning of what she saw, Wilhelm quietly turned his back.

"With a lapsed blessing, I expect the dragon carriage shall rock rather fiercely. Make sure not to let go of the children."

"Sir Wilhelm, I…"

"Lord and retainer truly are alike—your eyes are just like his."

Wilhelm parted with that deeply felt murmur, breaking off from the dragon carriage column with other guards.

Emilia did not know the true intent behind the murmur. But she had no time to pursue the matter. Immediately, at the instructions of a different knight, the dragon carriage convoy resumed its evacuation. And with the blessing no longer functional, the dragon carriage set out, its rocking robbing Emilia of the luxury of immersing herself in thought.

And so, back inside the ferociously rocking carriage...

The children huddled with Emilia in the canopied wagon of the dragon carriage. She tossed several blankets over the children, held their trembling hands, and continued to pay attention to the situation outside, ready to act immediately no matter what was coming. And explaining the situation outside to Emilia was—

"That old man and the others are clashing with someone behind us. A battle is breaking out."

—a voice, reverberating in Emilia's head as it relayed the tactical situation outside. Somehow, Puck sounded very laid back, floating unseen as he watched the situation unfold.

"Do you know how many there are?"

"Twice as many as we have, but...mm, it's completely all right. That old man is incredibly strong, so there's nothing for you and me to do, Lia. Wow, he cut another one down..."

Emilia kept her fighting spirit and kept the tension off her face, nodding at her telepathic exchange with Puck.

As a spirit, Puck had ways to know what was happening outside even without materializing. Emilia was using a minute amount of power to listen to his words and keep apprised of the situation.

"It would be no laughing matter if I materialized for no reason and was out of energy when you really need me. Besides, if I come out now, I'll end up a toy for the children."

"I think that'd be a good thing. Your cuteness would make them forget all their worries."

"Hey, don't say such scary things, daughter of mine. Anyway, that's how it looks outside."

Even as they exchanged lighthearted telepathic banter, Emilia was a bit grateful to hear Puck's report. But the corners of her lips rose stiffly as she painfully rued her own powerlessness.

Puck had guaranteed Wilhelm's strength with the sword, but Emilia had power to fight with, too. Wilhelm had declined Emilia's aid out of consideration for her position. Even though she understood that, Emilia was still chagrined over merely being protected by others.

She was unable to bring about the results demanded by her station. Her authority was a paper tiger; she was seen as a figurehead candidate from inside and outside the kingdom, and no one would claim her capabilities were up to the task, even as fiction.

And in spite of that, she was shackled to her position, her authority placed in a yoke, the decision to wave her power around denied to her.

Then what in the world was she there for?

"...Subaru."

When, in a small voice, her lips invoked the name of the black-haired youth, Emilia shook her head at her own weakness.

She had no right to call that name, almost like she was pleading for aid. If, that moment, she was calling out his name, it was not for want of power. It was—

"Hey, everyone, don't worry! No matter what happens, your big sister will protect you!"

It was for want of courage, so that Emilia might do what Subaru would in her place.

When Emilia spoke those words to them, the huddled, curled-up children lifted their faces. Her words sent the children, shoulder to shoulder with tears in their eyes, looking at one another's faces, and their voices came all at once.

"W-we're all right!" "Don't you worry about anything, Big Sis!" "W-we promised, so it's okay! We're not letting go, so...!"

It was instantly obvious the children were putting on a brave front as they clung to Emilia's arms and legs. They wrapped around both arms, both legs, and even her hips and shoulders; Emilia's body went rigid from the heat from being touched by others. But it was by no means a disagreeable sensation.

It was just that, at the same time, something felt off about their words.

"Promised... Who did you make a promise with? To do what?"

"He said not to let go of Big Sis." "He said you'd do reckless stuff if he's not with you, so...!" "He said he's worried if no one's watching out for you!"

As each reply came in turn, Emilia was shocked by her own reaction. Emilia felt like it was extremely overprotective, and even that she was being looked down upon...but she felt strong consideration pouring out of the words.

"—"

That way of speaking sounds like...

Emilia felt a throb in her chest the instant she had the thought.

Once she noticed it, she could ignore the throb in her chest no longer. Its assertion grew stronger at an ever-increasing pace, and Emilia's eyes wavered with bewilderment as it gently clawed against her heart.

Led by that throbbing, Emilia opened her mouth to ask, "Who said...he's worried about me?"

"Ah, no, that's...!"

The question immediately made the color of Petra's face change. Her adorable cheeks reddened as she shouted, interjecting with a desperate voice, but she was not in time.

"Subaru!" "Subaru said it!" "He was worried you'd feel lonely!" "Subaru said... Ah, right, we weren't supposed to say that..."

The children scrambled to be the first to say his name, but the last speech resulted in a hand going to the mouth. Then they all realized they had misspoken. "Oops," Petra said quietly, clutching her head.

But as Emilia blinked her eyes, she didn't even notice the looks on the children's faces.

"Suba...ru...?"

She'd had a feeling. Emilia could sense him from the words out of the children's lips.

But it can't be, said her feelings of denial, and they had won out. After all, Emilia had hurt him, speaking terrible words and leaving him in the capital, far away.

There, where Subaru's greatest desire was to reach out and offer

Emilia his hand, she had turned her back on him. That had to have been a great betrayal.

Why, when Emilia yearned for someone to save her, had Subaru's name come out?

It couldn't be. It wasn't possible.

Emilia had lived a life of disappointments.

She had been betrayed, repudiated, estranged; to her these were natural, expected things.

She wanted to be trusted, accepted, sought; but to her these things were impossible.

That was why, when Subaru behaved kindly to her, she'd rejected even him, and all the kindness he offered.

It was not that she couldn't believe he was being considerate to her. That she was worthy of his compassion—this Emilia could not believe.

If she piled expectation upon expectation, the blow when it all came crashing down would be unfathomable. Therefore, if he would someday distance himself from her, it was better if she distanced herself from him…

…before the pile between them climbed high enough to come crashing down.

And yet, why—?

"Subaru…came to the village? He…came back?"

With the children maintaining an awkward silence, Emilia could only let out that dumbfounded murmur.

Even then, the dragon carriage rocked ferociously as the battle between the knights and the pursuers continued. Emilia had a duty to protect the children, and that duty came first.

Yet Emilia's heart was being rocked far harder than the carriage, swaying greatly to and fro.

If Subaru had returned to the village, a number of mysteries began to make sense.

It explained why Ram knew so much about the expeditionary force rendezvous. It explained why the villagers had been so cooperative with the order to evacuate. It explained why the members of the expeditionary force had so deftly handled the affairs of a domain of which they should have known little.

The simple presence of one person, Subaru Natsuki, neatly tied these mysteries together.

If Subaru was with the expeditionary force, she understood why Ram did not go against his word. To the villagers, Subaru was the savior of the village; it was natural that they would not reject his proposal.

More than anything, evacuating the villagers and Emilia, sending them ahead while he stayed behind with the expeditionary force to deal with the threat, was very Subaru-like. Too like him.

The actions were too like the Subaru Natsuki that Emilia knew—

"Why...?"

Her murmur was tinged with incomprehension and sorrow. The emotions welling into her violet eyes made them faintly tremble.

If this was all the result of Subaru's actions, they had changed little from before—far too little. She'd hurt him, pushed him away, and yet, even so, Subaru had stayed the same.

"I hurt him that much, and put that sad a face on him... Why did Subaru come again to...?"

She didn't know why he'd tried to save her.

She'd tossed the question his way after Subaru was deeply wounded in both body and heart at the royal selection conference and the training square. At the time Subaru had not given her an answer. And so Emilia still didn't know.

Even though she'd given up, breaking the relationship between them, bringing it to an end without ever knowing...

"Why...?!"

"That's obvious...!"

Emilia spoke, her voice breaking and on the verge of tears; it was the wild voice of a red-faced Petra that answered.

The reaction, which made it sound like the girl knew the answer to the question she harbored, made Emilia look at her, hanging on her words.

But before the two could open their mouths any farther, the dragon carriage was assaulted by the largest jolt to that point.

"—?!"

The dragon carriage wended its way forward with incredible force, flinging around the bodies of Emilia and the children within. Instantly Emilia grasped hold of the wagon, stretching her arms and wrapping them around the children to the greatest possible extent.

However, the dragon carriage continued wending its way, not leaving her a single moment to calm down; the movement was as if they were fleeing from something. Simultaneously, a voice echoed inside Emilia's brain.

"Lia, someone's coming from the rear at incredible speed—"

Prompted by Puck's warning, Emilia shifted her eyes toward the dragon carriage's rear. Beyond the curtain flapping in the wind, she caught a glimpse of the cause of the dragon carriage's meandering movements: Something was chasing them…and drawing nearer.

"I'll…!"

I have to face this, thought Emilia, instantly trying to move.

But when she tried to stand up, her body was held back by light weights, unable to move. When she lowered her gaze, she saw them: the children grabbing her arms and clothes, not letting her go for anything.

"We won't let go!" "You can't go!" "We promised!"

Emilia, firmly grasped by the children, could not escape.

They were bonds she could have shaken loose, but Emilia did not move. When Emilia hesitated, Petra glared sharply at her face, shouting with a tearful look, "Are you going to make Subaru cry this time?!"

"—?!"

The girl's shout sent a ferocious tremor—both through the meandering carriage and through Emilia's heart.

The dragon carriage braked all of a sudden, and centrifugal force struck, sending Emilia, still linked to the children, flying into the air. Reflexively, she oriented herself onto the blankets, safely protecting everyone from the impact.

Swallowed by the rocking and the blankets, Emilia somehow managed to shake her head loose and sit up.

"Just now, what was th—?"

"Lia, it's right behind us!"

Puck materialized beside her head, pointing behind the tilting dragon carriage.

Heeding Puck's voice and motion, Emilia swiftly rose up, shielding the children behind her. At the same time, she unleashed her magical energy, and cold air dropped the temperature inside the carriage with incredible force.

Just as Puck had said, someone had caught up to the dragon carriage. The next moment, someone raised the dragon carriage's curtain.

Then, when she saw who was standing there, Emilia was dumbstruck.

"Why…?"

With ragged breaths, his shoulders heaving up and down, a lone young man climbed into the dragon carriage.

The sight made Emilia's eyes shake fiercely in bewilderment.

Her lips trembled. Emilia forgot the circumstances, and with a frail, minute voice, she spoke his name.

"—Subaru."

She spoke his name.

8

When Subaru thought back, it was a horrible way to meet someone.

It hadn't even been an hour since Subaru had been summoned to another world, adrift and unable to tell left from right.

In that state, he'd walked into an alley, and according to script, he'd been surrounded and half-killed by punks. His trip to another world was about to end in death within the first few hours.

Subaru remembered every little thing from that time: her words, her demeanor, her grandeur.

He'd never, never, never, *never* forgotten.

It was because of her that Subaru Natsuki could live in that world, standing on his own two feet.

"Mr. Natsuki, that's—!!"

Having dispatched Petelgeuse's delusions earlier, the dragon carriage had been racing down the Liphas Highway when Otto, watching the horizon from the driver's seat, shouted to Subaru as he caught sight of their target.

When Subaru followed his gaze, spotting the wriggling silhouette at the edge of the horizon, he too shouted.

"There!! Otto, give it everything you've got!!"

"I've been giving it everything this whole time!!"

With a powerful flick of the reins, the two land dragons picked up speed.

The jet-black land dragon stared straight ahead, wringing everything out of her spirit as she raced to fulfill Subaru's wish.

—After she saved him in that first encounter, he learned about her as he forced his way into her life.

He knew she was stubborn, she was obstinate, she put on a strong front, and she was kind.

He knew that he was unworthy to gaze at the side of her face. The very shame of it rang shrill within his chest.

He knew that his own incorrigible foolishness had made those sweet feelings go to waste.

Back then, he'd sworn. Subaru had certainly sworn it.

"I'll...save you."

He'd striven to uphold that promise.

The deaths had piled up, he'd cut a hole open in Fate, and somehow making it past all that pain and suffering, Subaru had reunited with her, reforged their bonds, and earned her smiling face once more.

Subaru would never forget the flood of emotions that had struck his chest at the time.

"Wilhelm!!"

"Sir Subaru?!"

By the time they caught up with the silhouettes on the horizon, it was already a battlefield where knight and black figure clashed.

Already a number of corpses lay upon the ground. The gallant figures riding around responded to Subaru's voice. Wilhelm blinked hard at the sight of Subaru, for the speed of the dragon carriage atop which he rode did not relent. The Sword Devil gripped a bloody blade, and the question of what Subaru was doing in that place nearly came to his lips, but—

"Where's Emilia?!"

Subaru's next shout, and the emotion filling his black eyes, made Wilhelm instantly cast the question aside.

Then Wilhelm pointed the tip of his sword ahead of the galloping dragon carriage and spoke.

"There! Straight ahead! Toward the Great Tree!!"

Lifting his face, Subaru set his sights on an even more distant horizon. He realized that they'd already made it halfway across the Liphas Highway, reaching as far as the Great Flugel Tree, where they'd waged the decisive battle against the White Whale.

"—"

That much having been confirmed, the dragon carriage sped through the battlefield, never lowering its speed.

He didn't stop. He needn't inquire about their safety. That would be an insult to the brave fighting of Wilhelm and his men, and more importantly, they were words Subaru should have spoken when they'd parted ways.

Subaru had asked Wilhelm to put Emilia and the others' safety on his shoulders. Wilhelm was acting in accordance with the trust Subaru had placed in him. Accordingly, there was no need for Subaru to stop, nor for Wilhelm to question why he raced forward.

Their exchange of glances was over in an instant, whereupon Subaru and Otto's dragon carriage left Wilhelm behind. However, the Witch Cultists were not about to simply let him go. Several of the figures kept the knights busy while others kicked off the ground, chasing after the dragon carriage, when—

"*I* am your opponent."

Caught by surprise from behind, a Witch Cultist was sliced in half like a tall stalk of bamboo. Bathed in blood spatter, the Sword Devil swung his treasured sword as he shot the dragon carriage a satisfied smile as it raced into the distance.

"It is a perfect opportunity to repay my debt of gratitude. And even though he did not say the words, I am pleased the one who asked it understands—indeed, I am…honored."

With the treasured sword granted by his liege in his right hand, he accepted a cavalier's sword tossed by one of his men in the left. The Sword Devil poised the swords crossed as his glare shot through the Witch Cultists.

"As if I would let anyone stop a man who wants to meet his woman. You and I both stink too much of blood to be present at their reunion— You will all remain here…as corpses."

His pronouncement of their sentence of death made the Witch Cultists, purportedly shorn of emotion, tremble all over.

Amid that sense of tension pulled taut, the Sword Devil bent forward, racing onward with a smile carved onto his lips.

The expression was a complex one—both that of a happy devil bathed in blood and the strained smile of an old man reminiscing on the sins of his youth.

"Mr. Natsuki, I see them! The evacuating dragon carriages are over there!"

With the battlefield left behind them, Otto, in the driver's seat as the dragon carriage picked up speed, raised his voice. As he pointed forward, Subaru, sitting right beside him, caught sight of the dragon carriage convoy moving off in the distance. The throbbing in his chest strengthened as Subaru clenched his fist, his emotions astir.

As they closed the distance bit by bit, the dragon carriage convoy was thrown into confusion when it sensed Subaru's carriage catching up. The column of dragon carriages began to weave around, and Subaru earnestly raised his voice.

"Stop! It's me! Not an enemy! Stop, please stop—!"

"—?! Mr. Natsuki?!"

"Please stop! It's an emergency! I need to check inside the carriages!"

The knight in the driver's seat of the leading carriage realized it was Subaru pulling alongside and shouting to him; he rushed to bring his carriage to an urgent halt. At his command, the land dragon neighed, and one by one, the dragon carriages behind him lowered their speed with such force, they nearly rolled onto their sides.

And then—

"Ia, come on out! Otto, get Patlash loose from the dragon carriage, please!"

Time was precious. Subaru didn't even wait for the dragon carriage to stop before leaping down. He broke his fall with a pathetic-looking roll that was a far cry from a graceful landing. He instantly rose to his feet, the red quasi-spirit Ia floating right before his eyes.

"Ia, can you tell which dragon carriage is booby-trapped?"

The quasi-spirit did not reply. But she asserted her existence with an increase of heat, rushing ahead of Subaru toward the column of dragon carriages, and flew circles above a carriage with a canopy.

From Ia's reaction, Subaru rushed to the dragon carriage without the slightest doubt in his mind. He violently stripped away the curtain covering the wagon, squinting as he peered into the poorly lit interior, and—

"—Subaru."

When he realized a voice, clear as a bell, had called his name, Subaru was struck by a wave of anxiety that threatened to make him break down then and there.

Inside the wagon was a beautiful girl with silver hair and violet eyes, staring dumbfounded at Subaru.

It was the sight of the girl he had pursued over and over, hoped for over and over, bent and broken himself over and over in the process, yet even so, he had never once managed to give up.

He was overflowing with emotion. Irresistible urges welled up within him.

However, Subaru gritted his teeth, instantly cutting his indecision away.

"Ia! Where is it?!"

Trailing behind Subaru, the quasi-spirit emerged within the wagon, flying around inside like an illusion. Scattering her mana like tiny specks of fire, the red quasi-spirit strongly illuminated one of the wagon's corners.

"Puck! Can you let me strip only this part off without setting off what's behind it?!"

"An unexpected reunion, and already you're making dema...... Mnggh, so that's how it is?"

Puck, eyes wide at Subaru's presumptuous call, realized something was wrong under the floor. The little cat narrowed his eyes at the area indicated by the quasi-spirit, swishing his tail as he made use of his power. Gathering his mana, he froze the floorboards, whereupon Subaru violently stomped on them, shattering them. Then he thrust an arm into the hole thus created; when he felt his fingertips wrap around it, he yanked it out.

"—Found it!!"

With a shout, what emerged from under the floor was a sack made of unusual material with complex symbols written upon it. It seemed to be made of some creature's hide, but the repulsiveness of the feel of it instinctively made him ill.

"A sack of demon beast hide—"

As Puck put into words the cause of his distaste, Subaru opened the sack. The inside was jam-packed with glowing magic crystals, corroborating Otto's testimony.

But that very moment, the magic crystals grew hotter, like they'd just begun a countdown sequence.

"What timing...! Puck, can you stop this?!"

"I don't think I can. I can contain the blast, though."

Puck looked at Emilia as he shook his head, seemingly offering a glimpse of his final trump card. The gesture made Subaru realize that it probably meant Puck manifesting in his true form, overcoming the problem by brute force.

It was a crude measure, but certainly it was possible for Puck to minimize the damage. It was possible, but...

"No, you can't!"

Subaru turned that plan down.

Certainly that method would do to keep everyone safe. But it would come at the cost of revealing Puck's form as a Great Spirit, and awe at the sheer enormity of that power made the rupture of Emilia's relationship with the villagers inevitable—Subaru couldn't even stop himself from shuddering as he protested.

After all, just then, Emilia and the villagers were finally on the same stage, coming closer together bit by bit—

It wasn't like at the royal selection conference. Showing her power off like she had there would only be a hindrance to her relationship with the villagers. That was why he could rely on Puck like that only if it was truly the only way, the most final of final resorts.

"Think. Think, think, think…!"

If the magic crystals he'd retrieved lived up to their billing, they'd turn the entire prairie into a sea of flame when they exploded. There was practically no time left until they exploded. It would be difficult to toss them somewhere far away. But if he relied on Puck, it would leave a dark shadow over Emilia's prospects in the royal selection. He wrung all his cunning to think of something before he'd have to redo things at the cost of his life. This time, there had to be something he could do for Emilia—

"—That's…it."

He let out a murmur. Exactly one way had come to mind.

It was a ridiculous, laughable conclusion. He wasn't sure he could actually pull it off. However, within the current limitations, it was the one possibility he could think of that had miraculous prospects of victory.

The instant he thought of it, Subaru's body practically leaped into motion.

With difficulty he picked up the heavy sack, his arms and chest scorched by the incandescent magic stones. Subaru ignored the pain and leaped out of the dragon carriage. And behind him—

"Wait…!"

In a shaking voice, Emilia called for Subaru to stop.

His legs, which had no time to stop, stopped. His body, which had no time to turn around, did. He stared straight at the eyes into which he could not look. They did not have the time to exchange words, yet exchange words they did.

"Subaru, why…?!"

This *why* included the various *whys* apart from that moment.

There was the *why* of that instant, when he had come aboard the dragon carriage; there was the *why* toward his creation of this situation; and from long, long before…

She was likely repeating the question she had posed in that room in the royal palace, too.

At the time, Subaru had been unable to give Emilia an answer to her question.

At the time, numerous emotions had surged within him that he had yet to sort out. Taken individually and separately, it was not that they were mistaken…but they were not correct, either.

It was the place where he had been given only one chance to reach out to her, and he'd let it slip through his fingers.

That place was the one chance he had earned, and he'd lost even that, kicking everything down the road.

He'd reunited with Emilia, gaining the chance to talk with her, and he had a mountain of thoughts and feelings he wanted to share. No matter how much he tried, it would never be enough to cover it all.

Many, many words floated into his thoughts, filling his throat, but that's where they vanished.

Contained with him was a flood of emotions and ideas, but in that moment his entire body and soul yearned for one thing.

What to talk about? What to tell her?

What words to choose? How would he face her?

"Why…?"

She asked him once again.

He took a short breath. And then, in a single phrase, Subaru told her.

He told her the one and only thing that gave his life meaning, even when covered in all those wounds.

"—I love you, Emilia."

9

In one go, they passed through the curtain of the dragon carriage, practically ripping it as they leaped out.

The instant the dazzling light of the sun burned Subaru's eyes, a huge black frame stood before him, blocking the sun's rays. It was Patlash. Subaru's favorite dragon had predicted everything before he had even called her, offering him her back.

Subaru leaped on, placing the leather sacks emitting high temperatures between his own belly and Patlash's saddle. He proceeded to take the reins, and the land dragon galloped on a path in the direction of the sun.

Behind him Otto was surprised by Subaru's actions; the knight in the driver's seat was shocked as well. The children leaping out from behind the curtain raised their voices, as did Emilia.

Subaru heard them calling out to him. But he didn't look back. There wasn't time.

Every feeling he wanted to convey, every word he wanted to speak, it had all been summed up in that single phrase. There was nothing left for Subaru to do there. In that moment there was only one thing he needed to follow through on.

"—"

Patlash became the wind, instantly leaving the landscape behind them.

The effect of the wind repel blessing had expired, so the shaking and gusts assailed Subaru without mercy. But the land dragon's agile movements protected her master, and Subaru, trusting his favorite dragon in equal measure, left everything to her.

He could feel through the leather bag that the magic crystals were becoming white-hot. Quietly, that heat increased with every passing instant. They were on the very brink of exploding. Subaru's belly, and Patlash's back, sensed this as they desperately dashed forward.

As his eyesight darkened from pain, he saw their destination coming into view at the edge of his vision.

It was the legendary Great Tree, snapped at its base and lying on its side. Lying beside that legendary tree was the headless corpse of a demon beast that had grown over the course of a long, long time.

The expedition force had probably had its hands full just hauling the head of the enormous demon beast away. Due to their freezing the massive fallen body to hold back the onset of rot, there was a chill in the air all around it.

Patlash ran toward the frozen carcass as Subaru ran his eyes toward the center of the White Whale. There rested the fatal sword wound inflicted by the Sword Devil.

"—!"

Drawing up right alongside the corpse, Subaru leaped off Patlash.

Then, without hesitation, he raised the powerfully hot leather sack high and stuffed it into the demon beast's wound. The giant corpse's wound was large enough that, even in its frozen state, there was plenty of space to pack the leather sack into it.

"—"

Having disposed of the leather sack, he instantly turned back. Subaru leaped back onto Patlash and grabbed the reins to immediately turn away, then the two of them circled around the corpse, slipping under the fallen Great Tree's shadow.

Subaru was practically dangling from the saddle as Patlash raced onto the grasslands. By the time the land dragon had taken a second or perhaps third step, the magic crystals reached the point of ignition, and light surged up from them.

All Subaru could feel was the shaking and wind from their mad dash. With his body shaken all around, he lost sight of which way was up, but he knew from the impact he felt that they'd escaped to where he'd intended. Subaru fervently clung to the trunk of the tree while Patlash curled up her body, covering Subaru with it.

Immediately after that—

"—!!"

There was a ferocious shock wave and blast of wind, along with the sound of the explosion, which echoed over the highway so fiercely that Subaru thought his eardrums would burst. A torrent of heat streamed past the White Whale's remains and the Great Tree, singeing Subaru and Patlash's flesh.

The light from the explosion passed through his closed eyelids, searing his eyeballs. But Subaru clung firmly to his handholds, gritting his teeth as he endured the pain.

The shock wave churned up his internal organs, and it felt like even the powerful roots of the Great Tree would be ripped from the soil. However, the tide of destruction finally began to abate—

"—?"

Subaru, realizing that at some point he'd stopped feeling anything, lifted his head.

He tried raising his voice, but his ears were ringing so badly he couldn't hear a thing. When he opened his eyes, he couldn't see anything through the hanging blast cloud.

He reached out with his hand and felt the hide of the land dragon right beside him. He couldn't tell from warmth, but his palm felt the movements of a living creature. She was alive. His shoulders eased in relief.

"—?!"

The next moment, he felt something moist touch the surface of his unseeing face.

When it repeated over and over, he wondered if it might be Patlash's tongue licking his face. He made a strained smile at the doglike show of affection. Also, her tongue was so coarse, he felt like his face was being filed.

However, he didn't lift a finger to stop it, nor did he raise his voice.

It figured that he was tired. He was completely out of endurance, no longer able to move a single step.

He wondered if it would be such a sin if he gave his body a little break.

"—!"

When he felt the faint stirring of the air against his skin, Subaru somehow managed to move his head.

He could see nothing. He could hear nothing. But for some reason, it felt good.

He could hear nothing. At that moment, nothing at—

"—Subaru!"

Ahh, whaddya know. Turns out I can hear something.

The sigh of relief was the last thing Subaru did before his mind fell into a deep, deep sleep.

10

When Subaru came to, his mind had entered a world of darkness once more.

Having lost his body, Subaru Natsuki continued to hover in that vast, empty space as nothing but consciousness.

As usual, the world had neither ground nor a discernable sky.

Nothing but darkness spread out before him in an ephemeral dream, one he would forget when he awakened.

"—*I love you.*"

But in that blank, hollow world of nothingness, there was an charming "someone" he couldn't meet anywhere else.

Always it gave Subaru a soft, numbing throb, as if he were filled with joy at a painful embrace.

"—*I love you.*"

The darkness unwound, the shadow formed, and the captivating "someone" appeared, approaching Subaru as she whispered her love.

He could not see the expression on her face. However, that "someone" was likely spinning words of love with a face drenched with anguish.

He wanted to be touched. He wanted to be longed for. Reflexively, Subaru's heart was drawn in.

He wanted to respond to her love, to repay her for it. He would never be able to repay love granted to him with anything less than love of his own.

And yet—

"—Subaru."

He heard it. A lovely voice from other than "someone" was calling his name.

His thoughts alone understood. A lovely voice apart from the "someone" filling the dream with black shadow was calling him to the world of white light.

As he understood this, a white light, something that should not exist in the land of darkness, was born.

"—I love you."
"—Subaru."

Simultaneously, the voices were tossed his way. He wanted to respond to the shadow's love. He absolutely had to respond to the love of the light.

He realized that his mind was being drawn away from the voice of that "someone" toward she whose voice reached him from the land of light.

The voice of that "someone" held grief at the state of Subaru's heart, for she was being left behind.

Two arms woven from shadow stretched out, but they did not reach his incomplete body. As Subaru grew distant, he heard the voice tremble, sadly calling out as it sought him over and over.

"—*I love you. I love you, I love you, I love you, I love you.*"
"—Subaru, please."

The whispers of love repeated over and over, whereas the call of his name contained a simple plea.

Remember who you are.

Remember what you have to do.

Remember the words you must exchange, in the world where you belong.

He couldn't stay there.

So—

"Next time, I'll probably come to meet you."

With nonexistent lips, surely unable to convey his feelings, he spoke his farewell to the "someone" fading in the distance.

They were words of departure, an oath that they would meet again. That "someone" let out a small gasp.

Then Subaru's mind was enveloped by a light that blotted out the world of darkness as he slowly melted away.

"—*I'll be waiting.*"

That echo was the only thing left as Subaru Natsuki was torn from the ephemeral dream...

11

His mind floated up through the sea called sleep, breaking the surface called waking as his eyes opened.

The tears of his waking eyes stung them like poison. His blurry vision saw thin, wavering violet.

Her breathtaking beauty was so close that they practically

breathed the same air, truly close enough for the hot breath from her pink lips to reach him—making him nervous enough to die on the spot.

"Isn't your face a bit close?!"

"Wah! Ah, Subaru! You're awake! I'm glad, really I am."

The violet that was so near turned out to be Emilia's eyes; the realization that it was her face that had been close enough to breathe on him snapped his mind awake. As Subaru flew into a panic, Emilia watched him, patting her breast with a look of pure relief—the angle was odd.

"Emilia-tan was super close while I slept. So this heavenly feeling against my head is..."

"You don't need to say it out loud. It's a lap pillow. Not bad for...a good sleep?"

"How can I complain? There's no pillow that's more luxurious than this. It's a pretty nice reward for working so hard."

Subaru shot her a teasing smile as he let his head rest upon her without complaint. As he did so, Emilia pursed her lips in a small smile, quietly gazing upon Subaru's smiling face.

The mood had shifted. It had changed from each making sure the other was safe...to their exchanging the feelings lying beyond that.

"Errr, can I ask you about a few things? For instance... Right, is Patlash okay? I remember I felt like she was licking my face right before I passed out..."

"Goodness, and there's so many things I want to ask, too... That land dragon was licking you quite awhile after you passed out, too, Subaru. She really, really raised a fuss when people tried pulling you away, and if Otto hadn't had a word with her, she might never have left your side."

"Whoa, Patlash, how far are you gonna take this loyal dragon thing? I'm falling in love."

They'd known each other for only two days, but the number of ordeals they'd been through together was already unmatched. If Crusch was going to give him a reward for helping deal with the White Whale, he couldn't even conceive of one besides Patlash anymore.

"She was badly burned, but her life doesn't seem to be in danger. I conducted the initial treatment, but Sir Wilhem is having Ferris examine her right now, so…"

"Eh? Ferris caught up, too?"

Subaru was both relieved and surprised to hear Ferris's name come from Emilia's lips. The kingdom's greatest healer having joined up with them was good news. And the fact he was there meant—

"Does this mean I've been sleeping for a long while?"

"Two or three hours, maybe? Don't worry, thanks to conversation mirrors, Ferris and them were able to link up, so all the wounded people are all right."

Emilia smiled pleasantly. One of the conversation mirrors originally owned by the Witch Cult rested in her hand. It was the one Subaru had kept for communicating with the expeditionary force left back in the village. She'd used it to converse with Ferris and the others, which accounted for the smooth rendezvous.

"So everyone's gathered around here, huh?"

"Ferris is still treating people… Julius, too. I was surprised. I mean, I would never have imagined you and Julius together, Subaru."

"I had a reason for that bluer than the mountains and higher than the seas. Explaining the circumstances of that subject from part one would get really long and messy, y'see…"

The relationship with Julius that had surprised Emilia was difficult to explain with words. Or rather, that very moment, even Subaru didn't know how to describe it.

If he had to put his complex emotions into a few short words that represented his overall appraisal of the man—

"I will hate that guy forever."

"What's with saying that all of a sudden?"

"I was trying my best to express the feelings I have for him that are hard to put into exact words… So where is everyone right now?"

Not wanting to talk about that any further, he switched topics. "Let's see," said Emilia, making a small, strained smile at Subaru's demeanor as she spoke. "Ferris told everyone to take a break until he finished healing people, but he should be right about done. Once that's over, we'll be heading for the capital again. There's a lot of things I have to speak to Crusch about, after all. That's thanks to your hard work, Subaru."

"Yeah, it totally was hard. Seriously felt like a game as the away team. I got through it with bluff, bluster, and guessing right about some little things. Just thinking about it twists my stomach!"

"Yes. Really…thank you."

Emilia's sincere gratitude made Subaru, attempting to hide his blush, able to hide it no longer.

But credit was credit. There was no point hiding it any longer.

"That's, right…I've, finally gotten back, haven't I?"

When he finally looked around, Subaru saw that he and Emilia were all alone inside the canopied dragon carriage's wagon.

The surrounding area held no sign of people; only the sound of the wind broke the silence. It was as if they were the only two people in the whole world—it was just like back then.

Wounded all over, his mind hazy, he'd awakened to find the two of them all alone.

"I feel like I've been seeing a long dream…"

As a matter of fact, the events from the moment of their departure to that time around—the final loop—seemed unreal, very much like he'd been dreaming.

That was how extreme and prolonged a situation it had been. It had been nothing but a veritable nightma—

"A bad dream…… No, not that."

"Was it a good dream?"

Emilia cocked her little head slightly, and her question prompted Subaru to continue.

The question made Subaru close his eyes, reminiscing on the time he had nearly declared a nightmare.

He remembered the many despairing situations that had visited him, places that he wanted to drive out of his head many times over.

His string of foolish acts. His self-serving behavior. His overbearing arrogance. How he'd cruelly betrayed expectations. How his spirit had been pummeled and broken by loss and despair. How he had once been ruled by madness, enough that when he sank into clarity, he sought to throw everything to the wind—and how, at the end of that, someone saved him.

He couldn't pretend it hadn't happened. Were it not for all those things, the Subaru of that moment would not exist.

Therefore, even if those days had been like a nightmare, inflicting nothing but hardships upon him...

"—It was good, really."

That long, long, nightmarish time remained nowhere, save for inside Subaru himself.

He could treat it as the past. But he could not allow himself to treat it as a dream.

The tragic results created by his own actions, and the horrific results they'd courted, were all his to bear.

Subaru was prisoner of the supernatural power of Return by Death. He had used that power to blaze open a new future. So this cross was his to bear.

"...How much have you heard?"

"Almost nothing. Julius said I should hear it from you."

"That meddling piece-of-shit bastard."

Was this his idea of being considerate? Inside his brain, Subaru spit invective at the handsome young man.

Then Subaru gently sat up from Emilia's lap, meeting her gaze with his own...

...as if to continue his words where they'd left off back then.

"That day, you asked me why. Why did I come save you? Why did I try so hard for you with this and that? Why, you said."

"Yeah, I asked that. And also, why you claimed I had saved you... I never did anything like that. I haven't at all. It's been only you saving me... I haven't given you anything. And in spite of that, you get so hurt for my sake..."

"Nah, back then I was all messed up..."

A part of him could not dismiss himself as just *messed up.*

It wasn't that he was messed up at all. At the time, thinking of himself only in terms of foolishness and frailty, the human being called Subaru Natsuki had honestly believed those words.

He had been pushing his own conceited emotions onto her, and wanted only for her to accept them.

Subaru knew of a man who had loudly asserted such self-serving love in his final moments, for it was Subaru himself who had watched this while leading the man to his demise.

Properly speaking, the sight of the Sword Devil offering up proof of his love had also been burned into his eyes.

"At the time, I was thinking only about me. I accept that. I was saying it was for your sake, but I was just drunk with the idea of 'I'm doing this for you.' I put into my own head that if I acted drunk on that, you'd accept me."

"Subaru…"

"Sorry. I was using you, and drowning in my own joy. Everything you said back then was true. I was wrong…but I wasn't wrong about everything."

He conceded that he'd used Emilia for his own benefit. But there was one thing that he would not concede.

"I want to help you. I want to be there for you. That's serious, that's true, not a lie."

"…Yeah, I know."

Emilia nodded at Subaru's words. Then her violet eyes greatly wavered and, blinking once, she stared at Subaru.

And then—

"—Subaru, why do you help me?"

They were the words she had spoken then. It was a question she had also posed several hours before.

Then, like before, the words were offered in search of an answer. Subaru had but one to give.

"I want to be there for you, because I love you, Emilia."

Subaru looked straight back into Emilia's eyes and stated it plainly.

In the end, the summary of the basis of Subaru's actions was exceedingly simple.

Wanting to be there for her, to stand by her side, to render her aid, to see her smiling face, to walk beside her, to live with her from now on—

Every last part of it was because he loved Emilia with all his body and soul, from the crown of the head to the tips of his toenails.

That was why, even at the risk of death, and in fact numerous deaths, no matter how hurt or hated or anguished he might be, even if he had to crawl to do it, he'd come back.

Just how many opportunities had he missed, only belatedly coming up with that simple answer?

He was truly in awe at the extent of his own stupidity.

"—"

Listening to Subaru's reply, Emilia opted to close her lips and keep her silence.

But that silence did not last long. Abruptly her composure crumpled; she bit her closed lips, and her wide-open, violet eyes grew moist.

It was the look of a girl who might break into tears at any moment, a girl who didn't know how to cry.

"I…I'm…a half-elf…"

"I know that."

Emilia earnestly shook her head, replying in a shaking, halting voice.

"I'm a half-elf, with silver hair… I'm hated by all kinds of people because I look like the Witch, they hate me. They truly, truly hate me."

"I've realized. I know. And those guys are blind."

Judging from appearances alone, and on top of that, basing everything on a resemblance to an arch-criminal from the distant past was ridiculous. How did anyone who didn't know a single thing about Emilia's true nature have any right to hate her?

"I have almost no experience interacting with people, and I don't have any friends. I have no common sense, and I'm ignorant of how the world works. That's why I say weird things from time to time… and because of my pact with Puck, my hairstyle practically changes on a daily basis, and my reason for wanting to be queen is…really, really selfish…"

She lined up her shortcomings one after another, even including things she didn't need to mention, offering a glimpse at her deepest vulnerabilities. Yet that timidity, that frailty, that lack of confidence—in that moment, Subaru thought it was all lovely.

Hence, Subaru gently shook his head.

"Emilia, whatever anyone says to you, whatever you think of yourself, I love you. I really love you. I super love you. I want to be together with you, always. I want to hold your hand, forever."

"Ah…"

"If you tell me ten things you hate about yourself, I'll tell you twelve that I love about you."

When Emilia seemed to try to pull back into herself, Subaru wouldn't let her escape, keeping his eyes glued to her as he stated how he really felt.

Emilia closed her little lips, looking at Subaru, and as she continued to look, tears welled in her eyes. When they grew to the point of overflowing, she blinked, letting droplets fall, tracing paths down her white cheeks.

"That's the special way I want to treat you."

"…This is the first time since I was born that I've been so happy to be treated as special."

He reached out with his hand, gently suppressing the flow of tears. With Subaru's hand touching her cheek, Emilia put her hand over his, and the body warmth exchanged between the two felt intensely hot.

"Why…twelve?"

"Because one hundred percent ain't enough to express how I feel."

When Subaru laughed, face brimming with a wide grin, Emilia answered with a tearful smile. Her face was dazzling, as if each and every falling tear were a diamond. Subaru felt so satisfied from seeing just one charming smile that he had to laugh at himself for how easily content he was.

And so they smiled together, as Emilia rubbed her cheek against Subaru's hand.

"I'm so happy. Really happy. I never once thought the day would come that someone would tell me they loved me."

In the days until that point, *special* had meant something entirely different to Emilia. That was why she was extremely frightened of receiving special treatment from anyone. Subaru knew how she felt about it, but had given her special treatment despite it all.

Even if it wasn't from anyone else, even if it was only Subaru in that whole world, the way he treated her truly was...special.

"Is this really fine? For me...for someone like me to be this happy, to have such happy feelings, it feels like an indulgence..."

"It's absolutely fine. Let's indulge ourselves. No matter how happy you are, it doesn't bother anyone else, and you can always give some of the excess to other people."

Which was why—

"You can take it slow, Emilia. Slow, gentle, take your time falling in love with me. After all, I'll be walking right by your side, doing my best to make you weak in the knees."

"—!"

"Eep," went Emilia, making a little sound from her throat. She proceeded to grow red in the cheeks, lowering her eyes. Then she touched a hand to her breast, quietly staring at Subaru as he smiled at her. And then...

"Thank you, Subaru. For helping me."

...Emilia smiled pleasantly as she said those words to Subaru. They were words she had spoken once before.

Realizing that fact, Subaru laughed. Emilia, realizing the same, laughed, too. She laughed and laughed, and suddenly, tears began to flow from the corners of her eyes. Subaru reached his hand out to Emilia's long, beautiful silver hair, gently stroking it as if combing through it.

He remained by the adorable girl's side as she gently continued to cry.

*　　*　　*

Under the sky of the approaching dusk, a boy from another world and a silver-haired half-demon drew close to one another, sharing their mutual feelings.

There had been repeated tribulation and despair continuing for a very long time.

Having overcome these, they had finally earned a quiet, tranquil time for them alone.

This was a tale about earning that time, and nothing more.

This was a tale about missed opportunities, continuing along different paths, remaining lost, and nothing more.

Everything had happened so that a single insecure boy could share his feelings with a single insecure girl.

This was a tale of striving to do exactly that one thing—
—and nothing more.

INTERLUDE
A BRIEF MOMENT IN A DRAGON CARRIAGE

With a rattling sound, the dragon carriage quietly advanced along the highway.

Protected by the blessing, Subaru was truly able to enjoy a tranquil journey in a dragon carriage for the first time.

Subaru's dragon carriage experiences had always been messy, so it was the first time he was able to travel in such peace and quiet. The first "peaceful" journey to the royal capital had been ruined by Subaru's selfish excesses, so it didn't count.

And amid this first experience—

"Hey, Petra...aren't you kinda...close?"

"Isn't this fine, Subaru? After all, Big Sis has been hogging you the whole time until now."

Subaru strained a smile as Petra said that to him and looked up with big, round eyes. She was sitting to Subaru's left and had been nuzzled against him, never leaving his side, since they'd set out again.

"Er, that's not true, Petra. Earlier, Subaru and I had...yes, we had something really important to talk about, so..."

"*Pfft.* Just so you know, Big Sis, I am definitely not losing to you!"

A red-faced Emilia tried to make excuses, but Petra didn't heed her one bit. But they weren't acting like they seriously scorned each other; if anything, they looked like they'd been teasing each other forever, which brought a big grin to Subaru's lips.

"Emilia-tan, you're talking with a child. You need to laugh and let these things slide with a smile on your face."

"I will not. Even with a child, I cannot behave in such an off-the-cuff manner."

"No one uses *off-the-cuff* anymore…"

"*Grrr*, playing that game again…!"

Emilia's lips tensed in displeasure, and Petra, unhappy to be treated like a child, tugged on Subaru's sleeve with a look of dissatisfaction. "Sorry, sorry," begged Subaru, giving a little, pained smile as he apologized to both of them.

At present Subaru and the others were heading to the capital with the children in a carriage after they'd had to change from the one that had been booby-trapped. Other than Petra, the exhausted children were asleep, and to be blunt, their snores and Petra's pressing up against Subaru were like his salvation.

After all, he couldn't handle being alone with Emilia after what had happened earlier.

He'd confessed to her, making all kinds of embarrassing statements in the process. Now that he calmly thought back upon making all kinds of cool-sounding statements, like about patiently waiting for her answer, he was about ready to expect jets of fire to sprout from his face.

"Subaru, what is it? You're making a strange face."

"I was just thinking that Petra's been a big help. I mean, she kept her promise not to leave Emilia-tan alone. She's been a very good girl!"

"Eh-heh-heh-heh."

As Petra looked up at him, Subaru gently stroked her hair and explained the second thing he was grateful to her for.

If, by some chance, Petra and the other children had let go of Emilia, she might have done something reckless and gotten herself hurt again. This had been avoided, and Subaru was able to see all his efforts come to fruition thanks to Petra and the other children around them.

Truly he had been blessed; perhaps too much, even.

"Once things calm down, there's way too many people I need to thank…"

He owed Crusch's followers a big thank-you, then another to the Anastasia faction for the aid of the Iron Fangs, and though it pained him, Julius's assistance had been a godsend as well. Russel had helped out in regard to the White Whale, plus he still owed a debt to Otto for his aid at the very end. Subaru had a lot of things to do.

"There's a mountain of stuff I've gotta think about, huh…?"

There was the issue of credit being due to the expeditionary force for taking down both the White Whale and Sloth, plus the alliance that had been struck with the Crusch camp. There was also the matter of pressing the absent Roswaal to take responsibility for compensating Earlham Village and dealing with various other matters that remained.

Many difficulties lay before Subaru—especially the talk that loomed largest on that mountain-like pile.

"Um, er, Emilia-tan… There's…something really important I have to talk to you about."

"Mmm, what is it?"

As Subaru gingerly brought the matter up, Emilia looked over to him with eyes full of trust. When Subaru gazed at those eyes and the emotions resting within, the task he had to carry out truly sunk in. At the same time, to be blunt, it frightened him to ponder whether the look in those eyes would change after he cleared the air.

Naturally, the matter he could not avoid telling Emilia about concerned another girl—Rem.

During the current loop, there was no one who'd aided Subaru as wholeheartedly as Rem. It was Rem's deep love and devotion that had gently healed Subaru's broken heart, allowing him to summon the will to rekindle the fight against fate every time he had to start over.

Had it not been for Rem, the Subaru sitting before Emilia would not have existed.

That was why Subaru harbored deep feelings for Rem that were special in their own way. Even if they were different from those he felt for Emilia, nothing else could compare to their strength and size.

Accordingly, Subaru settled on framing it around that—he knew full well that it was an awful way of thinking.

"This is really hard to say, but please, listen to me. Of course, I'm resigned to Ram kicking my ass when I tell her about this, but…I wanted to tell you first, Emilia-tan."

"…Mm-hmm?"

Subaru's odd, halting preamble left Emilia with a perplexed expression on her face. Seeing that nearly dulled his determination, but he hardened his resolve, feeling his courage bolstered by the battle with the Witch Cult.

He worked the wheels in his brain at maximum speed, multiplying everything by Return by Death to reach the most optimal way to explain—

"Actually, I wanted to talk about Rem. Where I'm concerned, Rem, um…well, you must have figured it out, right? I mean, well, she said a fair bit about it…"

Sweat oozed from Subaru's brow as he desperately tried to find the next words. Now that he was faced with giving the most awful confession in history, his courage, resolve, and experiences from Return by Death all failed him.

With Subaru already devolving into rambling excuses, drenched with cold sweat as he found it hard to speak, Emilia raised a hand.

"Hold on a moment. Subaru, calm down. I don't understand what you're trying to say, and I know that you're trying really, really hard, Subaru. Be a good boy and take it slow."

"I'm not sure what to think about the good-boy part…! No, wait, I'm not being very manly here. Okay, I'll just spit it out! See, Rem told me that she loves me just as much as I love you, Emilia, so…!"

He meant to build on the momentum from where he had just left off, but his words died out.

Having put his feelings into it with all his strength, he was sure that Emilia would be shocked at exactly what he was confessing to.

The mere thought of how she might react terrified him. Very, very tenderly, he watched for her response.

"_____"

However, Emilia's reaction was completely different from what Subaru had expected.

Subaru's words made Emilia's brows draw up. She touched a finger to her lips as she silently sank into thought. Was she mulling over his words, her anger building toward Subaru? It didn't seem like that at all.

"Subaru."

"Yes?"

When Emilia called his name, Subaru looked straight her.

Emilia resolutely faced Subaru's determined eyes head-on. However, her gaze also contained bewilderment, and Subaru couldn't understand why.

Then, the next words she spoke were literally beyond Subaru's comprehension—

"Who's Rem?"

FRAGMENTS

REM NATSUKI

1

A loud, crying voice echoed under the clear, blue sky.

It was the crying voice of a baby girl. Already she was crying with all her heart and soul.

Displaying emotions with every bit of available strength was a privilege reserved for babes. As he embraced that sentiment, he was shocked with himself, for it was not the thought of the young.

"So this is longing for youth... Maybe I should cry like Spica and return to the innocence of childhood?"

"If an adult acts like that on a public street, there's nothing I can do to help, you know?!"

When Subaru, feeling the weight of his years, made that murmur, the boy beside him played the straight man. Upon that exchange, the baby in Subaru's arms—the girl named Spica—took a deep, deep breath and went, "Aa—!!"

"Whoa! Spica's crying! Hey, uh, Rigel, you're her older brother! Do something!"

"You say that, but the fact you yourself aren't doing anything about it is a lot worse!"

The two males of the household batted responsibility back in forth with the baby between them.

The uproar attracted the attention of nearby pedestrians, but when they saw which three people were making the ruckus, they all thought, *Same as usual*, and promptly lost interest. As a result, the crying baby girl and the two caretakers remained as they were.

Subaru, dead center amid that noisy, passingly amusing scene, covered his face with a hand.

"So we have a little girl crying like this, and not a single person offers a lifeboat... Shit, have people's hearts hardened that much?!"

"This ain't the time to philosophize about the world! At this rate she's gonna give us a lecture when she gets back..."

"When who gets back, Rigel?"

"Well, that's obvio—"

The young man named Rigel cut off his words there as he looked over his shoulder in shock. Subaru went, "Ohh" as he followed Rigel's gaze, raising his eyebrows as he arrived at the figure standing behind him.

"Done with your shopping?"

"Yes, there were no problems... It seems things did not go so well for you."

"Nah, Spica's super lively. This one's growing up to be the type who runs all around and keeps men wrapped around her finger. She'll grow into a little devil before you know it. My heart's all aflutter. I can't wait!"

As Subaru flapped his lips, Spica, the girl he held in his arms, extended a little hand toward the woman standing there who was no larger than a leaf. Subaru desolately realized she seemed to be saying, *Change me.*

"Well, all that being said, we can't have her crying again. With that, I'll leave her to you."

"Yes, leave her to me."

Though his tone remained mischievous, Subaru handed the baby over with exceptional gentleness. The woman made a charming little smile as she took Spica, handling her like a precious treasure.

Then she hugged Spica snugly against her chest, gently rocking the baby's body to put her at ease.

"Yes, Father and Big Brother are helpless, aren't they? Spica, you need to grow up soon so you can give them the proper scolding they deserve."

"Hey now, she can't understand words yet, so can we not give her the special tutoring?"

An image of the future came to mind: his mischief being followed by her and Spica sandwiching him, hands on their hips in a pronounced huff. That scene, with them angry at him and Rigel both, was just—

"Er, now that I think of it, that's not as bad as I thought, it's really not! If anything, it comes off as one hell of a happy image of the future, doesn't it?"

"Leave me out of it. Having a little sister angry at me makes me look bad as an older brother."

"Well, it wouldn't make you look bad if you're lumped in with me. Your future... I can see it, I can see it...! Too soft to the little sister you like too much, kept under her thumb forever...you will be the Siscon King!!"

"Hey, you're the one who's wrapped around a woman's finger! I'll never, ever be like that!"

Subaru wagged his finger to fan the flames; a vein bulged on Rigel's forehead as he protested. But Rigel's statement made the blue-haired woman holding Spica knit her brows together.

"Rigel—what is this manner of talking you've been using outside? It's intolerable," she said.

"Uh, but, I mean..."

"Mother hates hearing *but* and *I mean*. Besides, your earlier words are mistaken."

As Rigel hemmed and hawed, she scolded him without mercy; then she pressed her lips to Spica's cheek and spoke.

"Mother does not have Father wrapped around her finger. After all, Father is always Mother's Number One."

Her cheeks reddened as she uttered something far more embarrassing than a baby crying on a public street.

This time, confronted with a mother able to say that out loud, Rigel raised both hands in abject surrender. Even Subaru couldn't do anything but awkwardly scratch a cheek.

The reactions from her beloved family sent her happily passing a hand through her long hair.

The stroke left Rem's hair, blue and pretty like the sky, swaying gently in the wind.

2

In a corner of Banan City, part of the city-state of Kararagi, Subaru sat on a bench at the corner of a public park dotted with playgrounds, gazing absentmindedly at affairs inside the park.

Directly in front of him, Rigel, his blue hair combed backward and spiky, was running around the public park, having fun with his friends. He might be cheeky to his own father, but he was an adorable kid, as befitted his age.

"Now if only we could do something about those awful serial killer eyes..."

"We will do nothing of the sort. That nasty look is part of who Rigel is. No matter how much fun he has, no matter how joyful he may be, his face will still make first acquaintances flinch with discomfort—that's our Rigel."

"Hey, I can hear you. And Mom, your attempt to help hurt even more, you know?!"

Rigel was caught and frozen in a game of freeze tag—passed down by Subaru himself—as he raised his voice in anger. Subaru and Rem both waved to their adorable son, seemingly to fan the flames like a proper husband and wife.

The foul, vein-bulging look of dissatisfaction on Rigel's face made him a dead ringer for a young Subaru.

"In other words, I can already expect his future to go something like mine. I'd be in shock too if I were him... I mean, in twenty years he's gonna turn into me."

"Would that not mean...a future where he marries a valiant wife, skilled in cooking and capable of all domestic affairs, who is also a wonderful and ideal bride?"

"Hey, what's that normie sellout garbage about? That can go jump in a… Wait, you meant me!"

When Subaru put a hand against his head and stuck out his tongue, Rem couldn't keep herself from sighing a little.

"If you don't deny it even a little, your wife will get carried away from being smothered in praise."

"What this about smothering you in praise? It's just the truth. I seriously am a real-life sellout."

If Subaru were seriously trying to kill her with flattery, he would go much, much further. But they were in a public park in broad daylight. If he started saying sweet nothings to her, the idle chatter around them would drown out everything else. That wasn't such a bad thing, but he wanted to fully enjoy the moment.

His son was playing; his wife was gently holding their baby daughter. Subaru felt like falling asleep beside them. Sitting beside her was somehow making Subaru sleepy.

"Er…"

"If you wish to sleep, I will lend you my shoulder. Spica has monopolized my arms, after all."

When he opened one eye, he found that his head had come to rest on Rem's shoulder as they sat side by side. With Rem so close, he could smell her sweet scent and feel her warmth. Subaru's cheeks slackened as he looked Spica's way.

She had her father's black hair and her mother's adorable face. Her life was innocent, delicate, and so very lovely.

"Damn you, Spica. Beloved daughter you may be, you're one frightening schemer, taking over my holy ground like that."

"My breasts are occupied until evening, so please wait."

"Right now, we're in a park in the middle of the day, so we'd better watch what we say, you know…"

When Subaru's eyes bulged at the audacious statement, the woman who had said it turned beet red.

"Man, my family's super adorable."

"Because you love them all each and every day."

Their gazing at each other made him feel funny, so Subaru accepted Rem's offer and rested his head on her shoulder. The feel of her blue hair brushing against him felt amazingly good, making Subaru rub his face against it without thinking about it.

"Someone wants to be tickled."

"Ah, sorry, it just felt sooo good. I'll just learn from Spica and behave. Rigel can be the only one who can't calm down. Wow, Rigel's such a little kid!"

"I can hear you, stupid dad! Don't compare me to you!"

"Rigel, your sister is sleeping, so please be considerate."

"It just ain't fair!"

The still-frozen Rigel shouted at the absurdity, but no one in the family backed him up. Adding to his woes, no one came to rescue Rigel from his frozen state. He was in quite an isolated position.

Though he resembled Subaru in appearance and mannerisms, the surrounding children did not tease him about that, which Subaru thought was incredibly kind on their part, but...

"You can't turn out like that, Spica! Only Big Bro acting like that is enough. Well, you take after Mother, so your future is bright. I only pray you don't get caught by a no-good man like me."

"There is no substitute for you. My darling is the greatest in the whole world."

Subaru gave a strained smile at Rem's enthusiastic seal of approval. Silence fell between them for a time; but this was not an uncomfortable silence in any way. With the sun's rays behind them, he gazed wistfully at his son being teased by his friends as he cuddled up to his wife, holding their daughter in her arms, and rested—it was a sweet, happy time.

"—Subaru."

The abrupt calling of Subaru's name made him open his closed eyes. When he glanced upward, Rem's clear, light-blue eyes were gazing into his. Her moist eyes loosened Subaru's tongue.

"...It's been a while since you've called me that. It's been 'darling' and 'Father' for ages."

"___"

The words Subaru spoke upon waking made Rem purse her trembling lips.

He was looking at the face Rem had often worn several years ago, right after they ran away. Subaru could tell even when Rem tried to hide it. After all, he'd always had his eyes on her.

Bathed by the wind, Subaru narrowed his eyes. It had been Rem who'd invited him on a family outing that day. He'd guessed that she had a reason for that. After all—

"Today...it's been eight years since that day, huh?"

"...You noticed?"

"Well, to me...no, to us, that was the day everything changed, right? It's not that I noticed or remembered, it's that I can't forget—there's no way can I forget."

It was the day he had submitted to fate, the day he had thrown everything away and fled with Rem.

It was a day when he'd meant to give everything up, but there was one thing only he hadn't given up on.

On that day he'd had her love—and the Subaru sitting there existed thanks to that.

"Subaru, do you...?"

Rem had consciously stopped calling him by that familiar name since they'd fled to Kararagi. It was no doubt a ritual by which she'd left their old lives behind.

All that time, Subaru hadn't asked her to divulge the true intent behind it, nor had Rem told Subaru on her own. As for what led her to depart from the ritual she had continued for so long, that was—

"...regret it?"

"Regret?"

"Yes, that you ran away. That you gave up. That you threw everything away. That you—"

"If you're gonna say, picked me, I'm gonna be ultra mad. I'll grab Rigel and Spica and head back home right now! Ah, nah, I'll leave Rigel here."

He saw that Rigel was giving him a foul look, but Subaru spoke anyway—"Mother and I are having an important discussion"—thrusting his son's concerns into a bottomless pit. "Now look here," he said afterward, turning back toward Rem as he spoke. "That's quite something to ask all of a sudden after eight years, and I'm not sure how many dozens or hundreds of times saying this is gonna help, but..."

"Yes."

"I love you the most in the whole world. You're the only bride for me, and I'm the only man for you. You're not a cheap woman...a guy like me doesn't settle for someone like you."

As they gazed at one another, Subaru's fingertip gave Rem's forehead a light flick. Then he drew close to the surprised girl's face and spoke.

"It's like I swore that day. I'm yours through and through. I'll do anything for you. I'll give anything to you. I live for you alone—Well, nowadays I have to add our kids to that."

With Rem's eyes closed, he crinkled his nose and stole a kiss from her lips.

A smile came over Subaru just from the touch of their lips and being close enough to feel her breath. No matter how many years passed, that childish mischievousness of his always stayed the same.

"Can't you stop worrying now?"

"...I am sorry. I always worry. I mean, I love you more and more, Subaru. Even though I keep thinking...there can never be a happier time than this...I become happier and happier. I love, I rejoice, and so I worry."

Tears appeared in Rem's eyes. She shook her head a little, even as she professed her own happiness. After shaking her head, she touched her cheek to Subaru's, allowing their mutual warmth to flow between them as she spoke.

"I worry that you'll go away, and I won't be able to touch you like this anymore."

"Relax. I'm not leaving your side and I'm not going away. As long as you love me, I'm never pulling away from you."

"My love for you will never run out, Subaru—"

"We'll be together forever, then. I love you, Rem."

Rem didn't know what to do with her own feelings as Subaru kissed her again.

Frozen in surprise, she sank deep inside herself as their hot tongues intertwined once more. When she felt his tongue depart, savoring the sensation of his saliva on her front teeth, her breath was slightly ragged when Subaru continued, "Don't make me say stupid stuff like maybe I settled for you in the first place. So what then? Instead of love for Rigel and Spica I should pity them? Spica's the crystallization of our love all according to plan, and Rigel's the kid born from our youth and burning love running wild."

"...It was quite a time when Rigel was born."

When Subaru put a hand on his hip and lectured her, Rem smiled softly as she looked back at him, reminiscing.

"Even though we needed to find a house and a job here in Kara-ragi and set up a calm, stable life..."

"Well, um, hey, we were young, so we couldn't just hold off."

"And even though you were tired from work, you became very energetic in the evening, Subaru."

"Er, um, hey, when you're young you have energy to spare, right?"

"I got pregnant almost at the same time as getting full-time work, so my head was pretty much a haze at the time..."

"A man really doesn't like acknowledging the so-called mistakes of his youth..."

Subaru deeply felt Rem's vigorous counterattack as he gazed into the distance and murmured. On the other end, Rigel grimaced at being treated like Subaru's mistake, but he apparently read the mood and refrained from intruding. Not bad for a son of his.

"Well, um, I was happy, too. When you told me, at first I had just a little bit of blood dripping from my nose, and then when I tried to check if it was a dream or not, it was actually bleeding from after you slugged me..."

Rem had lost her temper a fair bit, too, so the haymaker punch he'd received had sent him crashing into the wall with enough force to make their temporary residence tilt. It had been bad enough he had resigned himself to possibly experiencing Return by Death once again after a long hiatus.

At any rate, Subaru was able to recall every detail of when Rem had informed him of her pregnancy, including the warm feelings welling up in his chest at the time...

However, Rem responded to Subaru's words with a shake of her head.

"You are mistaken. My happiness is likely a different happiness from yours. What I think of happiness is...happiness that I did not have to lose you, Subaru."

"—"

"Rigel is the tangible bond born between Subaru and Rem. It may be a poor way to say it, but a child born between us firmly tied you to me so that you would never leave my side... That made me happy."

Perhaps he'd been leaning on her ever since those days of uncertainty.

He'd thrown away anything and everything until that point, the two of them fleeing to a new land with nothing but each other. Back in those days, with nothing to cling to but each other, Rem had always been shaken by the irrational fear that she would someday lose Subaru again.

In Rem's lack of confidence in herself, Subaru had met his match.

To Rem, worth much more than her minimal appraisal of herself, her life with Subaru was one of maximal happiness and anxiety, nurturing both fortune and fear as two sides of the same coin.

And it was the new life between them that had served as the marker to put an end to that time.

"You didn't believe?"

"No. I believe you more than this entire world, Subaru."

"Not that. I don't mean believing me...I mean, you didn't believe in yourself?"

Subaru's words drew a small gasp from Rem; then she nodded toward him. Inside her, Subaru loomed disproportionately large. Rem, thinking she was very tiny in comparison, must have felt anxious on account of that.

Enough not to notice that Subaru had harbored the same worry all that time.

Subaru couldn't help a pained smile at how they were intensely self-deprecating, husband and wife both. The sight of that made Rem's cheeks puff up.

"It is fine. I am an idiot. You cannot be faulted for laughing…," she said.

"No, no. I was just thinking all over again that our personalities are a perfect match, that and yes, my wife really is the cutest in the whole world."

For but a single moment, the surprise confession made Rem blink and brought a flush to her cheeks. Subaru's breast warmed at the response; he had managed to make Rem truly feel his love for her.

He liked, and loved, Rem most in the whole world. He was capable of yelling that in a loud voice. In fact, from time to time, he did just that. It had made them locally famous as a particularly passionate husband and wife.

"—Rigel, Spica."

"Mm?"

All of a sudden, Rem spoke the names of their two adorable children. When Subaru cocked his head, Rem said, "It's nothing," gazing at Subaru with upturned eyes.

"Both are the names of stars, yes? Stars in your homeland, Subaru?"

"Yep. My dad had a fundamentally lousy personality, but I straight-up admire him for naming me Subaru. I like this name. Subaru's the name of a star, y'see."

When, during his elementary school years, he brought up the topic of the origin of his name, Subaru had learned that he was named for a star cluster in the nighttime sky. Subaru had held an interest in illustrated books about stars ever since. So he knew a whole bunch of star names, and when he needed to stick a name onto something—

"I was always taking names from stars. I used the name of a star for my handle on the net, and if I used an alias I'd usually take one from a star. So even in that sense, these names really shine!!"

"I am uncertain what you mean by that, but I do think names of stars are wonderful. If a third child is born, I am sure it shall be the same."

"Isn't it a little soon to talk about a third? Spica's not weaned yet."

"I was thinking 1 could leave everything but breastfeeding to Rigel. Why do you think I was so careful not to have the next child until he got bigger?"

"Hard to notice with me around, but you're pretty hard on Rigel, too, aren't you, Rem?!"

Subaru made a strained smile at Rem's routine treatment of their son as he got up from the bench, brushing his rear. Then, as Rem looked up at him, he extended a hand toward her.

"Let's head back. A man can only do so much flirting with other people's eyes on him, you know," he said.

"I suppose so. Right now, I feel like you want to flirt with me with all your strength in a way that you haven't in a while."

"Oh yeah. Right now, my libido might be enough to keep up with even a demon's endurance..."

With that nervous murmur, he used the hand Rem was grasping to pull her into his embrace. "Wah!" she exclaimed in surprise as Subaru hugged her, Spica and all, deftly conveying his warmth to his family.

"Well, let's head back, then—to our house."

"Yes, darling."

Subaru walked forward, a basket of groceries in one hand, Rem's hand in the other, with Rem, carrying Spica, cuddled up against him as she followed half a step behind.

That was how they walked close to their still-frozen son at the center of the public park.

"Hey, son, still stuck in WinterFest on your own? This is slow even for freeze tag, and I'm bored, so Mother and I are taking your sister back home. You can sleep over at a friend's house tonight."

"That's blatantly ditching me, damn it! And this is after having my parents be all lovey-dovey in a public park in broad daylight."

"You jelly? Sorry, Rigel. Rem here is *all mine.*"

"Shut up!"

Subaru fanned the flames, drawing an angry shout from Rigel, but he didn't play the jilted son for long. He immediately took a deep breath and spoke. "Stay calm, stay calm. Don't let Dad fling you around willy-nilly. Calm, I'm calm… OK, I've calmed down. So what were you and Mommy talking about?"

"Where your name came from. Come to think a bit, I think Vega was my first candidate for your name."

"That sounds strong! Why'd you drop it?"

"Nah, when I thought of the original backstory it seemed pretty rough for a name. No way am I raising a son who can only meet his lover once a year. Lovers are important…especially my bride, the cutest of all."

"Yes, I am Subaru's Rem."

"Would you stop using topics about me to act all sappy like that?!"

His parents' sweet marital exchange drove Rigel to stamp the ground as he vented.

The other children playing freeze tag noticed Rigel's antics.

"Aah, Rigel moved! You can't break the freeze tag rules!"

"Geh!"

The children who had abandoned Rigel to that point showered accusations of rule breaking upon him. As Rigel froze, his throat tight, Subaru patted him on the shoulder.

"He who breaks the taboo of freeze tag must be punished. You must face the hell of being tickled by demons until you are unable to either laugh or cry— Be strong."

"Don't make up rules as you go with a serious look on your… Hey, what do you guys think you're…! Wait a sec! Don't just take what he says at face value! Wa, uwaaa—!!"

Rigel desperately ran away as the various children pressed upon him. However, they headed him off. They proceeded to press Rigel to the ground as several sets of fingers closed in…

"Farewell, my son. Father and Mother have something very important to discuss, so don't you dare come back until nighttime. Also, use of your horn is forbidden. And make sure you don't tear your clothes."

"Y-you heartless parents, I'll remember this—!"

Fingers pressed upon Rigel from all directions, toying with him as they pleased; his laughing voice echoed through the public park like a cry for help. The laughs of her older brother made Spica go, "Kya-kya," laughing in obvious delight.

Subaru sensed fine future prospects. Probably Spica's growth would further solidify Rigel's place in the Natsuki family.

Having displayed his boundless love for their beloved son by tweaking his nose *just* a little, Subaru walked forward, leading Rem by the hand.

And so he headed toward his own house, the place where he lived with his precious family in tranquility and happiness—

"Subaru."

"Mm?"

When he abruptly felt his arm tugged, Subaru stopped and looked back.

That instant, a powerful gust of wind blew between Subaru and Rem. He unwittingly closed his eyes, slowly opening them again when the wind relented.

Rem's long, blue hair was fluttering in the wind, glittering as if it were making the sunlight melt.

Rem had grown her hair long. The current Subaru somehow understood that this was due to her rivalry with someone. And so too did he understand that when he thought of a woman with long hair, the first image that came to mind was the one before his eyes: that of the girl most precious to him in the whole wide world.

The long hair silently flowed as Rem smiled at Subaru, reembracing their beloved daughter in her arms.

To Subaru, that loving smile was the loveliest thing of all.

"Right now, I am…the happiest woman in the world."

INTERLUDE

LET US FEAST

1

As they traveled along the highway, Rem let the dragon carriage rock her as she thought of him alone.

Rem was lying down, eyes narrowed from the dazzling morning sun and the moist breeze, when she gently lifted her head.

Straight ahead of her was the convoy of dragon carriages in military formation as they headed back to the royal capital. The carriages were carrying the wounded from the battle to defeat the White Whale; many of them were gravely wounded and had received only the bare minimum of treatment.

But the atmosphere of the unit was far from somber; it was that of an overflowing sense that their earnest desire had been achieved.

To them, the current trek to the royal capital was a triumphant return. The pain of their wounds did not hold a candle to their sense of fulfillment from achieving the wish they had waited years for. Indeed, their hauling the severed head of the White Whale to the royal capital would surely be greeted by praise from the masses for their valiant efforts.

In contrast to their deeply held sentiments, Rem was concerned with a young man not present.

"Your face is downcast, Rem. It seems your worries indeed know no bounds."

"...Lady Crusch."

When Rem looked toward the voice, she saw Crusch Karsten sitting right beside her.

Though she was bandaged under her light armor, Rem did not sense that her demeanor was affected by her wounds in the slightest. But there were traces of fatigue upon even her gallant face. She was in precarious enough territory that she was riding a dragon carriage, not on her favorite land dragon.

However, as Rem nodded toward her, Crusch cast her fatigue aside in the blink of an eye.

"Ferris, Wilhelm, and the expeditionary force accompanying them are brave, highly trained warriors. He shall surely have Ricardo and the Iron Fangs aiding him... Besides, it is difficult to believe that Anastasia Hoshin does not have other measures prepared. The Witch Cult's numbers are unknown, but it is not a losing battle."

"I wonder if it is selfish of me to worry, even so?"

"Once the seed of worry has taken root, stepping on it is not helpful. If you are the cause, you must overcome yourself with devotion and resolve. But one finds the self to be a difficult opponent— Forgive me, helping others find peace of mind is not my specialty."

Seeing the gloom on Rem's face deepen, Crusch lowered her eyes, realizing that she had misspoken. That instant, Rem broke into a small, spontaneous smile at how the woman who had felt so detached to date suddenly felt very close to her. "Very good," said Crusch, drawing her chin in upon seeing that smile. "Subaru Natsuki said it well. That a smiling face suits you better, Rem. Hearing it from the side, I thought it mere flattery, but it is less idiotic than I expected."

"If you were to smile, Lady Crusch, the air you give off would surely change as well. You are always so imposing... I believe you would display a wonderful smile."

"...I wonder. I am a woman poor at smiling. I have always regretted it, and do so even now."

Rem's suggestion caused Crusch to avert her gaze and murmur thusly. There was a smile carved upon her lips, but this was a slight smile, one plainly at her own expense.

Rem was surprised to see Crusch display such disgust with herself. To Rem, lacking in confidence, Crusch, always valiant and composed, was one of the ideal images of womanhood. Though as far as Rem was concerned, Ram, her elder sister, was the most ideal of all...

But before she could press the issue, Crusch hid her smile and changed the topic.

"Concerning Subaru Natsuki and the others... This revolves around Emilia's lineage. I anticipated the threat of the Witch Cult from the beginning. Surely Marquis Mathers has prepared measures of his own?"

"I do not understand Master Roswaal's thinking. For that reason, it shall do you no good to pry."

"How strict. Now that we are allies, he surely would not mind your letting a few words slip."

Likely, her jesting manner of speaking was her being considerate toward Rem. As a matter of fact, Rem had managed not to sink into a swamp of worry thanks to Crusch's speaking to her like that.

Besides, Crusch's hypothesis made perfect sense. It was a certainty that Roswaal, of all people, would have some kind of countermeasure for the current incident. After Subaru's having fallen into misfortune, his actions to assist Roswaal would surely restore his good name.

No, his cooperation in the battle against the White Whale had already made his name echo far more than that.

The hero, Subaru Natsuki.

To Rem, it was natural to assess the man who had saved her heart and her future thus; there was no other appraisal fitting Subaru, who would surely perform other shining exploits thereafter. And if Rem could exist beside that shining light, have it turn toward her from time to time, Rem sought nothing more. Rem would be fulfilled by that alone.

When Rem thought about Subaru, her heart was always filled with complex emotions. It always made her feel warm and at ease. And yet at some point anxiety crept in, bringing anguish; she felt like worry was tearing her apart.

It was Subaru, and Subaru alone, who gave her heart such joy and distress, ceaselessly alternating between one and the other...

"Subaru...truly is a very vexing person."

With a small, wry smile, Rem whispered loving words toward the image of the man rising in the back of her mind.

Crusch watched the side of her face in visible relief. She let her long hair flow down her back as she silently shifted her eyes toward the dragon carriage on the road ahead—but her amber eyes abruptly narrowed.

"—Mm?"

Crusch let out a tiny murmur. Rem lifted up her face, for she had detected a jarring sound at nearly the same instant.

The dragon carriage in front caught by the amber eyes was in the same direction as the discordant sound Rem had noticed. The two discrepancies were linked to the same event, which occurred a moment later.

Namely, the sudden destruction of the dragon carriage directly in front of Crusch.

It was destruction in its purest form. Out of the blue, the dragon carriage's entire frame was swallowed up by an overpowering shock wave, which blasted it away in pieces. To Rem, the sound of the devastating blow was like that of rainfall.

Red mist spewed out as the dragon carriage was instantly transformed into a bloody spectacle. The land dragon, the carriage, and surely the wounded inside the carriage as well, had been pulverized by wholly merciless destruction.

"—! We're under attack!!"

Instantly, Crusch shoved all distress from the blow aside and called the formation to arms. The expeditionary force's warriors, immediately sensing something was very wrong, raised their weapons, girding against enemy attack. Rem, too, ignored her physical fatigue, rising up with an iron ball in her hand… Then she saw a figure on the other side of the bloody mist.

Unarmed. Unguarded. Unconcerned. Unmoved, unmerciful, unreserved malice—

"—Trample them!!"

Crusch shouted toward the driver's seat. Hearing this, the knight loudly snapped the reins in lieu of a nod. The neighing land dragon accelerated, and the dragon carriage became a weapon, charging to run over its foe. And so they would score a direct hit on their target, the figure standing rooted to the spot, making no move to avoid it, sending him flying—

"Lady Crusch—!"

Rem shouted as she grabbed Crusch by her slender hips and leaped, escaping to the dragon carriage's side. The knight on the driver's seat was beyond her reach. Rem clenched her teeth in regret, and just after, she heard a voice.

"Goodness, could you not? I think running over someone who's done nothing is slightly beyond what decent people would do."

It was a gentle voice speaking with all the urgency of someone taking an early-afternoon stroll in a public park. In fact, if she'd heard such words in a public park, Rem would have been far less shocked. Yet that voice had unleashed the destruction that had shattered a dragon carriage in a tragic spectacle of blood spatter.

At a glance, he was an utterly unremarkable individual.

He was of medium height, with a medium build, and he had naturally white hair that was neither short nor long. The white suit that he wore to match the hair on his head was neither extravagant nor shabby, nor did his face have any defining characteristics; he looked like a completely average man.

Yet as a matter of fact, the land dragon coming into contact with him forcefully cried out as half of it was torn asunder; the knight on the driver's seat and the smashed dragon carriage were destroyed together to the point that it was impossible to tell them apart.

And what shocked Rem the most was not the man's demeanor as he treated the awful spectacle like it was nothing, but the fact that the man who had assuredly destroyed the dragon carriage had simply stood there. The man had done nothing. Merely by standing, he had taken a head-on collision from a dragon carriage, and won.

"I thank you, Rem. You saved me…but it seems the situation has improved little."

As Rem stood frozen, Crusch, embraced in her arms, rose to her own feet. She remained wary of the still-unarmed man as she turned a painful eye toward the bloody remnants of the dragon carriage.

"How dare you inflict such cruelty on my retainers…? Who are you?"

Razor-sharp will to fight rested in Crusch's eyes as she posed the question to the man in a hard voice. Upon receiving Crusch's question, the man touched his own chin, nodding multiple times as he spoke.

"I see, I see. That means you do know nothing about me. But I know all about you. Right now, the royal capital…no, the entire nation is astir where you are all concerned, candidates to become the next ruler. Even if I have little interest in titles and the affairs of the world, I can imagine it takes a great deal of resolve to bear such burdens. It must be so hard for you."

"Enough idle chitchat— Answer my question or I shall strike you down."

"What a terrible thing to say…but perhaps arrogance of this level is mandatory if one is to support a nation on her shoulders…not that I can understand even a smidgen of that emotion, mind you. Well, I suppose I could never understand the thoughts of someone who actually wants the throne and having that responsibility piled upon her. Ah, not understanding does not mean I am putting them down. You see, unlike you, I simply lack such arrogance…"

The man continued to ignore Crusch's demand as he spoke glibly at length. But—

"—I told you there would not be a third chance."

Crusch made that calm statement at the same time that she waved her arm, unleashing a blade of wind. This was Crusch's technique, One Blow, One Hundred Felled—the product of wind magic and her blessing of wind reading.

The man was slashed by the invisible cutting attack, able to slay a person, before he even realized he had been sliced. It was this might with the sword by which Crusch had protected the Duchy of Karsten in her first sortie, preventing damage when the demon beast known as the Great Hare appeared, causing rumors of the Valkyrie to quickly spread.

It was a hearty sword blow that could even rend the thick hide of the White Whale, sending a beast of that size crashing to the ground—a man's flesh, with a mass greatly inferior to that of the demon beast's, could not possibly withstand such a blow.

And yet—

"…Who raised you to cut a man down in the middle of a pleasant conversation?"

Tilting his head, the man stood there, his body showered with the slicing blow, only to easily shrug it off.

The cutting attack that had rent even the White Whale hadn't even made him twitch. There was no sign of the man's flesh—no, not even of the man's clothes having been cut.

It was thanks to an unknown phenomenon that did far more than merely defend against Crusch's invisible blade.

Crusch gasped; Rem's body froze up from the work of a different abnormal phenomenon. Looking at the two in front of him, the man sighed and pushed up his forelocks in annoyance.

"Now hold on, I'm speaking. I'm speaking, okay? Isn't it strange to interrupt a man when he's speaking? Not that I feel like asserting the right to speak, but it's common sense not to bother a man when he's trying to say something. Now, you're free to listen or not, so I won't complain about that part, but you deciding not to let me speak, that's just…I mean, how self-centered is that?"

The man spoke rapidly as he began to scuff the ground with the tip of his shoe. The pair maintained an awkward silence as the man pointed at them, clicking his tongue in further annoyance.

"And now silence. What's up with you people? You heard me. I know you heard me. I asked questions, didn't I? Then answer me. That's how it works. And you won't even do that. You don't want to. Ahhh, liberty. This is your liberty at work. This is how you employ your own liberty. That's fine, do as you please. But you know what that means, don't you?"

The man leaned forward as the mad glint in his eyes grew stronger. Then—

"It means that you're belittling my rights...the very few things I personally own, yes?"

A chill raced up Rem's spine. The next moment the man moved. Without warning, he listlessly raised his dangling arms, and a faint vortex of wind erupted.

Right after, in a line directly above the man's arms—the ground, the air, the world, broke.

"—"

Around and around, around and around, Crusch's left arm, severed at the shoulder, danced in the air.

The arm, still posed as if it were holding the invisible blade, flew, scattering blood droplets all around as it fell to the earth. The blow sent Crusch's body crumpling down; she began to convulse from the bleeding and intense pain.

"Lady...Crusch—"

After spending several seconds dumbfounded, Rem snapped back and leaped toward Crusch. Putting her hand against Crusch's bleeding wound, Rem wrung out the scant mana she had to stop the bleeding and treat it with all her strength.

Crusch's arm had been cleanly severed—flesh, bone, and nerves sliced through. No matter how out of place, Rem couldn't help but admire the terrifyingly perfect cut.

"Ferr...is... Uaa...u?"

In Rem's arms, Crusch's vision wandered as she spoke those

words. Her right hand gripped Rem's foot hard enough to make her bones creak.

Rem bit down, enduring Crusch's struggle to live. She glowered at the wicked deed of the man before her.

Rem had absolutely no understanding of the indecipherable man's means of attack and defense. As she pondered how to shield the wounded Crusch and get her away from the man, Rem suddenly realized that something else felt off.

During all of this, the other knights had strangely not joined the battle.

"Aaah… No matter how much I eat, it's still not enough! This is why we can't stop livin'. Eat, eat, bite, chew, swallow, swallow more, tear, crush, drink! Gorge! Aaah, that was a feast!"

The same time the insight hit her, the high-pitched voice of a youth reached her from behind.

A chill equal to that caused by the man before her caused Rem to look back in fright. And behind her, at the center of the stopped convoy of dragon carriages, she saw a blood-smeared youth kicking the knights who had fallen before him.

He was a short youth with light-brown hair that went down to the knees. His height was equal to Rem's or even lower; he was probably twelve or thirteen years of age. Under his unkempt hair, he wore tattered clothes over his diminutive frame. His bare limbs were covered in dirt and grime, and stained from large amounts of blood spatter.

Not one of the knights tumbled at his feet was moving. The youth had wiped out the surrounding knights while Crusch was battered in the white-haired man's attack.

"You…are…?"

Rem's lips quivered, for she was dumbfounded that she had not even sensed the combat taking place.

Hemmed in by bizarre opponents to the front and the back, Rem picked Crusch up and slowly backed away. Blood flowing from Crusch's wound was staining the grassland red; the air felt chill, as if to mock Rem's fearful heart.

Rem's trembling question prompted man and boy to glance at each other's faces. Then the pair nodded, as if giving each other a signal, whereupon devilish smiles came over both, as if such violent acts were deeply familiar to them; then they introduced themselves.

"Archbishop of the Seven Deadly Sins of the Witch Cult, Regulus Corneas, charged with Greed."

"Archbishop of the Seven Deadly Sins of the Witch Cult, Lye Batenkaitos, charged with Gluttony."

2

They were members of the Witch Cult—and archbishops at that.

Ignoring Rem, who froze when their titles reached her ears, the excitable-looking youth—Lye Batenkaitos—looked around at the fallen knights, fondly licking his lips.

"Oh yeah, coming here for a bite like this was a great idea. Considering that they took out our pet, this is…a rich harvest. It's nice, it's great, it's neat, it's all right, it's good, it's good, it's great, isn't it, of course it's great! It's been a while since we've been able to eat our fill!"

"To be honest, I just can't understand that part about you. Why can you not be satisfied with what you have right now? You know, people can only carry what will fit in the two hands they are born with. Why can't you understand that and hold your own cravings in check?"

"We hate lectures, and we don't need any. We don't care if what you say is right or wrong, either. To us, nothing matters besides the feeling of an empty stomach."

Batenkaitos of Gluttony slurped his saliva as Regulus of Greed let his shoulders sink.

With two Archbishops of the Seven Deadly Sins having appeared simultaneously, Rem desperately searched her nearly stalled head, earnestly hammering out a plan to break out of the situation.

With the combat ability present, it was impossible to crush the two men who had appeared before them.

Crusch's bleeding had stopped, but she was in nearly as precarious a condition as before. As it was unclear if the knights were dead or alive, Rem could not count on them to bolster her fighting strength. Rem herself had depleted her tiny reserve of mana by treating Crusch; even if she went into demon mode, she could not picture an outcome where she was triumphant.

"—"

When she glanced around the area, she could not see any sign of the Iron Fangs. One of their units was transporting the wounded beast men and hauling the recovered head of the White Whale. Likely their commander, Hetaro, had seen an opportunity and beat a hasty retreat. Perhaps, if she bought some time, they might return with reinforcements.

Even if that was true, she doubted they would arrive in time.

"Are you here because…we defeated the White Whale? To avenge the demon beast…?"

"Ahh, don't misunderstand. We're not interested in the dead White Whale. We're interested in the people who killed the White Whale. Somehow it did whatever it liked for four hundred years, but you managed to kill it. I hoped you all would be ripe for the slaughter…but it turned out even better than I expected!"

Batenkaitos bared his very sharp teeth as he wildly shook his head in vigorous excitement.

"Love! Chivalrous spirit! Hatred! Tenacity! Triumph! All bottled up and simmering for such a long, long time! Just having them passing down my throat makes me feel full! Is there a more beautiful food in the entire world?! No, no, nay, nothing, surely nothing, certainly nothing, absolutely nothing!! Drink! Gorge! That is what brings joy to our hearts, and our stomachs!!"

Rem couldn't understand anything he said.

Batenkaitos continued to writhe as if he'd dined to excess. As his laughs reverberated for a time, Rem silently shifted her gaze; that gaze caused Regulus to wave a hand with an exasperated look.

"Relax. I'm not anything like him. I'm just here by pure coincidence. You think I hunger and thirst like that? I have nothing to do with such vulgar behavior. Unlike him, always pathetically unfulfilled, I would be satisfied with, well, you, even as you currently are."

Regulus motioned to Crusch's lopped-off arm, wearing a sunny expression as he stood before Rem.

"I dislike...conflict and the like. If times remain ordinary, peaceful and gentle, that is enough for me. That is best. I have no ambitions greater than what I can reach with my meager hands. As an individual, my hands are full simply protecting what little I call my own."

Regulus closed his fist, drunk on his own performance. Rem wondered how someone who could take the lives of a land dragon and several humans, or inflict a grievous wound on a single woman, could speak like that.

On the one hand was Batenkaitos, who writhed from incomprehensible hunger, immersed in self-satisfaction while waving around his pet self-serving theories; on the other was Regulus, a strange man through and through. They truly had to be Witch Cultists.

Simmering anger welled up within Rem as she rose to her feet.

Rem laid Crusch, sleeping like the dead, down on the ground; she lifted up her own weapon in Crusch's place. Rem's little remaining mana swirled around, and a number of icicles rose in the air around her.

Seeing this, the expressions on Batenkaitos and Regulus changed.

"Have you listened to a single word I said? I told you, I don't want to fight. After hearing that, if you're going to act like this, that would be...ignoring my opinion. That would be infringing upon my rights. That is something even my unselfish heart cannot forgive."

"Is that all you have to say, Witch Cultist?"

As Regulus inclined his head, Rem spoke thus, her demeanor resolute. In contrast to Regulus, taken aback by the sight, a strong glint rested in Rem's eyes as the chain of her iron ball rang out.

"Someday a hero shall appear—a hero to destroy you all. However self-serving you are, however much misfortune your self-satisfaction creates, that man, the only hero Rem loves, shall surely bring you what you deserve."

"Heh, a hero? Well, that's more fun. If you trust him that much, that'll make him all the tastier for us!!"

Batenkaitos clapped his hands in delight as he stared at Rem, seeming to assess her. He was looking at her neither as an enemy nor as a woman. There was but a single, undiluted sentiment resting in that gaze: that of a hungry beast licking its chops in front of its food.

They were an ego run amok and a violent hunger demon. Rem boldly faced them both with pride.

"I am a senior servant of Marquis Roswaal L. Mathers…"

As Rem made her introduction, she stopped halfway after speaking her title, shaking her head.

At that moment, for that instant only, Rem introduced herself the way she truly wished her name to be known:

"Now I am but a woman in love—I am Rem, the woman assisting Subaru Natsuki, the man I love most, the man who will become a hero."

A beautiful white horn jutted out of Rem's forehead, granting Rem vigor as it collected the mana stored in the air around her. Power filled her entire body as she moved the hand gripping the iron ball's handle in a rhythmic motion and called forth more and more icicles.

Her eyes were wide open. She was aware of the whole world around her. She felt the air around her. But the only thing traced by the back of her mind was an image of him.

"Prepare yourselves, Archbishops of the Seven Deadly Sins—Rem's hero shall surely come to strike you down!!"

Raising her iron ball high, Rem leaped, her body shooting out, pounding the icicles home the same instant. Batenkaitos seemed set to strike them down as he opened his fang-filled mouth wide and spoke.

"Ahh, that's the spirit… Then, without holding back, let us feast!!"

Something struck her. Something struck her. And in that instant, she thought...

I hope that when he learns that I am gone, it sends a ripple through his heart.

In her final moment, that was Rem's only wish.

CHAPTER 6

TO EACH THEIR VOWS

1

As she lay on the bed, her face was tranquil, enough to make someone think she was merely asleep.

When he looked at the lashes on the borders of her closed eyelids, he could absentmindedly think, *Wow, it's been a while.* Her expression while awake was usually taut, but one could catch a true glimpse of her age on her face when she slept.

Now that he thought of it, he'd never once had a chance to see her sleeping face.

She was always waking up Subaru, always being strict with him, and only now did he realize just how lovely she looked when she let that hardness soften.

He'd seen her surprised face, her blushing face, her pouting face, her crying face, and the smiling face she showed him when they'd made up. He'd had so many chances to realize it before.

"—Rem."

Rem was not sleeping in the maid uniform she usually wore. There was no flower adornment for her pretty blue hair. To a maid, those were armor for battle—now she needed those things no longer.

"So this is where you were."

Subaru was idly spending his time in that quiet, unmoving room when someone spoke to him.

When he slowly turned around, he saw a woman standing at the room's entrance wearing a light-purple dress. The woman had long, beautiful hair, and behaved with refined elegance as she walked over.

But there was a faint bewilderment to her gait, as if she sensed something awry that did not match the nobility she had been born with. And when she approached, that discordant feeling spread to Subaru as well.

"Is she...?"

"Nothing's changed at all. It's not like I can do anything, so I'm just sticking around. It's kind of pathetic how I'm clinging to her like this..."

"I wonder if that might not...make her happy, somehow."

As Subaru hung his head, the woman timidly offered words of consolation. But those words, which could not possibly put his mind at ease, made Subaru unwittingly glare at her.

"...I am sorry. It seems I went too far and offended you."

"...I'm sorry, too. I'm just frustrated. Rem would be angry with me. She'd say, 'Subaru, you must not take things out on other people' or something."

Subaru lowered his head to the apologetic woman, weakly smiling as he mimicked Rem's manner of speech.

In the back of his mind, he could hear her voice saying those exact words. And yet her voice reached no one. There was no one to point out that Subaru's act was nothing like the real thing.

Subaru's hollow, farcical action made the woman before him don a pained look, covering her eyes. Without thinking, she shifted that right hand to her own left arm—holding it as if to support the freshly reattached limb.

Silence descended on the room, and Subaru shook his head, knowing he could not allow it to continue. When you're feeling despondent, continued silence becomes comfortable, and it is easy to become apathetic and stop your legs. But that was not what the man Rem believed in ought to do.

"Did you...need something from me?"

"Yes. The others have assembled in the office for some kind of discussion. It would be good to have...uh..."

The woman looked like she'd been rescued by his prompting as she continued her words about the business he'd surmised. But halfway through those words, her cheeks awkwardly tensed. Seeing this, Subaru pointed to himself and spoke.

"I'm...Subaru Natsuki."

"...I am sorry. Master Subaru Natsuki, is it? I shall properly remember. I am very sorry to have been so rude to you after all I have heard you have done for me."

"It can't be helped. There's way too many things you have to keep track of right now, so don't worry about it."

The woman's demeanor was genuinely apologetic—but the ill feeling from that very graceful, feminine behavior tore at his chest. He wasn't rude enough to actually say that, though.

"Well, I'll see you later, Rem."

Turning his head back, Subaru gave the sleeping Rem a gentle pat on the head. Her chest faintly rose and fell; her body was warm to the touch. Her living, physical body was firmly present.

For her, lost to the memories of others, that was the only thing that remained.

"The office, you said. It's bad to keep everyone waiting, so let's go, I guess?"

"Yes, let us do so, Master Subaru Natsuki."

The woman smiled charmingly as she addressed him by name. The fleeting femininity of the gesture really rubbed him the wrong way.

Recognizing his distaste, Subaru turned his face aside, making an amiable smile to conceal what truly lay in his heart as he spoke.

"Sorry to make you come all this way to get me...Crusch."

He addressed her by name, even though she already seemed to be another person entirely.

2

It was all over by the time Subaru arrived back at the royal capital.

"Who's Rem?"

Emilia had spoken those words to Subaru, turning her head to the side quizzically.

Perhaps, if the words and gesture had given the slightest hint of Emilia making a bad joke, Subaru would have followed suit and said something flippant in turn.

But Subaru had not seen even a single smidgen of such hope from Emilia's demeanor, and as shock overtook Subaru, Emilia never broke into a *Just kidding!* no matter how long he waited.

It was the same for Petra and the other children. None of them remembered Rem.

Faced with that fact inside the dragon carriage, Subaru desperately had it race to the capital.

It can't be. There has to be some mistake. That was what he believed.

After all, everything should have turned out all right. Subaru ought to have grabbed hold of the best possible outcome. He'd accomplished his objectives, protected the people precious to him, and overcome sadness and anguish, carrying on the struggle in spite of his heart being scarred many times over.

And yet—

"___"

When Subaru's feet stepped into the office, the gazes of those already in the room gathered upon him. He imagined the uncomfortable feeling he got from them was damage wrought from the blame they harbored toward themselves.

The three people in the office were Emilia, Ferris, and Wilhelm. Adding the recent arrivals Subaru and Crusch, that made five people participating in the discussion.

"...Ah, I'm glad you're back. Lady Crusch, sorry I made you run an errand."

"Not at all. It's quite all right, Master Ferr—"

"—Ferris is fine. We've been together far too long, it'll make me feel lonely if you add *Master* or anything else at this point, *meow*. No labels, okay?"

Greeting Crusch upon her return, Ferris spun his words with a reassuring tone of voice. He'd stripped off his royal guard uniform in favor of a feminine outfit with a short skirt.

Led by Ferris's hand, Crusch looked conflicted when she sat beside him and spoke.

"I cannot guarantee it will be like before, but I shall try, Ferris... Mm, Ferris."

"You don't need to rush. Ferri will always be your ally, always by your side. Besides, it feels like the current Lady Crusch has discovered a new way to be beautiful."

Ferris held her hand just as he had always done with the more valiant Crusch before. Ferris's behavior made Subaru harbor complicated feelings inside himself.

Even though Crusch had changed so much, Ferris's approach to her had not. He couldn't even begin to imagine how much melancholy Ferris was hiding underneath that smile.

"Subaru..."

Then, as Subaru stood still, Emilia shifted her considerate gaze toward him. The sorrowful gaze made Subaru's breath catch; he sat beside her as if it was the only natural thing to do.

"It's all right, Emilia. I've calmed down now—I'm all right."

His voice sounded all right. He maintained his calm. But he could not meet Emilia's gaze; he was so busy acting nonchalant that he didn't notice his hands were shaking.

"—Now that Sir Subaru and Lady Crusch have returned, let us begin our discussion."

In a low voice, Wilhelm spoke, cutting short the awkward silence about to fill the air.

It was rare for Wilhelm to lead a discussion. Ferris, deducing that this was the Sword Devil clumsily trying to be considerate, reluctantly took up the role of guiding the conversation and spoke.

"Well, let's do as Old Man Wil said… First, how about we go over the situation again?"

With those words, they began to discuss the events that had occurred after the fall of the White Whale and the Archbishop of the Seven Deadly Sins of Sloth.

The situation that had befallen Rem, Crusch, and the expeditionary force members with them had been very simple.

Having split from Subaru and his group, Rem and the others were in the middle of returning to the royal capital with the head recovered from the defeated White Whale when they had come under attack by separate Witch Cultists. As a result, half of the expeditionary force had been slain during its return journey—and according to the tale, the Iron Fangs, instantly separating at the direction of their lieutenant, had managed to escape losses of their own.

"The Iron Fangs that had fled returned with reinforcements from the capital, but…the Archbishops of the Seven Deadly Sins were gone, and all that remained were the dead and…"

"…Those in circumstances similar to mine, yes?"

Crusch finished off Ferris's words, furling her brow with chagrin. The anguish of the expression that came over her was doubtless caused by how helpless she felt inside. After all, she couldn't help but feel like what they were talking about had happened to someone else—

"Their own memories erased…was it. You think this is the work of the Archbishops of the Seven Deadly Sins, too?"

"I'm all but certain of it. There've been all kinds of reports of people with memory damage long before Lady Crusch and the others. They stated that the victims' memories had suddenly vanished, and even healing spells could not restore them. The cause had been unknown until now, but considering Sloth…"

"—There is surely no doubt this is the Authority of a Archbishop of the Seven Deadly Sins of the Witch Cult."

Wilhelm crossed his arms as he nodded grimly. The old man had a grave look on his face as he shifted his blade-like gaze toward Crusch. The gaze made Crusch unintentionally cringe.

"No, Lady Crusch, you are blameless. I am very sorry to have frightened you."

"…It is I who am sorry for being such a timid liege. Master Wilhelm, I have striven to remember you as well, but…"

A faint tremor of pain passed through the side of the aged swordsman's face when Crusch called him *Master Wilhelm*. No doubt he felt responsibility as the shameful retainer causing the lord to which he had offered his sword to put on such a painful display. Subaru felt similar regret, for now he knew painfully well just how deep Wilhelm's loyalty ran.

"We finally took care of Sloth, only to have other Archbishops of the Seven Deadly Sins appear right after. That's just the worst, *meow*. Well, we knew the Witch Cult would make a fuss as soon as Lady Emilia entered the royal selection, though…"

"…So it really is…my fault…?"

Emilia cast her eyes down slightly when Ferris pointed the conversation her way. "I suppose it is," said Ferris, agreeing with Emilia's faint murmur without the slightest hesitation. "Lady Emilia is a half-elf, so there was no way the Witch Cult would let this go. After all, they went from their usual creepy quiet act to causing this huge ruckus, so it's definitely linked to that."

"These people…hurt others because they hate half-demons…?"

"Hatred is painting it too softly. They're obsessed with exterminating Lady Emilia…with exterminating all half-elves. This was just…a fraction of it."

"A fraction, and they did such terrible things. Subaru, do you—?"

Emilia's voice shook as she called Subaru's name; her words caught in her throat. However, when her eyes met his, the interrupted words were conveyed to him nonetheless. Emilia was probably going to ask him…

Subaru, do you hate me too…?

"—! This is ridiculous. Ferris, think more carefully about how you phrase things. Don't say it like Emilia's at fault. It's those scumbags at fault through and through."

Seeing Emilia racked by guilt, Subaru felt hurt by the implication and rose to defend her. He glared at Ferris, rebuking him for his barbed demeanor toward Emilia throughout.

"Don't blame the wrong person. Hurting your allies by mistake doesn't help anything."

"Hmm, that sounds convincing when Subawu says it. Guess you have prior experience?"

"—!"

The sarcasm contained crystal clear malice toward Subaru. Hence Subaru grit his teeth and unwittingly began to get up. But a moment before he did so—

"Ferris—I cannot ignore what you have said just now. Apologize."

Before Subaru could put strength into his knees, it was none other than Crusch who scolded Ferris.

Wearing her dress, Crusch, who was so frail until that moment, tightened her expression; she sternly rebuked her own knight for his rudeness, training a bold, sharp gaze upon him like the Crusch of old.

"As Master Subaru Natsuki has stated, it is clear who should bear the blame for this matter. Also, you have no standing to mock him for stating an opinion that is correct. You understand, yes?"

"…Yes, Lady Crusch."

The current Crusch softened her stern speech slightly at the end. Her words and actions were very much like her, something that surprised Subaru.

Ferris, not yet able to hide the surprise on his own face, bowed his head toward Subaru and Emilia.

"Lady Emilia, I apologize for my rudeness. And Subawu, sorry, 'kay?"

"You litt— Nah, it's fine. More importantly, let's get back on track. I pretty much understand Crusch's…memory-loss incident. That leaves Rem……the people wiped from other folks' memories."

Subaru responded to Ferris's apology, farcical to the bitter end, by moving on to Rem's situation, the main issue—or at least the main issue to *him*.

"Mind you, Rem's not just some delusion on my part. She's a... very important girl to me. We wouldn't have beaten the White Whale without her, either."

"Sir Subaru..."

Wilhelm, too, lowered his voice as Subaru rued the difference in how the memories had been consumed.

Unlike Crusch, who had lost her own memories, Rem had been erased from the memories of others. The memory damage of the attacked expeditionary force's victims was split between those two symptoms. But where the latter case was concerned, Subaru and the others knew of similar previous cases.

"Like the effect of the White Whale's mist, *meow*. The people erased by that mist are erased from everyone's memories."

"According to Sir Subaru's information, the White Whale is associated with Gluttony. If that demon beast could do it, the Archbishops of the Seven Deadly Sins that attacked Lady Crusch and the others are connected to Gluttony as well."

"So the Authority of an Archbishop of the Seven Deadly Sins... huh... Ferris, you've examined Rem's body, I take it?"

Rem, sleeping in bed that very moment, had already had all her external injuries healed. When Subaru asked if Ferris had diagnosed anything other than external wounds, Ferris shook his head.

"To put it bluntly, I found nothing unusual—even though the result certainly is. The same goes for how the body continues to sleep, not waking no matter what anyone does. It's Sleeping Princess symptoms through and through."

"...What'd you say?"

Subaru raised an eyebrow at the abrupt metaphor. But in Ferris's place, Emilia lifted up her face and spoke.

"I've heard of it before. Certainly the symptoms are sleeping and never waking up...aren't they? Also, the people affected never hunger, nor do they age."

"It is an illness rarely seen even in this large a kingdom. There have been various reports of people falling into a Sleeping Princess state, but I have never heard of any of them awakening. Besides the issue of disappearing from memory, the symptoms match."

Wilhelm added to what Emilia had to say, but his voice sounded far more grounded in reality. Perhaps an acquaintance of his had fallen into a Sleeping Princess state.

Either way, nothing related to the Sleeping Princess condition, or Rem's situation in general, was beyond the realm of speculation.

"So short of asking Gluttony, there's no way to know the details. In the end, there's no avoiding slamming into the Witch Cult again. I was prepared for that, though…"

Subaru glanced at the side of Emilia's face as he verbally renewed his determination to oppose the Witch Cult.

The Cult's obsession with half-elves would doubtless cast a shadow on Emilia's path thereafter. Even without the Rem issue, they couldn't avoid clashing again. Hence, in his own thoughts, he became even more resolved than before.

"So, Subawu, your side is planning to be all gung ho and face the Witch Cult, *meow*… I see."

Ferris seemed tired somehow as he sighed.

And then—

"In that case, can we just…forget about that alliance agreement, *meow*?"

"—"

Ferris's nonchalantly tossed words brought a silent chill to the air.

For a moment Subaru didn't understand just what had been said. However, the instant comprehension caught up inside him, his insides grew hot with rage.

"What do you mean by that? How does what we were talking about lead to talk of scrapping the alliance?"

But despite his anger, Subaru asked the question in a calm voice that belied the burning in his chest. Ferris was not someone who would speak out of turn without a thought. At the very least, Subaru trusted that he would not do such a thing.

Subaru hadn't shouted in anger, and Ferris put on a surprised look as he spoke.

"I said exactly what I meant. An alliance is formed out of mutual benefit…but the pros are now outweighed by the cons, right? So I thought that cooperating now is meaningless, *meow.*"

"What about the mining rights for the forest? Maybe you think that all debts are paid for helping with the White Whale and the Witch Cult, but…"

"—You're telling us to cooperate even when the Witch Cult will keep going after Lady Emilia? Subawu, can you promise me that Lady Crusch won't be hurt even more in the process?"

"Th-that's…"

When Ferris asked him that, Subaru hesitated to continue. Seeing the drastic change in Crusch, he could not reject Ferris's concern out of hand. After all, Subaru bore wounds at least as deep as his.

Accordingly, the task of telling Ferris he was wrong did not fall to Subaru.

"Ferris, I must disagree."

Still sitting in his chair, Wilhelm glanced at the side of Ferris's face as he spoke. Ferris glared at the Sword Devil for raising a dissenting voice from within.

"Why are you against this, Old Man Wil? With Gluttony attacking Lady Crusch like this, what's the point of cooperating with Lady Emilia's side any longer?"

"In doing so…an opportunity to avenge our liege against Gluttony shall surely come."

"—! Are you saying that's more important than Lady Crusch's life?!"

Wilhelm, calm in his rebuttal to the end, caused Ferris's emotions to finally explode. Ferris looked down at his own palm as he bit his lip in regret before he continued.

"If we involve ourselves with the Cult again, more things like this will happen. When that time comes, the current Lady Crusch won't be able to defend herself—and I won't be able to help her."

"Ferris…"

Subaru understood that Ferris felt something close to hatred when he looked at his own pale fingers. Coming into contact with a small portion of that anger had made Subaru finally comprehend the feelings of remorse behind them.

Subaru harbored a sense of powerlessness just like the one tormenting Ferris.

Ferris hated himself for not having the strength to protect Crusch, someone so dear to his heart. Even his healing magic, purported to be among the best, was unable to aid Crusch as she was now—

"It must be very hard for Lady Crusch, too. Not being able to remember anything, understand anything…so she wouldn't even think of fighting like this. Right? …Right?"

When Ferris looked back at Crusch, seemingly clinging to her, his expression crumbled. He lost the usual, everyday look he'd maintained until moments before, having hidden the frailty of that face, on the verge of tears at any moment, behind a paper-thin shell.

Everything he did, he did because he wished with all his heart not to let Crusch get hurt—

"When it comes to your memory, I'm sure I'll manage to fix it somehow. Even if my magic is useless at the moment, I'll figure it out eventually. So please, don't do anything dangero—"

"Ferris, thank you for worrying about me."

When Ferris pleaded with her, showing how he truly felt, Crusch smiled gently toward him.

However, what lay behind that smile was not the look of a liege acceding to her retainer's request to pull back from danger. What lay behind it was firm will and resolve.

Faced with Ferris's heartfelt plea, she still had the will to gently but strongly reject it, and the resolve to fight.

The memories inside her might have vanished, but the will of Crusch Karsten persisted.

Even Subaru could tell. There was no way that Ferris, her very own knight, could not.

Crusch put her own hand over Ferris's shaking hand; then she firmly looked at Subaru and the others.

"There is still much I do not understand. I cannot remember a single thing about who I once was. I believe that you will all find contact with me to be bewildering... Even so, let me first thank all of you for holding me so dear."

"Lady Cruuusch..."

"Ferris, I understand that your words are founded in genuine concern. I understand the path you wish to lead me down by the hand... To follow your words means to walk a path of safety...but..."

One by one, Crusch looked between Subaru and the others, finally gazing gently at Ferris, whose voice was tearful.

"I do not wish to know nothing, understand nothing, and simply be swept away. If a choice must be made, I want to make it on my own, and not do as others say—I intend to continue striving for that."

Even without her memories, she still had the utmost respect for free will.

Perhaps a person's will and character rested not in memories, but somewhere else. Crusch had lost her past, yet even so, Subaru couldn't help but think that the Crusch he saw before him was strong.

Perhaps this was the soul that the old Crusch had once spoken about.

"—Uu, ngh, haafh!"

"Now that Lady Crusch has spoken, it would seem we do not desire to break off the alliance."

"Correct. Lady Emilia, Master Subaru Natsuki, we have caused you a great deal of trouble."

Ferris, who had broken into tears, was no longer in any state to continue the conversation. In his place, Wilhelm carried on, Crusch apologizing as she cradled Ferris in her arms.

"No, that's all right... We are in no position to complain. We must reunite with Ram and those who evacuated to the Sanctuary and discuss things thoroughly with Roswaal."

"You have my thanks. Master Subaru Natsuki, are you satisfied with this conclu—"

"—Yeah, it's fine. Besides that, what's happening with Anastasia and her people?"

Subaru agreed with Emilia and Crusch that they should uphold their alliance; at the end he invoked yet another name. This was the name of someone not participating in this final meeting, even though she was directly involved with both the White Whale and Sloth—for dealing with Anastasia Hoshin was a difficult issue for both camps.

"…Julius is one thing, but there's no way Lady Anastasia won't use this to her advantage, *meow*."

Ferris sniffled, and his eyes were red as he murmured resentfully from within Crusch's arms.

In point of fact, Crusch's position in the royal selection—she had been deemed the most powerful royal candidate by the public—had been deeply shaken. That was an enormous issue, even compared to the honor of defeating the White Whale, and there was no way Anastasia would not exploit it.

"But she wants to share the credit for the White Whale, too, right? How about hiding what happened with Crusch?"

"That's what…I was going to say. Subaru, can you…keep things secret until we decide how to deal with this? This is an extra condition for the alliance, okay…?"

Ferris said the last part rather quickly, as if trying to shoo Subaru away. Subaru almost felt like complaining about how self-serving he was, going from trying to erase the alliance to adding new conditions, but—

"Yeah, got it—since you asked with a crying face and all."

That invective was probably fitting, given the relationship between Subaru and Ferris.

For Subaru knew painfully well how it felt to be powerless and consoled by the person most precious to you.

3

"Wilhelm, thanks a ton for the supporting fire earlier."

With the conversation in the office complete, Subaru left the sobbing Ferris and the consoling Crusch behind as he flagged down Wilhelm in the corridor.

"No," said the Sword Devil as he looked back, unable to conceal his fatigue from the string of battles as he continued, "It was nothing at all. If anything, I was of little help at critical junctures."

"That's not true at all. We couldn't have beaten the White Whale without you, and after, there was no one I could trust to keep Emilia and the others safe more than you. I'm grateful, Wilhelm."

It wasn't that everything had gone off without a hitch. But these were Subaru's true feelings.

However, Subaru's gratitude made Wilhelm's expression darken. He was the type of person who had a deep sense of duty and felt responsible when others got hurt. Subaru somehow managed to form a smile toward the all-too-kind Sword Devil.

"The situation hasn't calmed down that much, but you're going to visit your wife's grave or something, right? It's too early to relax, but you did avenge her, and that's important, right?"

"—!"

Subaru's words, an attempt to change the topic, made Wilhelm's cheeks faintly stiffen. As the reaction made Subaru's eyes go wide, his bewilderment was redoubled when Wilhelm did something even more surprising—he suddenly bowed his head deeply in Subaru's direction.

"Sir Subaru, I must thank you again."

"H-hey, hold on a sec! I'm seriously trying to thank *you* here, Wilhelm…"

"No, truly I must. Until now, I have not thought of you as my ally. At the very least, in stating we should continue the alliance with Lady Emilia, my viewpoint was founded upon my own personal reasons. After the fact, I am ashamed at my own audacity in hiding my true thoughts."

Subaru, not understanding the reason for Wilhelm raking himself over the coals, could only watch as a question mark rose over his head.

In front of Subaru, Wilhelm abruptly pulled an arm out of the sleeve of his jacket. His left shoulder was bandaged; blood slowly oozed out of it that very moment.

"That looks painful. But Ferris should be able to heal a wound like..."

"This wound cannot be healed. It is an untreatable wound inflicted by the blade of one with the blessing of the grim reaper."

"Untreatable... But, Wilhelm—!"

As Wilhelm shook his head with a grave look on his face, Subaru gaped at him in disbelief. Even Subaru could imagine the terror of a wound that would never close. If gradual blood loss was not stanched, it was the same as putting a countdown on a person's life.

Subaru was racked with feelings of nervousness, but Wilhelm appeared quite calm.

"My life is not in any jeopardy from this."

"There's no way that it isn't! What the hell can you do about a wound like...?"

"This is not a wound borne from the events of today or yesterday. It is an old wound from much longer ago that has simply reopened—and that fact weighs very heavily upon me."

Subaru listened to Wilhelm speak in a quiet voice when he realized that his own body was shaking. The shaking had begun with his limbs, but at some point it had spread to even the roots of his teeth. Then he immediately realized the cause: the frighteningly dense aura of hostility given off by the Sword Devil before his eyes.

The Sword Devil continued in a quiet voice. "The power of a wound inflicted by the blessing of the grim reaper increases the closer the victim is to the one who carries the blessing. If they come near one another, even a closed wound will reopen... Such is the nature of the injury."

"Then the one who gave that wound to you was close by..."

"The one who wounded my left shoulder is the previous Sword Saint."

Those words made Subaru's breath catch as he looked at Wilhelm.

A quiet fire was burning in the eyes with which he looked at Subaru. He continued, "This sword wound was opened by my wife,

Theresia von Astrea. I must continue to pursue the Witch Cult in order to uncover the truth."

4

He'd meant to walk without thinking of anything, but before he knew it, he'd once again ended up standing in front of the room where Rem slept.

His feet took him toward her whenever free time allowed it. He knew full well that he was just indulging himself, clinging to Rem as she continued to slumber.

"You told me to be strong, but…it's like, now that you're gone, Rem, I can't find that strength anywhere."

Morning, noon, or night, the sight of Rem lying there never changed.

She breathed in her sleep. Her heart continued to beat. But beyond those things, there was not even a single proper sign that she was alive. She was there, and yet she was not. By that time, Rem didn't exist except in Subaru's heart.

"—"

Subaru sat at Rem's bedside, looking at her sleeping face as he thought back…

…and remembered when, in an effort to bring Rem back, he'd used a dagger to pierce his own throat.

He could not remember the exact instant in time. But the fact remained that he'd overcome various obstacles, grasping the best possible result for everyone with both hands—and hadn't hesitated to throw it all away.

If it meant losing Rem, if it meant advancing into a future without her, he didn't care how many times he had to fight Sloth, how many hells he had to go through…or so he had thought.

After the dagger punched through his throat, he felt himself fading in the face of blood, pain, passion, and loss— Then, when Subaru came to after Returning by Death, the sight of Rem sleeping in bed lay before him.

"...Shit. I never thought there'd be an auto-save just before committing suicide. That's really messed up."

Subaru, thinking that the change in restart points must have been some kind of mistake, tried to take his own life again. But when the paradox sank in that, even if he Returned by Death, he could not save Rem, he stopped his impulsive behavior; the dagger fell from Subaru's hand as he crumpled to the floor.

Even if, via Return by Death, he somehow managed to return to the point before the decisive battle with Petelgeuse, Rem and the others would have already gone their separate way hours before—which meant that no matter what he did, there was no way catch up with Rem before they were attacked on the return journey.

And supposing, by some miracle, he had caught up to them, he had no plan for defeating new Archbishops of the Seven Deadly Sins. Besides, if he went back and left Petelgeuse to his own savage devices, it would mean losing Emilia.

If he tried to save Rem, he'd sacrifice Emilia; if he tried to save Emilia, he'd sacrifice Rem—without sacrificing one, he couldn't even put his finger on the merest possibility of saving the other.

When Subaru realized the cruel choice facing him, he couldn't even kill himself anymore.

And so he remained without a plan, doing nothing but lingering close to Rem in the time since—

"—So this is where you were."

A voice, clear as a bell, abruptly reached Subaru from behind; his shoulders jumped as he looked back. There stood the girl precious to him gazing at him with a thin smile on her lips—a girl he'd left alone for the last several hours.

Even he wasn't pathetic enough to say something like, *What are you doing here? I'm busy.*

"Emilia...? You need something?"

"Do I...need anything in particular to come? I'm supposed to be close to that girl...to Miss Rem, as well, right?"

"Miss Rem, huh?"

Emilia walked to the bed and peered at Rem from Subaru's side.

It felt odd hearing Emilia add an honorific to Rem's name as she stroked her own silver hair.

"Ah, that's right," murmured Emilia in response to Subaru's words. "I called her just by her name, didn't I?"

"You were Roswaal's guest, Emilia-tan. She's Ram's little sister, so no need to explain, right?"

"Mm, I understand that much. I mean, she looks just like Ram. There's no way you could be wrong."

The image of Ram was probably in the back of Emilia's mind as she gazed at Rem's sleeping face. The twin sisters were two peas in a pod. Aside from their hair and eye colors, facial expressions, and the sizes of their breasts, they looked exactly the same.

The very late realization that Ram had no doubt forgotten Rem as well tore deeply at Subaru's chest.

"Subaru, you haven't slept at all, have you? You really should rest a little."

"I'm not tired, really. It's not like I'm actually doing anything."

"But you really want to do something, don't you? If you keep your mind tense like that, your body will be the next to go. So please."

The echo of her heartfelt plea finally made Subaru look in Emilia's direction. When their gazes met, for the first time since she had entered the room, Subaru's breath caught at the sullen look in her violet eyes.

Then he finally understood just why Emilia had come.

"I'm pretty pathetic, huh?"

"No, not at all. You've been a reeeally huge help to me. Really-really."

Emilia shook her head at Subaru's self-deprecation. From the beginning she'd been concerned about Subaru running himself ragged. With Subaru pushing himself too hard, she'd come to give him a gentle touch.

With Subaru seated in his chair, Emilia sat down herself; their gazes met as she earnestly tried to weave her words.

"I won't say something like *I'm sure it'll all work out*. I can't promise such a thing. I want to understand your feelings, Subaru…but I don't know anything about a girl I've forgotten, so if I say anything, I think it'll just hurt you."

"—"

"But I do know this—you can't worry about Rem and shoulder that burden alone. Subaru, let me share that burden with you."

"Emilia…"

Emilia's surprising words made Subaru's eyes widen in astonishment.

To Subaru, Emilia was truly speaking completely beyond his expectations.

"But you don't even remember anything about her…"

"Is it wrong to want to do something, even if I don't? She's a precious-enough girl to you to give you such a sad face, isn't she? Subaru, is it so strange that I want to help?"

"—"

"I want to help you in the same way that you helped me. If you're hurt, I want to do something for you. That's normal, isn't it?"

He could trust those feelings and approach them without hesitation; that affection needed no doubts.

For the first time, Subaru's stubbornness fell away, dissolved by the words Emilia had gone out of her way to speak. When he realized that, he thought himself a real idiot for having been so obstinate in the first place.

"…You really are something, Emilia-tan."

"Really? I feel like you're reeeally amazing, too, Subaru."

"Nah, no way— I'm glad you're here, Emilia."

Emilia's face went blank when Subaru slipped that last part in. Subaru made a strained smile at her demeanor, looking like she almost understood, but not quite. And when it dawned on Subaru that his lips were forming a smile, he finally realized…

—This was the first heartfelt emotion he'd experienced since he learned that Rem was asleep.

"Emilia, there's something I'd like to ask of you…"

"What is it?"

"Can you turn around? I'm gonna cry a bit."

"Mm-hmm, got it."

Emilia asked nothing more, turning her back to Subaru as he had asked.

Her consideration was a relief to Subaru as his gaze fell to his own knees. He gave in to the emotions surging inside him; he sniffled, and tears fell.

As Rem continued to sleep before him, he'd wasted time, beating himself up over his own powerlessness. Emilia, too, was concerned for Rem, yet he'd never even noticed.

Because he was the only one who remembered Rem, he'd convinced himself that he was the only person concerned about her, and that only he could save her.

Subaru continued sniffling at his own stupidity.

And then…

"_____"

In that quiet room, filled only with the sound of his own sobbing, Subaru's throat caught from the abrupt sensation of warmth.

From behind, over the back of the chair, Emilia embraced Subaru, gently stroking his head.

"_____"

She said nothing. She didn't have to.

Saved by her simple act of kindness, Subaru stanched the flow of both his tears and his whining.

And then, in that moment, he made an oath.

"I'll bring you back. Count on it, Rem."

He had told her before.

He, the man she'd fallen in love with, would stand before her as the greatest hero of all.

Wasn't he still only partway down that road?

"I'll definitely… Your hero is definitely coming for you—just you wait."

This was both a promise to himself, and his declaration of war against the enemy called fate.

Any who stood before Subaru Natsuki while doing evil, encroaching upon that which was not theirs to sully, would be pounded flat.

And it would be Subaru Natsuki who would do it.

"There's no doubt—no doubt!!"

In the time starting from zero, losing someone precious like you…is unthinkable.

That's why I'll get them back.

The days lost. The time I spent walking with you. The time I wanted to spend walking with you.

I'll bring them back again with my own two hands, so just wait, Rem…

AFTERWORD

Celebrate! Arc 3 is finally complete! It took a while!

Yes, hello, this is Tappei Nagatsuki/Mouse-Colored Cat, in your debt as always.

The third arc, beginning with *Re:ZERO -Starting Life in Another World-*, Vol. 4, is finally complete!

Since some of you readers *might* read the afterword first, authors tend to write about the contents of the novel without particular spoiler warnings, so if you haven't read the novel, leave this for later!

So based on the premise that you *really did* leave this for later, let's get into the nitty-gritty.

Within the story of this work, *Re:ZERO -Starting Life in Another World-*, the contents of the third arc, beginning with Volume 4, were things I wanted to do from the very beginning. I've probably mentioned this in Volumes 3 or 4, or maybe it was 5 or 6, but as an author, it's an indescribable feeling to have reached this point.

Actually, a lot of things happened during the time this third arc was completed. It gained a comic version, talk of an anime came up, the anime was hammered out, the anime was broadcast, and here we are at virtually the same time the anime comes to a close! There are few experiences quite like this one as a whole.

Thanks to all this, the anime came out great, and I've received many messages saying, "I found out about *Re:ZERO* from the anime!" Even with the anime finished, the *Re:ZERO* book series will continue. Just after the defeat of the powerful foe Sloth, a new, powerful enemy emerges! There are still so many mysteries to be revealed! With both reunions and farewells, the tale of Subaru Natsuki continues!

Well, since I went out of my way as a creator to stuff in an especially large cliffhanger, I'd like to think that a lot of people are looking forward to Volume 10!

I am eagerly waiting to hear how everyone feels about "what comes after," the parts not included in the anime!

Now then, with a broad smile on my face, allow me to follow the established custom of flattery!

To senior editor I., the third arc is probably what caught your eye most back in the web novel days. I can humbly state that my having arrived this far is due to your strenuous efforts. Developments hereafter will bring especially large headaches, so please lend me your shoulder and your best regards going forward!

Otsuka the illustrator, I know this is old news by now, but the characters truly blossomed splendidly in the anime. Otsuka, I think it is safe to say that your character designs are what made the anime so popular! Next arc, the cast of characters increases again, so as the author, I have the highest hopes of all! It'll be lots of fun!

To others, such as MF Bunko J's editorial department, Daichi Matsuse and Makoto Fugetsu for the comic versions, Kusano the designer, everyone involved on the bookstore and the business ends, and to many, many others, thank you for all the help!

And allow me to borrow this space to thank everyone who poured their strength into the *Re:ZERO* anime.

Masaharu Wanatabe the producer, WHITE FOX for animation work, Tsunaki Yoshigawa, Shou Tanaka P, Masahiro Yokotani the scenario writer, Yoshiko Nakamura, Eiji Umehara, Kyuuta Sakai the character designer, Kenichirou Suehiro for music, Koyomi

Suzuki for the OP and ED, and MYTH&ROID—and, to be blunt, far too many people to record in this space, I thank you from the bottom of my heart.

Of course, words cannot suffice to thank the entire cast performing these characters' roles. Thank you very much!

And finally, my greatest thanks to all of you readers who have stuck with me through this book and this tale.

Even with my dream of an anime version fulfilled, I shall strive so that new dreams might be granted henceforth—be it novel, manga, or anime, please give me your best regards and support!

Well then, let us meet again for the next novel—and the start of a new story arc!

Thank you!

Tappei Nagatsuki
August 2016
(The anime is over, but Re:ZERO *is in its middle acts and*
still has a long way to go!)

Creating the Natsuki Subaru Household

*** They're wearing kimonos because they live in Kararagi.**

Rem — Grew her hair long with Emilia in mind.

Subaru — Grew his hair long. Hairstyle is homage to Wilhelm(?)

Spica — Good thing she didn't take after Subaru.

Rigel — The spitting image of a young Subaru. Hair color same as Rem's.

Shinichiro Otsuka

"There, there, Lady Emilia…Arc 3 is over. Thank you for your hard work."

"Yeah, it really is. It was a *really, really* tough story, though."

"But Subaru was wonderful and very cool. And adorable."

"I *really* agree with you! I have to hang in there just as much as he does!"

"Yes, I suppose so. So with that too in mind, let us eagerly engage in the next volume preview in Subaru's place!"

"All right…! Err, first of all, with Volume 9, the third arc of *Re:ZERO* is done. Also, Volume 10, which begins Arc 4, was printed right after…and actually goes on sale *next month*!"

"Volume 9 neatly ties into the end of the anime, so it seems they are being very kind to readers who want to continue reading right away. I would have expected such consideration."

"And the anime came out *really* nicely, too. Also, Volume 1 of the *Blue Rays* and the *Dee Vee Dees* will come out the same month, apparently with novellas written by the original author added to them! He seems to be a very hard worker."

"These are must-see stories that appear neither on the Web, nor in the main novel series, but here alone. They touch on Lady Emilia's past and, I am embarrassed to say, on Rem's and Sister's pasts as well. Others touch on the daily lives in the camps of rival candidates, and that might be fun, too."

"After that…Oh, right! This is important, too! *Re:ZERO -Starting Life in Another World-* is going to be a video game! The details are yet to be released, but…"

"Activities of Subaru taking place in neither the anime nor the novels…I shall buy a hundred."

"It won't just be Subaru, it will probably be me, Rem, even Ram, I think. Sounds like fun."

"Yes, seeing Sister's activities will be fun, as well. I shall buy two hundred."

"Tee-hee. Your room will get pretty full if you buy that many."

"That is how fun it shall be—Lady Emilia, we should finally…"

"Mm, got it. All right, this ends the next volume preview. See you again for Volume 10."

"Yes, Volume 10—Take care of Subaru and Sister for me, Lady Emilia."

HAVE YOU BEEN TURNED ON TO LIGHT NOVELS YET?

IN STORES NOW!

SWORD ART ONLINE, VOL. 1–15
SWORD ART ONLINE, PROGRESSIVE 1–5

The chart-topping light novel series that spawned the explosively popular anime and manga adaptations!

MANGA ADAPTATION AVAILABLE NOW!

SWORD ART ONLINE © Reki Kawahara ILLUSTRATION: abec
KADOKAWA CORPORATION ASCII MEDIA WORKS

ACCEL WORLD, VOL. 1–16

Prepare to accelerate with an action-packed cyber-thriller from the bestselling author of *Sword Art Online*.

MANGA ADAPTATION AVAILABLE NOW!

ACCEL WORLD © Reki Kawahara ILLUSTRATION: HIMA
KADOKAWA CORPORATION ASCII MEDIA WORKS

SPICE AND WOLF, VOL. 1–20

A disgruntled goddess joins a traveling merchant in this light novel series that inspired the *New York Times* bestselling manga.

MANGA ADAPTATION AVAILABLE NOW!

SPICE AND WOLF © Isuna Hasekura ILLUSTRATION: Jyuu Ayakura
KADOKAWA CORPORATION ASCII MEDIA WORKS

Read the light novel that inspired the hit anime series!

Also be sure to check out the manga series!

AVAILABLE NOW!

 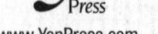 

www.YenPress.com